Praise for the story that began the sensation

BASTARD

An ambitious intern.
A perfectionist executive.
And a whole lot of name calling.

"Smart, sexy, and satisfying, Christina Lauren's *Beautiful Bastard* is destined to become a romance classic."

—Tara Sue Me, author of *The Submissive*

"*Beautiful Bastard* has heart, heat, and a healthy dose of snark. Romance readers who love a smart plot are in for an amazingly sexy treat!"

—Myra McEntire, author of *Hourglass*

"*Beautiful Bastard* is the perfect mix of passionate romance and naughty eroticism. I couldn't, and didn't, put it down until I'd read every last word."

—Elena Raines, *Twilightish*

ALSO BY CHRISTINA LAUREN

Beautiful Bastard

Beautiful STRANGER

A Novel

CHRISTINA LAUREN

GALLERY BOOKS

NEW YORK • LONDON • TORONTO • SYDNEY • NEW DELHI

G

Gallery Books
A Division of Simon & Schuster, Inc.
1230 Avenue of the Americas
New York, NY 10020

First Gallery Books trade paperback edition May 2013

GALLERY BOOKS and colophon are registered trademarks of
Simon & Schuster, Inc.

For information about special discounts for bulk purchases,
please contact Simon & Schuster Special Sales at 1-866-506-1949
or business@simonandschuster.com.

The Simon & Schuster Speakers Bureau can bring authors to your
live event. For more information or to book an event contact the
Simon & Schuster Speakers Bureau at 1-866-248-3049 or visit our
website at www.simonspeakers.com.

10 9 8

Library of Congress Cataloging-in-Publication Data
Lauren, Christina.
   Beautiful stranger / Christina Lauren.—First Gallery Books
trade paperback edition.
      pages cm
   I. Title.
   PS3612.A9442273
   [B47 2013]
   813'.6—dc23
                                                        2013001432

ISBN 978-1-4767-3153-7
ISBN 978-1-4767-3154-4(ebook)

Beautiful
STRANGER

Prologue

When my old life died, it didn't go quietly. It detonated.

But to be fair, I'd been the one to pull the pin. In just one week I rented out my house, sold my car, and left my philandering boyfriend. And though I'd promised my overprotective parents that I'd be careful, it wasn't until I was actually at the airport that I called ahead to let my best friend know I was moving her way.

That's when it all seemed to sink in, in one perfectly clear moment.

I was ready to start over.

"Chloe? It's me," I said, voice shaking as I looked around the terminal. "I'm coming to New York. I hope the job's still mine."

She screamed, dropped the phone, and reassured someone in the background that she was fine.

"Sara's coming," I heard her explain, and my heart squeezed just thinking about being there with them at the beginning of this new adventure. "She changed her mind, Bennett!"

I heard a sound of celebration, a clap, and he said something I couldn't quite make out.

"What did he say?" I asked.

"He asked if Andy was coming with you."

"No." I paused to fight back the sick feeling creeping up into my throat. I'd been with Andy for six years and no matter how glad I was to be done with him, the dramatic turn in my life still felt surreal. "I left him."

I heard her small, sharp inhale. "You okay?"

"Better than okay." And I was. I don't think I realized exactly *how* okay I was until that moment.

"I think it's the best decision you ever made," she told me and then paused, listening as Bennett spoke in the background. "Bennett says you're going to shoot across the country like a comet."

I bit my lip, holding back a grin. "Not too far off, actually. I'm at the airport."

Chloe screeched some unintelligible sounds and then promised to pick me up at LaGuardia.

I smiled, hung up, and handed the counter attendant my ticket, thinking a comet was too directed, too driven. I was really more like an old star, out of fuel, my own gravity pulling me inward, crushing me. I ran out of energy for my too-perfect life, my too-predictable job, my loveless relationship—exhausted at only twenty-seven. Like a star, my life in Chicago collapsed under the force of its own weight, so I was leaving. Massive stars leave behind black holes. Small stars leave behind white dwarfs. I was barely leaving behind a shadow. All of my light was coming with me.

I was ready to start over as a comet: refuel, reignite, and burn across the sky.

One

"You're wearing the silver dress or I'm stabbing you," Julia called from the kitchen zone, as I'd begun calling it. It certainly wasn't big enough to be labeled a full-fledged kitchen.

I'd gone from an echoing, rambling Victorian in the Chicago suburbs to an adorable East Village apartment roughly the size of my former living room. It felt even smaller once I'd unpacked, put everything in its place, and had my two closest friends come over. The living room/dining room/kitchen area was framed by giant bay windows, but the effect was less palatial and more fishbowl. Julia was only visiting for the weekend, for this night of celebration, but she'd already asked me at least ten times why I'd chosen such a tiny place.

The truth was, I chose it because it was different from anything I'd ever known before. And because tiny apartments were pretty much what you were going to find in New York when you moved there without first securing a place to live.

In the bedroom, I tugged on the hem of the miniature, sequined dress and stared at the extreme amount of blindingly pale leg I was offering up tonight. I hated that my first instinct was to wonder if Andy would think it was too revealing, while my second instinct was to realize I loved it. I'd have to delete all of those old Andy programs, immediately.

"Give me one good reason why I shouldn't wear this."

"Can't think of one." Chloe walked into the bedroom wearing a deep blue number that flowed around her like some kind of aura. She looked, as usual, unbelievable. "We're drinking and dancing, so showing some skin is requisite."

"I don't know how much skin I want to show," I said. "I'm dedicated to my freshly minted single-girl card."

"Well, some of the women there will be showing bare ass, so you won't stand out if that's what you're worried about. Besides," she said, pointing to the street below, "it's too late to change. The limo's here."

"*You* should be showing bare ass. You're the one who's been naked-sunbathing and day-drunk in a French villa for the past three weeks," I said.

Chloe gave a little secret smile and tugged my arm. "Let's go, gorgeous. I've spent the past few weeks with the BB. I'm ready for a night out with the girls."

We piled into the waiting car and Julia popped the champagne. With just one tingling, bubbling gulp, the entire world around me seemed to evaporate until we were just three young friends in a limo barreling down the street to celebrate a new life.

And this night we weren't just celebrating my arrival: Chloe Mills was getting hitched, Julia was visiting, and the newly single Sara had some living to do.

◆

The club was dark, deafening, and filled with writhing bodies: on the dance floor, in the halls, against the bar. A DJ spun music from a small stage, and flyers plastered all across the front promised that she was the newest and hottest DJ Chelsea had to offer.

Julia and Chloe seemed entirely in their element. I felt like I'd spent most of my childhood and adult life so far at quiet, formal events; here it was as if I'd stepped out of the pages of my quiet Chicago story and into the quintessential New York tale instead.

It was perfect.

I shoved my way up to the bar—cheeks flushed, hair damp, and legs feeling like they hadn't been properly used like this in years.

"Excuse me!" I shouted, trying to get the bartender's attention. Though I had no idea what any of it actually meant, I'd already ordered slippery nipples, cement mixers, and purple hooters. At this point, with the club at maximum density and the music so loud it shook my bones, he wouldn't even look up at me. Admittedly, he was slammed and making such a small number of tedious shots was annoying. But I had an intoxicated, newly affianced friend burning a hole in the dance floor, and said girlfriend wanted more shots.

"Hey!" I called, slapping the bar.

"Sure is doing his best to ignore you, in't he?"

I blinked up—and *up*—at the man pressed close to me at the crowded bar. He was roughly the size of a redwood, and nodded toward the bartender to indicate his meaning. "You never yell at a bartender, Petal. Especially not with what you're going to order: Pete hates making girly drinks."

Of course. It would be just my luck to meet a gorgeous man just days after swearing off men forever. A man with a British accent to boot. The universe was a hilarious bitch.

"How do you know what I was going to order?" My grin grew wider, hopefully matching his, but most likely looking a lot tipsier. I was grateful for the drinks I'd already had, because sober Sara would give him monosyllables and an awkward nod and be done with it. "Maybe I was going to get a pint of Guinness. You never know."

"Unlikely. I've seen you ordering tiny purple drinks all night."

He'd been watching me all night? I couldn't decide if that was fantastic, or a little creepy.

I shifted on my feet and he followed my movements. He had angled features with a sharp jaw and a carved hollow beneath his cheekbones, eyes that seemed back-lit and heavy, dark brows, a deep dimple on his left cheek when the grin spread down to his lips. This man had to be well over six feet, with a torso it would take my hands many moons to explore.

Hello, Big Apple.

The bartender returned, then looked at the man beside me expectantly. My beautiful stranger barely raised his voice, but it was so deep it carried without effort: "Three fingers of Macallan's, Pete, and whatever this lady is having. She's been waiting a spell, yeah?" He turned to me, wearing a smile that made something dormant warm deep in my belly. "How many fingers would you like?"

His words exploded in my brain and my veins filled with adrenaline. "What did you just say?"

Innocence. He tried it on, smoothing it over his features. Somehow he made it work, but I could see from the way his eyes narrowed that there wasn't an innocent cell in his body.

"Did you really just offer me three fingers?" I asked.

He laughed, spreading out the biggest hand I'd ever seen on the bar just between us. His fingers were the kind that could curl around a basketball and dwarf it. "Petal, you'd best start with two."

I looked more closely at him. Friendly eyes, standing not too close, but close enough that I knew he had come to this part of the bar specifically to talk to me. "You give good innuendo."

The bartender rapped the bar with his knuckles and asked for my order. I cleared my throat, steeling myself. "Three blow jobs." I ignored his irritated huff and turned back to my stranger.

"You don't sound like a New Yorker," he said, grin fading slightly but never leaving his constantly smiling eyes.

"Neither do you."

"Touché. Born in Leeds, worked in London, and moved here six years ago."

"Five days," I admitted, pointing to my chest. "From Chicago. The company I used to work for opened an office here and brought me back on to head up Finance."

Whoa, Sara. Too much information. Way to enable stalkers.

It had been so long since I'd even looked at another man. Clearly Andy had been a master in this kind of situation, but unfortunately I had no idea how to flirt anymore. I glanced back to where I expected to see Julia and Chloe dancing, but I couldn't find them in the tangle of bodies on the floor. I was so rusty in this ritual I was practically revirginized.

"Finance? I'm a numbers man myself," he said, and waited until I looked back at him before turning the smile up a few notches. "Nice to see women doing it. Too many grouchy men in trousers having meetings just to hear themselves say the same thing over and over."

Smiling, I said, "I'm grouchy sometimes. I also wear trousers sometimes, too."

"I bet you also wear pants."

I narrowed my eyes. "That means something else in British, doesn't it? Are you giving me innuendo again?"

His laugh spread warm across my skin. "Pants are what you Americans so blandly call 'underwear.'" When he said this, the "un" sounded like a noise he might make during sex, and something inside me melted. While I gaped at him, my stranger tilted his head, looking me over. "You're rather sweet. You don't look like you come to these kinds of establishments very often."

He was right, but was it that obvious? "I'm really not sure how to take that."

"Take it as a compliment. You're the freshest thing in this place." He cleared his throat and looked to where Pete was returning with my shots. "Why are you carrying all these sticky drinks out to the dance floor?"

"My friend just got engaged. We're doing the girls' night out thing."

"So then you're unlikely to leave here with me."

I blinked, and then blinked again, *hard*. With this frank suggestion, I was officially out of my depth. *Way* out of my depth. "I . . . what? No."

"Pity."

"You're serious? You just met me."

"And already I have a strong urge to devour you." His words were delivered slowly, almost a whisper, but they rang through my head like a cymbal crash. It was obvious he wasn't new to this kind of interaction—the proposition of no-strings-attached sex—and although *I* was, when he looked at me like that I knew I was bound to follow him anywhere.

Every shot I'd had seemed to hit me all at once and I weaved a little in front of him. He steadied me with his hand on my elbow, grinning down at me.

"Easy, Petal."

I blinked back into awareness, feeling my head clear slightly. "Okay, when you smile at me like that, I want to climb you. And God knows it's been forever since I've been properly manhandled." I looked him up and down, all pretense of polite society apparently gone. "And something tells me you could more than do the job—I mean, holy *hell*, look at you."

And I did. Again. I took a steadying breath and was met with his amused grin. "But I've never just randomly hooked up with some stranger at a bar, and I'm here with friends, celebrating the awesome marriage they're going to have, and so"—I gathered up my shots—"we're going to do these."

He nodded once, slowly, his smile turning a little brighter, as if he'd just accepted a challenge. "Okay."

"So I'll see you later."

"One can hope."

"Enjoy your three fingers, stranger."

He laughed. "Enjoy the blow jobs."

I found Chloe and Julia at the table, collapsed and sweaty, and slid the shots down in front of them. Julia put one in front of Chloe and held her own aloft.

"May all of your blow jobs go down so easily." She wrapped her mouth around the rim, held both hands up in the air, and tipped her head back, swallowing the entire shot without blinking.

"Holy balls," I mumbled, staring at her in awe, as Chloe broke into laughter beside me. "Is that how I'm supposed to do it?" I lowered my voice, looking around. "Like an *actual* blow job?"

"It's a miracle I still have any gag reflex." Julia rather

indelicately wiped her forearm across her mouth and chin, explaining, "I did a lot of beer bongs in college. Let's go." She nudged Chloe. "Bottoms up."

Chloe bent to the table and took the shot hands-free, as Julia had, and then it was my turn. Both of my friends turned to look at me.

"I met a hot guy," I said without thinking. "*Really* hot. And, like, seventeen feet tall."

Julia gaped at me. "Then why are you standing here doing *fake* blow jobs with us?"

I laughed, shaking my head. I had no idea how to answer that. I could have left with him, and it really could have gone to BJ territory in someone else's far more daring life. "It's a girls' night out. You're only here for two days. I'm good."

"Fuck that noise. Go get some."

Chloe came to my rescue: "I'm just glad you met someone you thought was hot. It's been forever since you had this sort of happy boy-related smile." Her own smile vanished as she reconsidered. "Come to think of it, I've never seen you with a happy boy-related smile."

And with that truth placed so plainly on the table, I picked up my shot, ignoring Julia's protest about my bad form, and downed it. It was sweet, delicious, and just what I needed to clear my head of the jerk in Chicago and the beautiful stranger at the bar. I dragged my friends out to the dance floor.

Within seconds I felt boneless, mindless, deliciously untethered. Chloe and Julia bounced around me, yell-sang the songs, lost themselves in the mass of sweaty bodies all around us. I wanted my youth to linger a little bit. Away from my routine, overscheduled life in Chicago I could see I hadn't enjoyed it properly. Only here, with the DJ melting song to song, did I see how I could have spent my early twenties: under the lights, dancing in a scrap of a dress, meeting men who wanted to devour me, watching my girlfriends be wild and silly and young.

I didn't have to move in with my boyfriend when I was twenty-two.

I could have lived a life outside the straight-and-narrow world of society functions and glad-handing.

I could have been *this* girl instead—dressed to the nines, dancing her heart out.

Lucky for me, it wasn't too late. I met Chloe's elated smile and returned it.

"I'm so glad you're here!" she yelled over the music.

I started to reply with some similar screaming drunken oath of friendship, but just behind Chloe, set into the shadows off the dance floor, stood my stranger. Our eyes met, and neither of us looked away. He was sipping his three fingers of scotch with a friend, but I could tell by how unsurprised he seemed to be caught staring that he'd been watching every move I made.

The effect of this realization was more potent than the alcohol. It heated every inch of my skin, burned a hole directly through my chest and lower: down past my ribs, and deep into my belly. He lifted his glass, took a sip, and smiled. I felt my eyes rolling closed.

I wanted to dance for him.

Never in my life had I felt so sexy, so completely in control of what I wanted. I'd made it through my master's degree, found a well-paying job, and even redecorated my house on a budget. But I'd never felt like a grown woman the way I did right now, dancing like crazy with a beautiful stranger standing in the shadows, watching me.

This—*this* moment was exactly how I wanted to start fresh.

What would it mean to be devoured? Did he mean that as explicitly as it sounded—his head between my thighs, arms wrapped to my hips, holding me open? Or did he mean over me, inside me, sucking my mouth and my neck and my breasts?

A smile spread across my face, my arms stretched up to the ceiling. I could feel the hem of my dress inching up my thighs and didn't care. I wondered if he noticed. I *hoped* he noticed.

If I thought he'd walked away, it would have deflated the moment, so I didn't look over his way again.

I was unaccustomed to bar flirtation protocol; maybe his attention lasted all of five seconds, maybe it lasted all night. It didn't matter. I could pretend he was there in the darkness for as long as I was here in the strobing lights on the floor. I'd grown to never expect much of Andy's attention, but with this stranger, I wanted his eyes burning through my skin to where my heart thrashed against my ribs.

I lost myself to the music, and memories of his hand on my elbow, his dark eyes and the word *devour*.

Devour.

One song bled into another, and then another, and before I could come up for air, Chloe's arms were around my shoulders and she was laughing into my ear, jumping up and down with me.

"You've attracted an audience!" she yelled so loud above the music that I winced, pulling back.

She nodded to the side, and only then did I notice we were surrounded by a group of men wearing tight, dark clothes and grinding suggestively at the air near them. Looking back at Chloe, I saw that her eyes were bright and so familiar, this take-no-prisoners woman who had worked her way to the top of what was now one of the world's largest media firms and who knew exactly what this night meant to me. Suddenly cool air spread over my skin from the fans overhead and I blinked back into consciousness, still giddy that I was actually in New York City, actually starting over. Actually enjoying myself.

But behind Chloe, the shadows were dark and empty; no stranger stood there watching me.

My stomach dropped a little. "I need to hit the ladies'," I told her.

I wormed my way through the circle of men, off the dance floor, and followed the signs to the second floor, which was essentially a balcony overlooking the entire club. I walked down a narrow hallway and into the bathroom, which was so bright that a pulse of pain spiked from my eyes to the back of my head. The room was eerily empty, and the music downstairs felt like it was coming up from underwater.

On my way out, I fixed my hair, mentally high-fived myself for putting on a rumple-free dress, and touched up my lipstick.

I walked out of the door and right into a wall of man.

We'd been close at the bar, but not this close. Not my face to his throat, the smell of him surrounding me. He didn't smell like the men on the dance floor, awash in cologne. He just smelled clean, and like a man who did his laundry, and who also had a touch of scotch on his lips.

"Hello, Petal."

"Hi, stranger."

"I was watching you dance, you tiny, wild thing."

"I saw you." I could barely catch my breath. My legs felt wobbly, like they weren't sure if they should collapse or go back to rhythmically bouncing across the floor. I chewed my bottom lip, suppressing a smile. "You're such a creepster. Why didn't you come out and dance with me?"

"Because I think you rather liked being watched instead."

I swallowed, gaping up at him and unable to look away. I couldn't tell what color his eyes were. At the bar I'd assumed brown. But there was something lighter gleaming here in this part of the club, just above the strobes. Greenish, yellow, something mesmerizing. Not only had I known he was watching me—and liked it—but I'd danced entirely to the fantasy of him devouring me.

"Did you imagine I was getting hard?"

I blinked. I could barely keep up with his bluntness. Had men like this always existed, who said exactly what they—and I—were thinking without sounding scary, or rude, or pushy? How did he manage it?

"Wow," I gasped. "*Were* you . . . ?"

He reached down, took my hand, and pressed it firmly to where he was erect, already arching into my palm. Without thinking, I curled my fingers around him. "This is from watching *me* dance?"

"Are you always such a performer?"

If I hadn't been so thunderstruck, I would have laughed. "Never."

He studied me, the smile still in his eyes but his lips fixed into something more thoughtful. "Come home with me."

This time I did laugh. "No."

"Come to my car."

"*No.* There is no way I'm leaving this club with you."

He bent and pressed a small, careful kiss to my shoulder before telling me, "But I want to touch you."

I couldn't pretend that I didn't want it, too. It was dark, with flashing arrhythmic lights, and music so loud it felt like it hijacked my pulse. What harm could come from one wild night? After all, Andy had so many.

I led him past the restrooms, farther down the narrow hallway, to a tiny abandoned alcove overlooking the DJ station. We were trapped at a dead end, secluded around a corner but by no means hidden. Other than the wall forming the back of the club, the rest of the space around us was open, and only a waist-high glass wall kept us from falling to the dance floor below. "Okay. Touch me over here."

He raised an eyebrow, ran a long finger across my collarbone, from one shoulder to the other. "What exactly are you offering?"

I met those strangely backlit eyes that seemed so

amused by everything around him. He looked normal, so sane for someone who followed me through a club and bluntly told me he wanted to touch me. I remembered Andy, and how rarely—outside of keeping up appearances—he ever wanted my touch, my conversation, my *anything*. Is this how it happened for him? A woman would pull him aside, offer herself, and he would take whatever he could before coming home to me? Meanwhile, my life had become so small I could hardly remember how I used to fill the long nights alone.

Was it greedy to want it all? A career to die for, and a crazy moment here and there?

"You're not a psychopath, are you?"

Laughing, he bent to kiss my cheek. "You're making me feel a touch crazy, but no, I'm not."

"I just . . ." I started, and then looked down. I pressed my hand flat against his chest. His gray sweater was unbelievably soft—cashmere, I thought. His jeans were dark, and fit him perfectly. His black shoes were unscuffed. Everything about him was meticulous. "I only just moved here." It seemed a fitting explanation for how much my hand was shaking against him.

"And a moment like this doesn't feel very safe, does it?"

I shook my head. "Not at all." But then I reached up, wrapped a hand around the back of his neck, and pulled him to me. He moved willingly, bending down and smiling just before our lips met. The kiss was both the perfect kind of soft and the perfect kind of hard, with the scotch warming his lips against mine. He groaned a little when I opened my mouth and let him in, and the vibration set me on fire. I wanted to feel every one of his sounds.

"You taste like sugar. What's your name?" he asked.

With that, I felt my first real pulse of panic. "No names."

He pulled back to look at me, eyebrows inching up. "What'll I call you?"

"What you've been calling me."

"Petal?"

I nodded.

"And what'll you call me when you're about to come?" He gave me another small kiss.

My heart jerked hard in my chest at the thought. "I don't think it matters what I call you, does it?"

Shrugging, he conceded, "I don't suppose so."

I took his hand, brought it to my hip. "I've been the only person to give myself an orgasm for the past year." Moving his fingers to the edge of my dress, I whispered, "Can you change that?"

I could feel his smile against my mouth when he bent to kiss me again. "You're serious."

The idea of giving myself to this man in this dark

corner scared me a little, though not enough to change my mind. "I'm serious."

"You're trouble."

"I promise you, I'm not."

He pulled back just enough to examine my eyes. Back and forth his gaze moved until his eyes curved into that amused smile. "The fact that you have no idea how you come off . . ."

He turned me, pressed my front to the edge of the glass wall so I was looking over the balcony at the mass of churning bodies below. Strobe lights pulsed down from iron beams that extended across the club just in front of me, lighting the floor beneath while keeping our upstairs corner virtually black. Steam began to blow up from vents in the dance floor, covering the partiers up to their shoulders; waves broke out in the surface as they moved through it.

My stranger's fingertips teased at the back edge of my dress, and then he lifted it, slid a hand down the back of my underwear, over my backside and between my legs to where I positively ached for him. Even the vulnerable position didn't embarrass me as I arched back into his hand, already lost.

"You're drenched, sweetheart. What's it you like? The idea that we're doing this here? Or that I watched you think about fucking me while you danced?"

I didn't say anything, too afraid of what the answer

might be, but I gasped when he slid a long finger inside me. Thoughts of what I *should* do blurred along the edges as I thought about boring Sara in Chicago. Predictable Sara who always did what everyone expected of her. I didn't want to be that person anymore. I wanted to be reckless and wild and young. I wanted to live for myself for the first time in my life.

"You're a tiny little thing, but when you're slippery like this, I'm quite sure you could easily take those three fingers." He laughed into a kiss he pressed to the back of my neck as a broad fingertip circled my clit, teasing and slow.

"Please," I whispered. I had no idea if he could hear me. His face was pressed to my hair, and I could feel his cock pressed to the side of my hip, but other than that, I was unaware of anything beyond his long finger sliding back into me.

"Your skin is amazing. Particularly here." He kissed my shoulder. "Did you know the back of your neck is perfect?"

I turned, smiled up at him. His eyes were wide open and clear, and when they met mine, they curved into a smile. I'd never looked someone so closely in the eye when they were touching me like this and something about this man, and this night, and this city, made me immediately sure this was the best decision I'd ever made.

Dear New York, You are brilliant. Love, Sara.

P.S. This is definitely not the alcohol talking.

"I don't have many chances to look at the back of my neck."

"A shame, really." He pulled his hand away and I felt a mild chill where his warm fingers had been. He dug into his pocket and pulled out a tiny package.

A condom. He just happened to have a condom in his pocket. It would never have occurred to me to bring a condom with me to some random club.

Turning me to face him, he swiveled us, pressed me back against the wall and bent to kiss me, first soft and then harder, hungrier. When I thought I'd lose my breath, he wandered away, sucking at my jaw, my ear, my neck, where my pulse hammered wildly. My dress had fallen back down my thighs, but his fingers teased at the edge, slowly lifting.

"Someone could walk down here," he reminded me, giving me one last out, even as he lowered my panties enough for me to step out of them.

I didn't care. Not even a little. And maybe even a tiny part of me wanted someone to wander up here, to see this perfect man touching me like this. I could hardly think of anything other than where his hands were, how my skirt was over my hips now, how he pressed so hard and insistent against my stomach.

"Don't care."

"You're drunk. Too drunk for this? I want you to remember it if I fuck you."

"So make it memorable."

He lifted my leg, spreading me, exposing my bare skin to the cool air-conditioning blowing from just above us, and hooked my knee around his hip, making me grateful for my four-inch heels. Reaching between us, I unbuttoned his jeans, pushed his boxers down just enough in front to free him, and wrapped my hand around his erection, rubbing it across my wetness.

"Fuck, Petal. Let me get this on."

His pants were open but slung over his hips. From the back we could even appear to be dancing, maybe just kissing. But he pulsed in my palm, and the reality of the situation made me wild. He was going to take me, right here, overlooking the crowd below. In that crowd were people who knew me as Good Sara, Responsible Sara, Andy's Sara.

New home, new job, new life. New Sara.

My stranger was heavy and so long in my hand. I wanted him and was also a little terrified that he might impale me. I wasn't sure I'd ever held a man who got this hard.

"You're big," I blurted.

He smiled, a wolf truly about to devour me, and quickly tore the condom package with his teeth. "That is the best thing you can say to a man. You could even tell me you're not sure I'll fit."

I swept the tip across my opening, and trembled from it. He was so warm: soft skin, hard beneath.

"Fuck. I'm going to come all over your fist if you don't stop that." His hands shook a little with urgency as he pulled himself from my grip to roll on the condom.

"Do you do this a lot?" I asked.

He was right there, poised against me, his smile aimed at my face. "Do what? Sex with a beautiful woman who won't tell me her name and prefers me to fuck her in a public hallway rather than in a proper place like a bed, or a limo?" He started to push in, achingly slow. The light burned in his eyes, and—*holy crap*—I didn't think sex with strangers was supposed to be intimate like this. He watched every reaction cross my face. "No, Petal. I must admit I've never done this."

His voice was tight, and then his words fell away because he was deep inside me, here in this chaotic club with living, breathing lights and music pulsing all around us, where people walked past unaware only fifteen feet away. And yet, my entire world reduced to the place where he filled me, where he rubbed firmly against my clit with every stroke, where the warm skin of his hips pressed to my thighs.

There wasn't any more talking, only small thrusts that grew faster, and harder. The space between us filled instead with quiet sounds of praise and urging. His teeth pressed into my neck and I gripped his shoulders for fear I might fall over the edge or even somewhere else, not onto a dance floor but into a world where I couldn't get enough of being so exposed, having my pleasure so visible to anyone watching—especially this man.

"Christ, you're gorgeous." He leaned back, looking down, and sped up a little. "I can't stop looking at your perfect skin and—*fuck*—where I'm moving in you."

Light was clearly on his side because to me he was backlit, just the silhouette of my stranger. I could see nothing when I looked down but dark shadows and the suggestion of movement: him into me, and out again. Slick and hard, pressing against me with every pass. And, as if to emphasize that I didn't really need to see anyway, the lights dimmed almost to black as a lazy, oscillating beat filled the club.

"I took video of you dancing," he whispered.

It was a few, long moments before his words registered above the feeling of him moving in me. *"Wh—what?"*

"I don't know why. I won't show it round. I just . . ." He watched my face, slowing down enough presumably so I could think. "You were so fucking possessed. I wanted to remember. Bloody hell, I feel like I'm confessing my sins."

I swallowed, and he bent closer, kissing me before I asked, "Is it weird that I like that you did that?"

He laughed into my mouth, moving in and out of me again with slow, deliberate strokes. "Just enjoy it, right? I like to watch you. You were performing for me. There isn't anything wrong with it."

He lifted my other leg, wrapping both around his waist, and then, for the span of several perfect seconds in the darkness, he started to really move. Fast and urgent, he let out the most delicious grunts and there would be no question what was happening if someone happened upon our little corner of this balcony. With that thought alone—where we were, what we were doing, and the possibility that someone could see this man taking me so roughly—I was lost. My head rolled back against the wall and I could feel it

feel it

feel it

building in my belly so low and heavy, an aching ball rolling down my spine and then out, exploding along my sex so hard I cried out, not even caring a little if anyone could hear me. I didn't even need to see his face to know he was watching me come apart.

"Holy fuck." His hips grew jagged and rough and then he came with a low groan, fingers digging hard into my hips.

He might bruise me, I thought. And then: *I hope he bruises me.*

I wanted a reminder of this night, and *this* Sara when I left, to better differentiate the new life I was so determined to have from the old one.

He stilled, leaning heavily against me, with his lips planted gently against my neck. "Good Lord, little stranger. You've wrecked me."

He pulsed in me—aftershocks of his orgasm—and I wanted him to stay buried deep like this for eternity. I imagined how we looked from across the club: a man pressing a woman to a wall, the hint of her legs around his hips visible in the darkness.

His broad hand smoothed up my leg from my ankle to my hip, and then with a small moan he pulled out, set me on my feet, stepped back, and unrolled the condom.

Holy hell, I had never even come close to doing something this insane. My grin took over my entire face as my legs shook almost to the point of collapse.

Don't freak out, Sara. Don't freak out.

It was perfect. Everything about this had been perfect, but it had to end right here. *Do it all differently. No names, no strings. No regrets.*

Straightening my dress, I stretched on my toes to kiss his lips once. "That was unbelievable."

He nodded, humming a little into the kiss. "It was. Shall we—?"

"I'm going to go downstairs." I began to back away and gave him a small wave.

He stared at me, confused. "You're—"

"Good. I'm good. You're good?"

He nodded, dazed.

"So . . . thanks." Adrenaline still buzzing in my veins, I turned before he could respond, and left him standing with his pants unbuttoned, his lips twisted in a surprised grin.

Minutes later I found Chloe and Julia, both of them ready to head home. Arm in arm we left the club, and only after we were in the limo, and I was silently reliving every second of what had just happened with that strange, powerful man, did I remember: I'd left my underwear on the floor at his feet, and the video of me dancing on his phone.

Two

Saturday my life was perfect: blazing career, orderly flat, several women available for play whenever and wherever. Sunday and Monday: a fucking mess. I was unable to concentrate, obsessively watching that damn video, and had a stranger's knickers burning a hole in my bedroom bureau.

Shifting in my chair, I ran my thumb over the screen, turning my phone on for the thousandth time today. The lunch meeting had veered off-topic again, and I'd tried my best to look like I gave even the slightest fuck what anyone was going on about, but as soon as the topic of American football came back up, I was done.

All I could think about was her anyway.

I glanced down, making sure the volume was muted and hesitating for only a moment before pressing play.

The screen was dark, the image was blurry, but I didn't need to make out every detail to know what came next. Even without the sound I could remember the throbbing music, the way her hips moved to the beat while her skirt slipped further and further up her thighs. American women didn't appreciate the value of perfectly pale, unfreckled skin, but my stranger had the most exquisite skin I'd ever seen. Fuck, I would've licked her from ankle to hip and back again if she'd given me the chance. I knew now that she was dancing just for me, that she knew I was watching.

And she fucking loved it.

Christ. That tiny slip of a dress. Her messy chin-length caramel hair and those enormous, innocent brown eyes. Those eyes made me want to do very, very bad things to her while she watched.

Her perfect arse and tits didn't hurt, either.

"You're a terrible lunch date, Stella." Will reached over and pulled a chip from my plate.

"Mmm?" I murmured, eyes still down, careful not to react in any way. "You're discussing American football. I'm over here killed by boredom. I am sitting here, quite literally dead."

If there's one thing I'd learned in this business, it's that you never, ever show your cards, even when you're holding the worst hand imaginable. Or a video of a girl dancing just before you fucked her against a wall.

"Whatever you're looking at on that phone is obviously a hundred times better than how the Jets are gonna look this year. And you're not sharing."

If only he knew.

"Taking a peek at the market," I said with a small shake of my head. I almost whimpered as I closed the video, slipping my phone into the inside pocket of my suit jacket. "Boring stuff."

Will drained the last of his drink and laughed. "I hate that you're such a good liar." If we hadn't been best mates since opening one of the most successful venture capital firms in the city three years ago, I might have actually believed him. "I think you're looking at porn on your phone."

I ignored him.

"Hey, Max," James Marshall, our head tech advisor, piped in. "Whatever happened with that woman you were talking to at the bar?"

Normally when my best mates asked about a random woman I'd met, I'd shrug and say, "Quick shag," or even simply, "Limo." But for some reason, this time I shook my head and said, "Nothing."

Another round of drinks arrived at our table and I thanked the server absently even though I hadn't yet touched my first one. My gaze moved restlessly around the room. It was the typical lunchtime crowd: business meetings and ladies who lunch.

I wanted to crawl out of my skin.

James groaned, closing the file he'd been looking over as he slipped it into his briefcase. He lifted his glass to his forehead, wincing. "Is anyone else still paying for the weekend, though? I'm too old for that shit anymore."

I lifted my scotch to my lips and immediately regretted it. How could a drink I'd had practically every day since puberty suddenly remind me of a woman I'd seen exactly once?

I looked up at the sound of a throat clearing.

"Hey," Will said. I followed his gaze to where a man was crossing the dining room. "Isn't that Bennett Ryan?"

"Well, I'll be damned," I said, as the tall shape of my old friend moved across the restaurant.

"Do you know him?" James asked.

"Yeah, we went to uni together; he was my flat mate for three years. Called a couple of months ago, wanted to borrow my place in Marseilles to propose to his girlfriend. We talked about Ryan Media's expansion to the New York office." We watched as Bennett stopped at a table on the far side of the room, smiling like an idiot before bending to kiss a stunning brunette.

"I'm guessing France did the trick." Will laughed.

But it wasn't the future Mrs. Bennett Ryan who had my attention. It was the beautiful woman who stood beside her, reaching for her purse. Caramel-honey hair, the same red lips I'd been kissing at the club, the same wide brown eyes.

It was all I could do to stay in my chair and not go straight to her. She smiled at Bennett, and then he said something that made both women laugh as the three of them left the restaurant and I could do nothing but stare on.

I supposed it was time to pay my old friend a visit.

"Max Stella." Large metal doors separating an inner office from Ryan Media's outer reception area opened, and The Man Himself walked out to meet me. "How the hell are you?"

I stepped away from the floor-to-ceiling windows overlooking Fifth Avenue and shook Bennett's hand. "Brilliant," I said, glancing around.

The space itself was at least two stories high in the atrium, and the polished marble flooring gleamed in the full sun. A small seating area was set off to the side, with leather couches and an enormous glass-bubble chandelier hanging from at least twenty feet up. Behind the broad reception desk, a smooth waterfall was built into the wall, the water cascading over slate-blue stone. A small cluster of employees hurried from the elevators to various offices, throwing Bennett nervous glances.

"Looks like you're settling right in."

He motioned for me to follow him inside. "We're slowly getting things rolling. New York is, after all, still New York."

He led me into his office, a corner suite with seamless windows and a breathtaking view of the park.

"And the fiancée?" I asked, nodding to a framed photograph on his desk. "I'm guessing she liked the Mediterranean. Why else would she agree to marry an arrogant twat like you?"

Bennett laughed. "Chloe is perfect. Thanks for letting me take her there."

I shrugged. "Just an empty house most of the time. I'm glad it did the trick."

Gesturing for me to sit, Bennett sat himself in a large wingback chair, his back to a wall of windows. "It's been a while. How are things?"

"Fantastic."

"So I hear." He scratched his jaw, studying me. "I'd love for you to come over sometime now that we're moved in. I've told Chloe all about you."

"I hope that's a slight exaggeration." Of anyone in New York, Bennett Ryan probably had the most dirt from my wildest days.

"Well," he conceded, "I've told her just enough to want to meet you."

"I'd love to catch up, any time." I glanced at the buildings out the window behind him, hesitating. Bennett wasn't easy to read in these kinds of situations; it was one of the things that made him so good at what he did. "But I'll admit that I'm here to ask a favor."

He leaned forward, smiling. "I figured."

I'd comfortably worked with some of the most intimidating people in the world, but Bennett Ryan never failed to make me take the time to choose my words carefully. Particularly when asking about something this . . . delicate.

"I've been a bit preoccupied with a woman I met the other night. I let her go before getting her number, and have been kicking myself ever since. As luck would have it, I spotted her having lunch with you and your lovely Chloe yesterday afternoon."

He considered me for a moment. "You're talking about Sara?"

"Sara," I said, perhaps a bit too triumphantly.

"Oh no," he said, immediately shaking his head. "Not a chance, Max."

"What?" But with Bennett I couldn't maintain an innocent expression for long. The man knew me only from my university days. Maybe not my best representation of good behavior.

"Chloe will have my balls if she finds out I let you anywhere near Sara. No way."

I pressed a hand to my chest. "I'm wounded, mate. What if my intentions are honorable?"

Bennett laughed and stood to walk over to the window. "Sara's . . ." He hesitated. "She's just come out of a bad breakup. And you're . . ." He looked at me and raised an eyebrow. "You're not her type."

"Come on, Ben. I'm not a nineteen-year-old wanker anymore."

He threw me an amused smirk. "Okay, but you're talking to the man who saw you successfully hook up with three women in a single evening, without any of them knowing about the others."

I grinned. "You've got it all wrong. They were all very well acquainted by the end of the night."

"Are you shitting me?"

"Just give me her number. We'll consider it a thank-you for the loan of my gorgeous villa."

"You are such an asshole."

"I believe I've heard that before," I said, standing. "Sara and I, we had . . . an interesting conversation."

"A conversation. *Sara* had a *conversation* with you. I'm skeptical."

"A rather enjoyable one, yes. She's intriguing, that little one. Unfortunately, we were interrupted before I could get her name."

"I see."

"What luck I had, running into you lot and all." I raised my eyebrows expectantly.

"Lucky, yes . . ." Smiling, Bennett took his seat again, looking up at me. "But I'm afraid you'll have to find your luck somewhere else. I'm quite fond of my testicles; I'd like to keep them. I'm not going to smooth the way for you here."

"You always were a prick."

"So I've heard. Lunch Thursday?"

"You bet."

I left Bennett's office intent on having a look around the company's new quarters. They'd taken over three floors of the building and I'd heard they'd already had quite a bit of work done. The spacious atrium was breathtaking, but the office areas were just as lush, with wide hallways, travertine floors, and plenty of natural light coming through windows, glass block walls, and skylights. Each office seemed to have a small sitting area—nothing to match Bennett's, but perfect for sit-downs that didn't call for the formality of a conference room.

That said, the conference room was breathtaking: a wall of windows looking out on midtown Manhattan, a wide polished walnut table that seated at least thirty, and state-of-the-art technology for presentations.

"Not bad, Ben," I murmured, walking back into the hallway and staring up at a large Timothy Hogan photography installment. "Good taste in art for a total wanker."

"What are you *doing* here?"

I looked up to find a very surprised Sara frozen halfway down the hall. I couldn't help breaking into a grin; this really was my lucky day.

Or . . . not, if her expression was any indication.

"*Sara!*" I sang. "What a lovely surprise. I was just at a meeting. I'm Max, by the way. Pleasure to finally put a name to the"—I dropped my eyes and studied her chest, and then the rest of her, through her snug black dress—"face."

Christ, she was hot.

When I looked back up, her eyes had grown to roughly the size of dinner plates. Honestly, the woman had the most enormous brown eyes. If they were any bigger, she'd be a lemur.

She grabbed my arm, pulling me down a hallway, her fitted knee-high boots clacking on the stone tiles.

"Lovely to see you again so soon, *Sara*."

"How did you find me?" she whispered.

"A friend of a friend." I waved my hand dismissively and looked her over. Her bangs were swept to the side and held in place by a tiny red clip, which matched her full crimson lips. She looked like she had stepped right out of some sixties photo shoot. *"Sara* is quite a lovely name, you know."

She narrowed her eyes. "I should have guessed you're a psychopath."

I laughed. "Not quite."

A young woman walked by, ducking her head and muttering a timid, "Good afternoon, Miss Dillon," before scampering away.

And we have a last name. Thank you, terrified intern!

"Aaah, Sara Dillon," I crowed. "Perhaps we could continue this conversation in a more private location?"

She looked around and dropped her voice. "I'm not having sex with you in my office, if that's what you're here for."

Oh, she was fantastic. "I actually just came by to welcome you properly to New York. But I suppose I could just do that out here . . ."

"You have two minutes," she said, turning on her heel and moving toward her office.

We turned corner after corner, finally reaching another smaller reception area lined in windows overlooking the city skyline. A young man sitting at a circular desk looked up at us as we passed.

"I'll be in my office, George," she said over her shoulder. "No interruptions, please."

With the door closed behind us, she turned to face me. "Two minutes."

"If pressed, I *could* get you off in two minutes." I stepped forward, reaching out to brush my thumb along her hip. "But I think we both know that you'd like me to take longer."

"Two minutes to explain why you're here," she clarified, her voice shaking slightly. "And how you found me."

"Well," I began, "I met this woman on Saturday. Fucked her against a wall, in fact. And I haven't been able to stop thinking about her. She was extraordinary. Beautiful, funny, sexy as hell. But she didn't give me her name, and she left me with nothing but her knickers. That could hardly even be considered a trail of breadcrumbs." I closed the distance between us, tucking her hair behind her ear and running my nose along the side of her jaw. "And when I came this morning, touching myself while thinking about how she felt, I still didn't know what name to say."

Clearing her throat, Sara pushed me away, moving to the other side of her desk. "That doesn't explain how you found me," she said, cheeks flushed.

I'd seen her under the strobe lights, head thrown back and eyes closed, but I wanted to see her bare, with the sunlight streaming in through her office windows. I wanted to know exactly how far that blush would spread down her body.

I dropped the teasing bit a little. This Sara was so starkly different from the flirtatious Chicago transplant I'd met at the bar. "I happened to see you at lunch yesterday with Ben. We go way back. I simply put two and two together and hoped I'd see you again."

"You told *Bennett* about Saturday?" she hissed, and the flush I'd been admiring drained from her face.

"God, no. I assure you, I don't have a death wish. I just asked for your number. He refused."

Her shoulders relaxed the smallest bit. "Okay."

"Look, it's a coincidence that I saw you, and I'm coming off a bit strong by being here, but I did want to see Ben regardless. If you ever want to have dinner . . ." I dropped my card on her desk and turned to leave.

"The video," she said abruptly. "What did you do with it?"

I turned back, and the urge to tease her became almost unbearable. But the longer I took to answer, the more panicked she appeared.

Finally she broke. "Did you put it on YouTube or PornTube or whatever sites people use?"

I burst out laughing, unable to keep it in. "What?"

"Just please tell me you didn't."

"God, of course not! I'll admit I've watched it approximately seven hundred thousand times. But, no, I would never *share* it."

She looked down at her hands in front of her, picking at her fingernail. "Could I see it?"

What was that in her voice? Curiosity? Something more?

I moved around the desk to stand behind her. She was still tense but she leaned back against me, her hands clenched in fists at her sides. I pulled my phone from my jacket and found the video, pressing play and holding it up for her to see.

With the volume up, the beat of the music played from the small speakers. She appeared on the screen, dancing with her arms above her head, and just like the first time I watched it in person, I felt myself begin to harden.

"That right there," I said against her neck, "is when you wondered whether I'd notice your dress hitching up. In't it?" I pressed my hips against her backside, leaving no question as to what she was doing to me.

I set my phone on the desk in front of her, placing my hand on her waist. "And there," I said, nodding to the video again. She picked up my phone and looked at it more closely. "The way you looked at me over your shoulder, that's my favorite part. That look on your face, it's like you're dancing just for me."

"Oh God," she whispered. I hoped she was remembering what it felt like, what it was like to have me watch her.

And then she picked up my hand and moved it slowly to the hem of her dress, which she lifted to her hip. Her skin was smooth beneath my palm, and I slipped my hand to her stomach, the muscles of her abdomen quivering under my touch.

"*Were* you dancing for me?" I asked, needing the reminder.

She nodded, pushing my hand lower. Christ, this woman was a tangle of contradictions.

"What else did you think about?" I asked. "Did you think about my face between your thighs, and my mouth?"

She nodded again, biting her lip.

"I wanted to touch you," I said, my hand moving down beneath her underwear. "Just like this."

Her body bowed beneath me, curving against my own to bend over the desk. "I want to feel how wet you are," I said, my breath ragged, my voice low and rough. "How wet you are knowing that I came this morning while watching you."

My fingers slipped lower.

She gasped.

"Are you watching?" I asked, pushing a single finger inside. She nodded and I slipped in a second, my thumb moving in circles over her clit. "You're so fucking *wet*," I said, my teeth dragging along her shoulder.

"We . . . shouldn't do this here," she said.

And still, she pushed farther into my hand. All around my steady rhythm, I could feel her begin to tighten, her breath coming out in tiny, sharp pants.

With a guilty wince, I removed my hand and turned her to face me. She looked practically drugged, eyelids heavy, lips parted.

"And unfortunately my two minutes are up."

I kissed her cheek, the corner of her mouth, and then each of her eyelids when she closed her eyes. And then I took my phone out of her hand and walked out of her office.

Three

A stranger took video of me dancing.

And then he found where I worked—because apparently he's buddies with *my boss*—and I asked him to show me the video.

Following that, I made him put his hands in my *underwear*—again, but this time in my new *office*—and proved to both of us how much the idea of him touching himself while watching the video turned me on.

"Oh, dear God."

"That's the tenth time you've said that in the past fifteen minutes, Sara. Come out here and spill." My assistant, George, leaned against the doorway. "Unless it's so scandalous I need to come in there and close your door."

"It's nothing. I'm just . . ." I straightened the pens in a cup on my desk, tapped some papers into alignment. "Nothing."

He curved his lips into a skeptical smile. "You're a terrible liar."

"Really. It's a huge, gigantic, regrettable nothing."

George walked into my office and collapsed in the chair across from my desk. "Did this Nothing happen at Chloe's engagement party on Saturday?"

"Possibly."

"And was it of the Male Nothing variety?"

"Potentially."

"Was the Male Nothing the slice of Max Stella that was just in your office?"

"What? No!" I lied without blinking. I'd high-five myself later for that bit of unexpected smoothness. George was right the first time: I was a terrible liar. But apparently my shame over the Public Wall Sex Situation was enough to tap into as-yet-unknown skills. "And how do you know who Max Stella is?"

George made careful study of local, hot men, but seeing as how he arrived only a week before I did— a New Yorker for all of thirteen days—I didn't think even he could work that fast.

"Let me ask you," he began, "what was the first thing you did when you arrived and had settled into your apartment?"

"Found the closest sources of wine and cupcakes," I said. "Obviously."

He laughed. "Obviously. But because my goal is not to be an old plump spinster, what *I* do is check out the scene. Where are the fun places to eat—dance—party?"

"To meet all of the men," I added.

He acknowledged this with a wink. "*All* of the men. I find out everything I can, and in so doing, I also find out about the Who's Who of the city." He leaned forward and gave me a wide, bright smile. "In this city, Max Stella is a Who."

"A *who*? How?"

He laughed. "He's a Page Six darling. City of London import a few years back. Brilliant VC mastermind, always fucking some hot celebrity or trust fund princess. Different flavor of arm candy every week. La la la."

Great. I'd managed to select the same slutty publicity hound make and model as my previous boyfriend. But here, not only was Max a well-known womanizer, he was a high-profile venture capitalist, whom I would no doubt cross paths with time and again for work. And who had video of me dancing like a stripper while I imagined his head between my legs.

I groaned again. "Oh, dear God."

"Calm down. You look like you're about to pass out. Have you had lunch?"

"No."

"Look. You're way ahead here. We only have four contracts that require any kind of attention and if what Henry told me about you is true, I'm guessing you've combed through them a hundred times already. Chloe hasn't even received any furniture for her office, her assistant isn't even in New York yet, and Bennett's only chewed out three people today. Clearly, nothing is on fire here that requires your attention. There's plenty of time for you to slow down and get some food."

I took a deep breath, smiling gratefully at him. "Henry trained you well."

George had been hired as Henry Ryan's assistant at Ryan Media after I finished my business degree and left for a big commercial firm. When Bennett called to offer me the Director of Finance position in the new branch, Henry emailed, telling me that if I did join the New York offices, he was going to make sure Bennett assigned me George, who was dying to relocate.

George smiled back and gave me a sweet little salute. "Henry told me you were impossible to replace and to not even try. I had something to prove."

"You're amazing."

"Oh, girl, I know," he said. "And I consider it part of my assistant duties to ensure you know where to go to have fun. Cupcakes, wine, or *otherwise*."

My mind immediately went to the image of the club on Saturday, packed with people and vibrating with the volume of music, voices, feet pounding. Again, Max's face flashed through my thoughts, the sound he made when he came, the sheer size of him in front of me, pressing me to the wall, lifting me, and gliding in and out.

I pressed my face into my hands. Now that I knew

who he was, and he wanted to see me again? I was screwed.

George stood up, walked around to my side of the desk, and pulled me up by my arm. "Right. Go, get some food. I'll pull the Agent Provocateur contracts and you can deal with them when you're back. Breathe, Sara."

Grudgingly, I went and grabbed my purse from my closet. George was right. Aside from the celebration with the girls two nights ago, and the sleepless nights I'd spent unpacking my new home, I'd spent a majority of my time at the office, trying to get everything up and running. Much of the three floors we rented in the shining glass and steel midtown building was still empty, and without the rest of my department or the marketing team here yet, we couldn't do our thing: the world's best media campaigns.

Chloe had stayed on at Ryan Media when I left, taking over several accounts in Marketing with Bennett. But it was her brilliant work on the enormous Papadakis campaign that had catapulted the company into overdrive, and it had quickly become clear that a New York branch would be needed to handle some of these larger accounts. Bennett, Henry, and Elliott Ryan had spent two weeks in the city to find the perfect office space, and then it was all under way: Ryan Media Group would have another home in midtown.

Michigan Avenue in Chicago was bustling, but it had nothing on Fifth Avenue, Manhattan. I felt buried by an endless grid of streets, hulking masses of architecture, and the constant people, traffic, and noise. Horns blared around me, and the longer I stood still, the more the sound of the city grew deafening. Did I go left or right to find the hidden little Chinese place Bennett liked? What was it called—Something Garden? I stood, struggling to get my bearings, while a stream of businessmen and women parted around me like water around a rock sitting dumbly in a river.

But just as I reached for my phone to text Chloe, I saw a familiar tall shape duck into a doorway across the street. I looked up at the name on the tiny storefront: HUNAN GARDEN.

The restaurant was dim, practically empty, and smelled amazing. I couldn't remember the last time I'd eaten anything more substantial than a granola bar. My mouth watered and, for a moment, I forgot that I was supposed to be on high alert.

I'd moved here to start fresh. Starting fresh meant putting my career first, finding *myself*—not falling into another messed-up Stepford relationship. And that settled that. I *would* get my lunch there, but I would do it after telling Max he needed to never, ever come into my workspace like that again. And that when I put his hand under my dress just now it was a total accident. Complete slip. Unintentional.

"Sara?"

My name was a quiet, erotic sound in his accent, and I turned toward his voice. He was in a booth in the corner, peeking around a tall menu in his hands. He lowered it, clearly surprised, but then he smiled and I wanted to smack him for how jittery that made me feel. His features were even more prominent in the low shadows of the restaurant. He looked even more dangerous.

I walked to his table and ignored the way he moved over to let me in beside him. His hair was cut short and left longer on top. It fell forward when he moved and I wanted to reach out, see if it was as soft as it looked beneath the cone of overhead light. Damnit.

"I'm not here to join you," I said, straightening my shoulders. "I just needed to get a few things straight."

He spread his palms out in front of him. "By all means."

Taking a deep breath, I said, "I had the most fun I can reasonably remember with you at the club the other night—"

"Likewise."

I held up my hand. "But I moved here to start over. I wanted to do something crazy and I did, but that isn't who I am. I love my job and my colleagues. I can't have you walking into my office to flirt with me. I can't ever act like that at work again." I leaned forward and lowered my voice. "And I can't believe you kept that video."

He had the presence of mind to look contrite. "I'm sorry. I really did intend to delete it." Leaning forward on his elbows, he said, "The thing is, I can't seem to stop watching it. Watching that is better than a shot of fucking whiskey for my nerves. Better than even the filthiest porn."

A low hum spread through my belly and between my legs.

"And I suspect that you like hearing that. I also suspect that the wild Petal I met at the club is a much larger part of Sara Dillon than you like to think."

"She's not." I shook my head. "And I can't do this."

"*This*," he said, "is simply a meal. Sit down with me."

I didn't move.

"Come on." He sighed quietly. "You let me fuck you on Saturday, you put my hand beneath your clothes a few minutes ago, and now you won't join me for lunch. Do you always make a point of being so confusing?"

"Max."

"Sara."

I hesitated for a long beat before I slid into the booth beside him, and felt the radiating warmth of his long, solid frame next to me.

"You look beautiful," he said.

I looked down at the simple black dress I wore. My bare legs peeked out below the hem and just above the knees. He ran a finger from my shoulder to my wrist and my bare skin broke out in gooseflesh.

"I won't come to your office again like that," he said, so quietly I had to lean a little closer to hear him. "But I do want to see you again."

I shook my head, staring at his long fingers on me. "I don't think that would be a good idea."

When the waiter stopped at our table, Max's fingers lingered on my hand, and when I was unable to think of anything to order, he chose meals for both of us.

"I hope you like prawns," he said, grinning.

"I do." His hand on mine, his leg so closely pressed to my thigh, what did I want? I didn't want to be continually distracted by a force of energy like Max, but I remained unable to pull out of his orbit. "Sorry, I'm a little distracted."

His other hand crossed over his body and slipped below the table. I felt the light brush of fingers along my thigh. "Distracted by me? Or by work?"

"At the moment, you. But I *should* be distracted by work."

"You have plenty of time for that. I'm going to wager your assistant sent you out to eat."

I leaned back to look at him. "Spying?"

"No need. He looks like a busybody, and you look like you rarely remember to take lunch." His fingers pushed the hem of my dress up higher, higher, higher to my hip bone. "This all right?" His accent dropped the last bit of his sentence into a whisper.

It was more than all right, but my heart pounded with a mixture of excitement and anxiety. Once again, I was letting him completely take my reason away, hide it in this dark corner where I couldn't find it.

"We're in a restaurant."

"I'm aware." He slipped beneath the soaked lace of my panties and slid his fingers over my clit, dipping down into my wetness. "Good God, Sara. I'd love to spread you on this table and have *you* for lunch."

For a brief pulse, my skin ignited. "You can't say things like that."

"Why? We're the only people in this place besides that old man in the corner, the waiter, and the cook in the back. No one can hear me."

"That isn't what I meant."

"I can't say things like that because of what it does to you?" he asked.

I nodded, unable to say anything when he slipped two fingers into me.

"We have maybe ten minutes before our food comes out. Think I could make you come that fast?"

It wasn't as if he didn't already have two fingers deep

inside me, but for some reason when he put it like that, I grew hyperaware of where we were. It was a torment: the knowledge of what I *should* do in a quiet restaurant like this—sip my tea, eat my lunch—and the desire to do something completely unlike me: have this man finger me where anyone could walk in and see.

It was the same crazy fantasy from the club, all over again: the potential of being caught with this beautiful, strange man, and getting away with it.

He began to move his thumb in small circles, but kept his fingers pressed deep, unmoving. His arm barely shifted above the table, but below where the tablecloth hit our hips, an explosion was building.

I stared at his arm, his dress shirt peeking out from his suit jacket, and could feel him watching my face, watching every single breath I took, every gasp and every time I bit my lip to keep from making a sound. His confident, firm touch built a heavy ache between my legs and I pushed into him, wanting more, and harder somehow. In the distance a dish crashed to the floor, but Max quietly moaning my name immediately eclipsed the sound.

Our waiter emerged from the kitchen and headed toward us.

"Look at you," Max said, leaning to kiss my neck just below my ear. His breath was warm on my skin, and I was torn between focusing on his touch and fretting about the man walking across the room toward our table. The combination of his touch and the fear of being caught almost made me fall to pieces.

As if he knew this, Max murmured, "No one in here knows you're about to come all over my hand."

I expected him to stop, to put his hands on the table, but Max simply stilled his thumb as the waiter stopped at our table, and refilled his water. Ice clinked against the glass, and a drop of condensation slid from the rim to the tablecloth, fanning out and growing larger and larger as more water fell. It was as if the glass were melting along with me. From above the table, it looked like Max had simply reached across his body and put his hand on my leg. He slid his thumb across my clit once, and I gasped.

"Your food should be out in just a minute," the waiter said with a bland smile.

Max pressed his thumb hard into my clit and I bit the inside of my cheek to keep from crying out. He smiled up at the waiter. "Thank you."

The waiter turned and walked away and when Max looked at me, with such barely concealed mischief, dizzying relief mixed with a vague stab of disappointment, and I felt myself fully melt in his hands.

"That's it," he whispered, rocking his palm against

me as he slipped a third finger inside. With this, he stretched me to the blissful edge of pain and I felt indecent, like I was doing something irrevocably filthy, but he just watched me crave more of it all. "Oh, fuck, Sara. That's it."

My nails dug into the leather cushion below me, and he risked being noticed by beginning to pump his fingers, his shoulders rocking. My head fell back against the booth and I let out the smallest moan, completely disproportionate to the shaking climax that tore through my body.

"Oh God," I groaned as he prolonged it with his long fingers pushing even deeper. I turned to press my face into the shoulder of his suit to stifle my cry.

He slowed, and stilled, before kissing my temple, and then pulled his fingers out. Lifting his hand from under the table, he pressed his fingers to his mouth once, briefly, before wiping them on his napkin.

And then he licked his lips, watching me. "Your tongue tastes like candy, but your pussy tastes even better." He leaned in and kissed me deeply. "I want it to be my cock inside you next time."

Yes, please.

Jesus, who was this woman possessing my brain? Because I wanted it, too. Even after what he'd just given me, I wanted to climb into his lap and take all of him inside.

Before that line of thinking could get me into even more trouble, my phone buzzed in my purse. I pulled it out: Bennett.

BACK FROM MY MEETING. LET'S SIT DOWN AT 2.

The clock on my phone read one forty-five. "I have to go."

"We're establishing a pattern here, Sara. You come, you go."

I offered him a half-smile, half-wince, but when the waiter came back with our food, I slid a twenty onto the table and asked him to put mine in a to-go container.

"I'd like your number," Max said, stuffing the money back in my purse.

"Absolutely not." I laughed.

I had no idea how this had unraveled. Okay, that was a lie, I knew exactly how it had unraveled—he'd started whispering in that hot accent and then fingered me—but I knew better than to let myself get involved with Max. For one, he was a player, and in no way did I want to go down that road again. And two, my job. It had to come first.

"I will eventually get it from Ben, you know. We go way back."

"Bennett won't give it to you without my permission.

Very few people want to punch my ex more than I do, but Bennett is one of them." I kissed Max's jaw, relished the sharp stubble, and got up. "Thanks for the appetizer. Delete the video."

"I'll consider it if you go out with me again," he answered, eyes shining with amusement.

I exited and crossed back over Fifth, biting back a smile.

Four

Three days after I'd given her an orgasm for lunch I wasn't any less obsessed.

"So who are you bringing tonight?" Will asked absently, eyes on the folded copy of the *Times* in his hand.

The drive back to the office from the tailor had been silent up to this point, broken only by the sound of the engine and the occasional car horn or shout from the street. I continued to go over the files I'd brought—photographs from a new exhibit in Queens—as I answered, "Going solo, actually."

He looked up at me. "You don't have a date?"

"No." I glanced over just in time to see his eyebrows inch up in surprise. "What?"

"How long have we known each other, Max?"

"Six years, I'd say."

"And in all that time, have you ever attended a social function without a date?"

"I really wouldn't remember."

"Perhaps we could check Page Six. I bet they'd know," he deadpanned.

"Very funny."

"It's unusual, that's all. It's our biggest event of the year and you don't have a date."

"It hardly matters, yeah?"

He laughed. "Are you serious with me right now? 'Who is Max Stella taking?' is one of the first things people ask when there's a party like this."

"I like how you play me up as the skirt-chasing wolf in contrast to you, all upstanding and virtuous."

"Oh, I never said anything about being virtuous," he said over the top of his paper. "I'm simply suggesting that people might wonder if you're meeting someone there, that's all."

I turned back to my files as I considered this. In truth, I hadn't made a date for the fund-raiser. I hadn't made a date because I wasn't interested in taking anyone.

Which was weird. Maybe Will was right. Ever since I'd met Sara, other women seemed predictable and tame.

Will was also right when he said the annual Stella & Sumner Charity Gala was our biggest event of the summer. It was held at the Museum of Modern Art, and everyone who was anyone in New York would be in attendance. With dancing, dinner, and the silent auction that followed, we managed to raise hundreds of thousands of dollars for a pediatric cancer foundation every year.

The dreary sky of the afternoon had cleared, but the

smell of a storm still hung in the air when my car stopped at the barricades in front of the museum. A valet opened my door and I climbed out, fastening the button of my tuxedo jacket as I stood. My name was called from several directions, the pop and flash of cameras erupting like a small lightning storm within the press area.

"Max! Where's the date?"

"Max, quick photo! Quick, over here!"

"Any truth to the rumor of a Smithsonian endowment?"

I smiled and posed for pictures, waving as I made my way inside. I felt like I was on autopilot, glad that I'd kept the press from inside the event tonight. I simply didn't have the energy.

Guests were directed through the museum and out to the garden, where the majority of the party would be held, where crowds of well-dressed people mingled while sipping cocktails and champagne, discussing money and each other and whoever happened to be the gossip of the day. A series of white tents had been erected, each of them lit from below by pools of brightly colored light. An orchestra sat at one end of the garden, a DJ booth for the after party at the other.

The air was heavy and humid, and the night clung to my skin almost uncomfortably. I crossed to a line of large tables dressed in white and dripping in crystal. Reaching for a flute of champagne, I felt someone come near beside me.

"Perfect as usual, Max. You've really outdone yourself."

I blinked over to see Bennett standing next to me.

"It's bloody hot out here, is what it is," I said, nodding toward the drink he held in each hand. "Here with your Chloe, I assume."

"And your date is . . ."

"Flying solo tonight," I answered. "Hosting duties and what have you."

Bennett laughed, bringing his glass to his lips. He didn't comment but it was impossible to miss the way his eyes shifted over my shoulder.

I turned just in time to see Chloe and Sara walking back from the restroom. Sara looked stunning in a light green gown with beading covering the bodice and trickling into the skirt. Silver stilettos peeked out beneath the hem of her dress.

It took a moment before I could speak.

"She's here with someone, Max."

I turned and gaped at Bennett before looking around our immediate vicinity to try to spot who she might have come with. "She is? Who?"

"Me."

"Wait, what? No way."

"Christ, I'm kidding. Look at your face." He scratched his jaw and waved casually at someone across the room and I legitimately wanted to punch him.

"Max," he said, voice low and serious now. "Sara is Chloe's best friend and an important member of my team. I trust your business sense more than I trust almost anyone's, but your history with women is not exactly pristine.

I'm the last person to point fingers, trust me, but don't do anything stupid."

"Calm down. It's not as if I'm planning to drag her off for a romp in the coat closet or anything."

"Wouldn't be the first time," he said with a smile, draining his glass.

"For you, either, mate," I answered.

Bennett looked almost relieved as I left him at the table, and for the briefest of moments, I felt almost guilty for lying to him. The truth was that while I *did* want to drag Sara off to the nearest coat closet, I also wanted a moment to just watch her.

I made my way across the garden, shaking a few hands and thanking others for their donations, keeping Sara in my peripheral vision as I went. I stopped to the side of the large Lachaise nude sculpture and watched her from a distance, captivated by how beautiful she looked tonight.

Her gown was long and fitted, displaying every curve perfectly and emphasizing some of my favorite ones.

I remembered the way she'd looked that night on the dance floor, wild in her too-short dress and too-high shoes, and compared that to the sophisticated woman here tonight. I could tell even then that what we'd done had been out of character for her. But I don't think I'd understood exactly how much until tonight. She was poised and delicate . . . though, still, there was something else, some neglected recklessness beneath her prim exterior.

My eyes moved along the line of her throat and across her collarbone, and I wondered what she was wearing under her gown. I wondered what had brought forth the woman who had fucked me against a wall in a club full of people.

I was fairly certain Bennett hadn't been joking when he'd suggested I stay away from Sara. Or that his fiancée would have his balls—and mine, too—if she found out. Bennett was obviously aware that I had more than a casual interest in Sara, but he was tight as a vault and, despite his protests, would never interfere if this were what Sara wanted.

But Chloe—she was a different matter altogether. She seemed too smart, her gaze too knowing. I didn't know much about the future Mrs. Ryan, but I was sure that if Bennett had finally met his match, I did not want to be on her bad side.

And despite that, I was quite enjoying this little game Sara and I seemed to be playing.

When the orchestra shifted into a slower song, I watched as a few people excused themselves from their circles and ventured out onto the dance floor. I walked around the edge of the garden, stepping behind Sara and tapping her on one bare shoulder.

She turned, her smile slipping from her face when she saw me.

"Well, hello to you, too," I said.

Sara took a long sip from her champagne flute before addressing me. "How are you tonight, Mr. Stella?"

Mr. Stella, was it? I smiled. "I see you've done a little checking up on me. I must have made quite an impression."

She returned a polite smile. "A quick Google search gives a girl plenty of information."

"Hasn't anyone ever told you the Internet is full of rumor and falsehood?" I stepped closer, brushing the backs of my fingers along her arm. It was soft and smooth, and I noted the way goose bumps spread along her skin. "You look stunning tonight, by the way."

She met my eyes, sizing me up. Even as she put a little distance between us, she murmured, "You don't look so bad yourself."

I feigned shock. "Did you just compliment me?"

"I may have."

"It would be a shame for both of us to have gotten all dressed up and not share a dance. Wouldn't you agree?" Sara glanced around the garden and I added, "Just a dance, Petal."

She emptied her glass and set it on the tray of a passing waiter. "Just a dance."

Placing my hand on the small of her back, I guided her to a dimly lit corner of the dance floor.

"I enjoyed our lunch the other day," I said, taking her in my arms. "Perhaps we could do it again. Maybe with a slightly different menu?"

She smirked, and looked past me.

I pulled her body flush to mine, eliciting that little quirk of her eyebrow I was beginning to like so much. "So how are you finding New York?"

"Different," she said. "Bigger. Noisier." She tilted her head, finally looking up at me. "The men are a little pushy."

I laughed. "You say that as if it's a bad thing."

"I suppose that would depend on the man."

"And what about *this* man?"

She blinked away, smiling politely again. It struck me that Sara behaved like a woman who was very much used to being watched in public.

"Look, I'm flattered by your attention, Max. But why are you so interested in me? Can't we admit we had a good time and leave it at that?"

"I like you," I said, shrugging. "I rather like your kink."

She laughed. "My kink? That's one I've never heard before."

"Well, that's a shame. Tell me, when you fantasize, what's it about? Is it about sweet, gentle sex in a bed?"

She looked up at me with a challenge in her eyes. "Sometimes, yes."

"But is it also about being touched in a restaurant, where anyone could see?" I leaned in, whispering against the shell of her ear. "Or fucked in a club?"

I felt her swallow, felt her shaky breath before she straightened, putting a socially acceptable amount of distance between us. "Sometimes, of course. Who doesn't have those fantasies?"

"A lot of people don't. And even more people don't ever act on them."

"Why are you so hung up on this? I'm sure you could turn that smile on any woman here and take her in any room in this museum."

"Because, unfortunately, I don't want any other woman here. You've become quite a mystery to me. How can you house such a paradox behind those big brown eyes? Who was that woman who fucked me in front of all those people?"

"Maybe I just wanted to see how it felt to do something crazy like that."

"And it felt amazing, didn't it?"

There was no hesitating when she looked up at me. "Yes. But look," she said, taking a step back. My arms fell to my sides. "I'm not interested in being anyone's plaything right now."

"I believe I'm asking to be yours."

Shaking her head, she fought a smile and looked up at me. "Stop being cute."

"Meet me upstairs."

"What? No."

"The empty ballroom adjacent to the restrooms. It's up the stairs and to your right." I stepped closer, then kissed her cheek as if to thank her for the dance.

I left her there just as the music came to a stop and they announced that dinner would be served inside, immediately followed by the auction. I wondered if she would do it. If she would risk being missed, if she felt the same buzz of adrenaline I felt.

The sound of conversation built as I stepped out of the humid night and into the air-conditioned museum. I climbed the wide staircase and meandered down the hall into the empty, unlit ballroom. The voices dimmed as I pulled the door behind me, leaving it open just a sliver.

I waited just inside for a beat, listening to the muted sounds of the party as it continued downstairs and outside, and listening to make sure I was truly alone in the dark room.

The occasional patron walked down the carpeted hall and inside the empty ballroom, making brief phone calls or looking for the restrooms. It felt as if every sound I made echoed out into the hallway, my shoes slapping on the wood floor as I took note of the layout. The room was longer than it was wide, and the city glowed through the windows on the long side of the room, the hum of traffic steady on the streets below. Along the far, short wall was a rectangular table partially hidden by an ornate screen. The room was otherwise completely empty. I walked over and leaned against the table, behind the screen and even farther out of sight as I waited.

Over fifteen minutes after I'd left her—and after I'd almost given up on waiting any longer—the slice of light through the door expanded and cut across the floor. I watched the shape of her body through the screen, backlit from the light in the hall. I knew that in the darkness, I remained invisible to her, and I took the opportunity to watch her as she scanned the room. I could imagine the pulse in her throat hammering with nerves and excitement. Stepping out from behind the screen, I finally let her see me, a silhouette against the light of the city.

She crossed the room, eyes on mine as she slowly closed the distance between us. Her expression was hard to make out in the dim lighting, and I waited for her to speak, to tell me to go to hell or even to ask me to fuck her again, but she said nothing. She paused with just inches between us, hesitating for only a moment before grabbing my jacket and pulling me to her.

Her lips were warm and insistent and she tasted of champagne. I imagined her downing a glass, hoping to find the courage to come up here and do exactly this. The thought made me moan, eyes fluttering closed as she opened her mouth to me, her head tilted back as her tongue pushed against mine. I palmed her breast with one hand, gripping her hip hard with the other.

"Take this off," she said, hands fumbling with my tie, fingers tugging at my buttons.

I walked us backward and unzipped her dress, watching it slip from her body to pool around her feet at the floor. She was completely naked beneath her gown.

"You've been like this the whole time?" I asked, taking one nipple into my mouth and looking up at her.

She nodded, lips parted as she twisted her hands into my hair, whispering words like *more* and *with teeth* and *please.* I guided her down to the table, gripping her behind the knees to pull her toward the edge.

My fingers trailed down her ribs and over her flat stomach. I met her eyes, lifting a brow as I ran my hands over the heels of her shoes. "We'll leave these on, I reckon," I said, looking down at her otherwise naked body. She was perfect: creamy skin, spectacular tits, and taut, pink nipples.

Bending over her, I licked a line down her neck to her breasts, pressing my thumb into a fading mark I'd apparently sucked into her skin on Saturday. "I bet you looked at this every day," I said, admiring my handiwork, pressing just a bit harder.

"Too much talking," she said, pushing open my shirt. "Too many clothes."

I grazed my teeth across her nipple, sucking, blowing across the hardened peak. "Touch me," I said, pressing her palm over my cock.

She squeezed and my head fell against her shoulder.

Her hands shook as she unfastened my trousers, hurriedly shoving them down around my hips. She leaned back on the table, her body stretched, the shadows dipping into the hollow of her collarbone, the curve of her breasts.

"Max," she whispered, eyes hooded as she looked up at me.

"Yeah?" I was distracted by her neck, her breasts, her hand curling around my cock.

"Do you have a camera?"

How did she do that? How did someone so contained, so naturally refined, let loose that completely? I reached into my jacket—still hanging open from my shoulders—and pulled out my phone, holding it up to her. "This'll do?"

"Will you take pictures of us?"

I blinked, and then blinked hard again. Was she kidding? "Fuck. Absolutely."

"No faces."

"Of course not."

A beat of silence passed as we both considered what I could do with this gadget in my palm. She wanted pictures of what we were doing. I reeled from the knowledge that she got off on this as much as I did. I could see it in the way her pulse beat wildly in her throat, at the fever in her eyes.

"Nobody else sees them," she said.

I smiled. "I don't relish the idea of sharing any part of you. Of course no one else sees them."

She leaned back and I brought the phone up, aiming at her. The first shot was of her shoulder. The second of her hand on her breast, her nipple caught between her fingers. A soft moan left her lips as I smoothed my hand up her thigh to slip between her legs.

Voices echoed in the hall, pulling us out of our dark corner and back into the reality of where we were, and how we both eventually needed to return downstairs. I rolled a condom down my length and reached up to press my thumb to her mouth, slipping it inside.

She answered wordlessly, wrapping her legs around my hips and trying to pull me closer. I watched myself slide into her just as the door to the ballroom creaked open.

As it had before, the brightness from the hall spilled into the room, filtering through the screen and painting her torso with its ribbon of light. Her breath caught but I didn't stop, instead lifting her chin and motioning for her to stay quiet as I pushed into her again. Heat spread from my cock up my spine at the feel of her around me.

She closed her eyes tight and I gripped her hip to steady myself, thrusting into her harder, pulling her farther down the table toward me. The light from the city was just enough for me to capture a sensual, dark photo of my hand on her skin. Footsteps crossed the room toward the window, and her legs tightened around me as if to keep me from pulling back and away.

I watched her nipples harden, her lips part in excitement. *Don't worry,* I thought with a smile. *I'm not stopping.*

My movements were shallow and I gripped her breast, pinching her nipple. "They're right there," I whispered, bending to kiss her neck and relishing the wild rhythm of her pulse under my lips. "They could see us if they wanted."

Her breath caught and I pinched again, rougher this time. "I'm not pulling back. I just want to push farther and farther and farther in."

"Harder," she begged in a whisper.

"My hand, or how I'm fucking you?"

"Both."

I swore against the skin of her neck. "You're fucking dirty, you know that?"

Her mouth opened in a silent gasp as I rocked into her, wishing I could get even deeper somehow. I felt her stomach tense against mine, her hips roll up with greater insistence. Fuck, she was warm and slick and if she didn't get there soon I was going to go before her. Thankfully, with a squeak, she dug her nails painfully into my shoulder, her body tensing as she came apart around me. I felt lightheaded, euphoric, as if something inside was about to explode.

The sound of footsteps returned, and then came to a quiet stop just on the other side of the screen. I felt my orgasm barrel down on me, white hot and enough to make me see stars. It went dark as I pushed one final time, my head buried in her neck as I let myself drown, lost to every other sensation as I came deep inside her.

And then silence, the collective moment when we struggled to contain our panting breaths, and nobody dared to move.

I became vaguely aware of the sound of breathing just beyond the screen, the stillness of someone waiting. Listening. I turned my head and saw Sara's wide eyes, her teeth buried into her bottom lip. A moment passed, and then another before the footsteps moved on, the light slipping along our sweaty bodies just as the door closed.

Five

Monday morning, I found Chloe in her suddenly cluttered office, staring out the window. Her furniture and all of her boxes had finally arrived, and her pacing and mumbling told me that she was more than a little overwhelmed at the prospect of unpacking.

I'd spent most of the weekend alternating between horror and celebration over what I'd done at the fundraiser, and had come in to work to get my mind to stop looping through and looking too closely at what my actions said about me. I stayed until midnight on Saturday and, unfortunately, made my way through all of the contracts and invoices I needed to get done this week. Other than a handful of phone calls, I had nothing to do, and these days an idle Sara was not a good thing.

"Need help?"

Chloe laughed, flopping down on her couch. "I don't even know where to start. We just finished unpacking our apartment. Plus, I feel like I just packed all of this up."

"Start with your bookshelf. I never feel organized until I can see the neat rows of books all set up."

Shrugging, she slid from the couch and crawled to where a few boxes were stacked against a wall. "Did you have fun at MoMA?"

I opened a box of supplies and pulled out a box cutter. "Definitely."

I could feel her look up at me, and her lingering attention pressed into the side of my face. I probably should have elaborated, but my mind turned completely blank when I struggled with what else to say. What else had happened? We arrived. Had some hors d'oeuvres. Max and I danced, and then I asked him to take pictures while he pounded me on a table.

By the time I remembered the rest—the dinner we'd missed, the silent auction he'd gone to attend, the beautiful garden I'd escaped to after our . . . *encounter*, too much time had already passed for me to add to my one-word answer.

"Good," she said, and I could hear the smirk in her voice. "I'm glad you decided to come. Max and Will apparently host that every year and they raise a ton of money for the charity. I think it's amazing."

"Amazing," I mumbled in agreement, remembering Max in a tux. Good sweet baby Jesus, the man was born for black tie. He looked pretty amazing half naked, too.

I looked out the window, remembered the throbbing heat of his breath on my neck.

"I'm not pulling back," he growled, spreading a huge hand over my breast. "I just want to push farther and farther and farther in."

My breasts weren't small but the size of his hand had made me feel tiny, like he could pick me up and snap me in half. Instead of feeling afraid, I had spread my legs wider, welcomed him deeper.

"Harder."

He pulled back to look at me. "My hand, or how I'm fucking you?"

"Both," I'd admitted, and he bent back low to my neck, biting me.

I found myself wondering about the pictures he'd taken and shivered slightly. I tried not to imagine him looking at them. Maybe even touching himself while he did . . .

Chloe cleared her throat and pulled a few periodicals from her box. I blinked, hard, and looked down at the journals in front of me. *Jesus, where was all this coming from?*

"I saw you talking to Max," she said. "You guys danced for, like, three songs, too. Did you just meet him that night?"

Was she a mind reader? *What in the actual hell, Chloe?*

I didn't look up, and instead mumbled, "Yeah, we just met at the"—I waved my hand in the air—"the thing on Friday."

"He's gorgeous," she said.

Poke. Poke.

I could feel her gaze on me. Chloe was the least subtle poker in the world. She dropped a hint like a strike fighter drops bombs. "Don't you think he's gorgeous?"

Finally I looked up at her and rolled my eyes. "Knock it off. I'm not going to swoon for you over Max Stella. He seemed nice, that's all."

She laughed and shoved a few books on the shelf. "Fine. Just making sure you weren't caught under his spell. He sounds like a great guy, but yeah, definitely a player. At least he's up front about it, though."

She watched me for a minute as I struggled to not react to that. It was a fair dig on Andy, and was the kind of thing she could say in a year or two and we'd both laugh and say, "I know, right?"

But for now her words just kind of dissolved into awkward silence.

"Sorry," she mumbled. "Bad timing. Did you know that Max and Bennett went to school together?"

"Yeah, he mentioned something about that. I didn't know that Bennett went to college in England."

She nodded. "Cambridge. Max was his flat mate

from their first day there. He hasn't shared many stories with me, but the ones he has . . ." She trailed off, shaking her head as her attention returned to the books in front of her.

I was supposed to be uninterested, completely uninterested in all of this, right? So I studied my thumb, and only then did I notice a fresh paper cut.

Get it together, Sara; your brain is so fixated on Max that you no longer sense pain? That's pathetic.

So how does one look when one absolutely does *not* care about the stories that Chloe may have heard? I mean, obviously the fact that he hasn't shared *many* stories means that he's shared *some.*

Right?

I alphabetized a giant stack of periodicals, pretending to be engrossed. Finally, the question felt like it was choking me and I relented. "Like, what kinds of things did they do?"

"Just guy stuff," she said, distracted. "Rugby. Brewing their own beer and the insane parties after. Taking the train to Paris and blah-blah escapades."

I wanted to strangle her. "Escapades?"

She looked up suddenly, as if she remembered something, and her dark eyes definitely had a mischievous shine to them. "Hey, this reminds me. Speaking of escapades . . ."

My stomach fell to my knees.

"You disappeared on Friday night, for like an hour! Where did you go?"

My face heated, and I cleared my throat, furrowing my brow as if I had to work to remember. "Oh, I just felt a little overwhelmed. I, uh, went for a walk around the grounds."

"Damn," she breathed. "I was hoping you ran into a hot caterer and got banged on a table."

A hoarse cough burst out, and my entire throat was suddenly so dry that I couldn't stop coughing.

Chloe stood and got me a cup of water from the cooler in the reception area, returning with a knowing grin. "You are so busted. You always start coughing when you're freaking out."

"I'm fine."

"Lies. Lying liar who lies all the lies. Tell me."

I absolutely refused to look at her. Something about Chloe's dark brown eyes and patient smile directed right at me made me spill everything. "There is nothing to tell."

"Sara, when you disappeared, you came back after being gone for an hour and looked . . ." She tucked a long lock of brown hair behind her ear to reveal a devilish smile. "You know how you looked. Freshly fucked."

I cut a box open and pulled out a stack of design magazines, handing them to her. "And it's too crazy to explain."

"Are you kidding me? You're talking to the woman who had sex with her boss in the eighteenth-floor stairwell."

My head shot up and a laugh burst out. I drank some more water to keep the cough at bay. "Holy crap, Chloe. I didn't know *that* detail." I considered this a little more. "God, good thing I never used the stairs. Gross. That would have been super awkward."

"We were ridiculous. Nothing could be crazier than that." She shrugged and turned her nonjudgmental face on me. "Or, could there be? You tell me."

"Okay," I said, leaning back against her couch. "The guy I met at the bar last week? The hot one?"

"Yeah?"

"He was there on Friday."

Her eyes narrowed, and I could see her gears cranking. "At the fund-raiser?"

"Yeah. He found me outside the restroom," I lied and looked out the window so she wouldn't see it in my eyes. "We hooked up. I guess that's why I looked . . . er, rumpled."

"When you say hooked up you mean . . . ?"

"Yeah. In an empty ballroom." I looked up and met her eyes. "On a table."

She let out a loud whoop and clapped her hands. "Look at you, you wild thing."

It was so like something Max would say to me, but delivered so differently, that for a moment it rendered me a little speechless. It was disorienting to ache for him like this, to wonder what he was doing, and whether he was presently looking at pictures of me spread out beneath him.

"Seriously, Sara, I knew you had it in you," she added.

"The thing is, I don't really want another relationship. And even if I did, I get the impression he isn't really like that." I stopped before spilling too much. If I alluded any more to Max's reputation on Page Six, Chloe would absolutely know who I meant.

She hummed, listening, as she sorted through a stack of journals.

"But he's fun, Chloe. And you know how things were with Andy."

She stopped sorting, but toyed with the corner of a page. "Well, that's the thing, Sare. I *don't* really. I mean, come on; in the three years you and I have known each other, I only had dinner with you guys maybe five times. I learned more about him from the papers than I did from any stories you told me. You hardly ever talked about him! I always just ended up with the sense that he was using your family's reputation to appear well connected and . . . wholesome."

I felt guilt and embarrassment settle in my chest like a lead weight. "I know," I said, inhaling and letting it out again slowly. It was one thing to imagine how people saw me, another to hear it straight out. "I always worried that if I said anything about him to someone, it would be misconstrued, and somehow break his public strategy. Plus, we weren't like you and Bennett. We didn't have a lot of fun together by the time I met you. Andy was a phony and an epic jerk and it took me a really long time to see that. This thing on Friday was just fun."

Chloe looked up. "Hey, it's fine. I knew it was something like that." She turned back to another box. "So this is good then, he's not like Andy."

"Yeah."

"So you mean he's *into* you."

"At least physically, which is fine for me right now."

"So what's the problem? It sounds like the perfect situation."

"He's kind of intense. And I don't really trust him."

Putting down the books in her hand, she turned to face me. "Sara, this is going to sound really weird, but just hear me out, okay?"

"Of course."

"When Bennett and I started . . . whatever it was we were doing, I was determined that every time it happened it would be the last. But I think I always knew it would keep happening until it had run its course. Luckily for us, I don't think we'll ever stop feeling what we felt those first few times. Even so, I didn't trust him. I didn't really even *like* him. Above all of it, he was my *boss*. I mean, hello, inappropriate." She laughed, and following her gaze over to her desk, I saw that the first and only thing she'd unpacked so far was a picture of the two of them at the house in France where he'd proposed to her. "But I think if I'd just given myself permission to enjoy it a *little* bit, it might not have consumed me so much."

I was starting to know exactly what she meant about being consumed. And I knew, too, that I was consciously fighting it with Max, with the *idea* of Max. But my reasons were different. It wasn't a boss-employee thing, or any other kind of power struggle. It was the simple fact that I didn't want to be anyone else's but my own for a while. And although this thing with Max was insane and completely different from anything I'd ever felt before—*I* was different—I liked it. A lot.

"I do like him," I admitted carefully. "But I don't think he's boyfriend material. In fact, I know he's not. And I am most definitely not girlfriend material right now."

"Okay, so maybe you just get together every now and then as fuck buddies."

I laughed, pressing my face into my hands. "Seriously. Whose life is this?"

She looked at me like she wanted to pat my head. "Sara, it's *yours*."

∾

George was reading a newspaper in my office with his feet up on my desk when I returned.

"Working yourself to the bone?" I teased, sitting on the corner of my desk.

"On my lunch break. And you had a package arrive, darling."

"You found it in the mailroom?"

He shook his head and lifted the parcel off his lap, waving it at me. "Hand delivered. By a very cute bike messenger, I might add. I had to sign for it and promise not to open it."

I snatched it from him and jerked my chin to the door, wordlessly telling George to scram.

"You're not even going to tell me what it is?"

"I don't have X-ray vision, and you are not going to be here when I open it. Get out."

With a noise of protest, he kicked his feet off my desk and left, closing my door on his way out.

I stared at the package for several minutes, feeling the rectangular shape of it beneath the padded envelope. A frame? My heart jumped in my chest.

Tucked inside were a wrapped parcel and a note that read,

Petal,

   Open this with discretion. It is my favourite.

Your stranger.

I swallowed, feeling a little as if I were on the verge of unleashing something I would no longer be able to contain. Looking up to ensure that my door was firmly shut, I unwrapped it, my hands shaking when I realized that it was indeed a frame. Made of deep, simply cut wood, it held a single photo: a picture of my stomach, and the curve of my waist. The black table beneath me was visible. Max's fingertips were also visible at the bottom, as if he was pinning me to the surface at my hips. A faint beam of light spread across my skin, a reminder of the door opening nearby, of the person wandering around the room just beyond the screen.

He must have taken that picture just as he'd buried himself in me.

I closed my eyes, remembering how it had felt when I came. I was like a bare wire, plugged into the wall and with the charge that would illuminate that dark ballroom running through me instead. He'd bared my clit with his fingers, stroked me just like that. I'd wanted to close my legs against the intensity of it, but he'd growled, held me open with his pounding hips.

I shoved the frame back in the mailing envelope and hid the entire thing in my purse. Heat spread like a clawing vine across my skin and I couldn't even turn up the air, couldn't open a window this high in the building.

How did he know?

I felt the weight of it pressing down on me, how much I'd wanted it to be a photo of us, how much I'd wanted to be seen. He understood, maybe more than I did myself.

Stumbling to my desk, I sat down and tried to take stock of the situation. But directly in front of me was today's *New York Post*, open to Page Six.

There, smack in the middle of the page, was a story titled, *Sex God Stella Goes Solo.*

> **The playboy millionaire venture capitalist tried something a little new Saturday night at MoMA.**
>
> **No, it wasn't looking at art, and it most certainly wasn't raising money (let's be honest: the man already raises money better than every slot machine in Vegas). Saturday night at his annual fund-raiser to benefit Alex's Lemonade Stand Foundation, Max Stella arrived . . . alone.**
>
> **When asked where his date was, he simply said, "I'm hoping she's already inside."**

Unfortunately for us, photographers were forbidden from the event.

We'll get you next time, Mad Max.

I stared down at the paper, knowing George had put it here for me to see and was probably now laughing to himself.

My hands shook as I folded it and shoved it in a drawer. Why hadn't it occurred to me that a photographer could have been in there? That there were no photographers in the event at all was a miracle. And although Max had certainly known this, I hadn't, and I hadn't even *thought to care.*

"Crap," I whispered. I knew, with sudden clarity, that this thing between us either needed to end absolutely, or I needed some semblance of control. Feeling relieved in hindsight was a slippery slope, and I'd already dodged three bullets in my first week.

I hit the spacebar on my laptop to wake up my computer and googled the location of "Stella & Sumner."

I couldn't help but smile. "Of course."

Thirty Rockefeller Plaza.

∾

Stella & Sumner took up half of the seventy-second floor of the GE Building, one of the most iconic buildings in the city. Even I recognized it from blocks away.

However, for such a well-known venture capital firm, I was surprised how little space it required. Then again, it took very little to run a company that basically just raised and invested money: Max, Will, some junior executives, and assorted math brainiacs.

My heart was hammering so fast I had to count ten deep breaths, and then duck into a bathroom just outside their office doors to get myself together.

I checked each stall to ensure it was empty, and then looked myself right in the eye. "If you're doing this with him, remember three things, Sara. One, he wants what you want. Sex, no strings. You don't owe him more. Two, don't be afraid to ask for what you want. And three"—I stood up straighter, taking a deep breath—"be young. Have fun. Turn the rest off."

Back in the hall, the glass doors to Stella & Sumner opened automatically when I approached and an older female receptionist greeted me with a genuine smile.

"I'm here to see Max Stella," I said, returning it. She had a familiar smile, familiar brow. I glanced down and read her name placard: BRIGID STELLA.

Holy crap, did his *mother* work as his receptionist?

"Do you have an appointment, love?"

Her accent was just like his. I jerked my attention

back to her face. "No, actually. I was hoping I could just get a minute."

"What's your name?"

"Sara Dillon."

She smiled—but not a knowing smile, *thank God*—looked at her computer, and then nodded a little to herself before picking up the phone. "I've got a Sara Dillon here hoping for a chat." She listened for barely three seconds and then said, "Right."

When she hung up, she was already nodding. "Straight down the hall to the right. His is the office at the end."

I thanked her and followed her directions down the hall. When I drew closer, I saw that Max stood in his doorway, leaning against the frame and wearing such a self-satisfied smile that I pulled up a good ten feet short of my destination.

"Get over yourself," I whispered.

He burst out laughing, turning and walking into his office.

I followed him in, closing the door behind me. "I'm not here for what you think I'm here for." And then I paused, reconsidering. "Okay, maybe I *am* here for what you think I'm here for. But not really. I mean not here, and not *today* here, when your mother is right out there! Oh my God—who hires their mother as their *receptionist*?"

He was still laughing, that damn dimple etched into his cheek, and with each rambling word I unleashed he seemed to laugh harder. Goddamn if he wasn't the most playful, adorable . . . infuriating . . . *ass!*

"Stop laughing!" I yelled and then slapped a hand over my mouth as the words echoed back to me from the walls all around us. He struggled to straighten his expression, walked over to me and kissed me once, so sweetly I literally forgot for a beat what I was here for.

"Sara," he said quietly. "You look beautiful."

"You always say that," I said. I closed my eyes, felt my shoulders slump. I couldn't remember a single instance in the last three years where Andy had complimented me on something other than the wine I chose for dinner.

"That's because I'm nothing if not honest. But what are you wearing?"

I opened my eyes and looked down at my white blouse, pleated navy skirt, and thick red belt. Max was staring directly at my chest, and I felt my nipples harden under his gaze.

He grinned. He could tell.

"I'm wearing . . . work stuff."

"You look like a naughty schoolgirl done right."

"I'm twenty-seven," I reminded him. "You're not being a pervert by checking out my boobs."

"Twenty-seven," he repeated, grinning. He acted

like every bit of information I gave him was a pearl he could string on a necklace. "How many days is that?"

I narrowed my eyes at him. "What? It's . . ." I looked up for a few seconds. "About nine thousand, eight hundred fifty. But more, actually, since my birthday is in August. About ten thousand."

He groaned and pressed a dramatic hand to his chest. "Fuck. Numbers queen and stacked like that. I'm helpless against your charm."

I couldn't help but smile back at him. He'd never been rude or sharp with me, and had given me more orgasms in a week and a half than any other man had in . . . *ugh, Sara. Depressing. Move on.*

He looked me over once more before saying, "Well, I certainly can't wait for you to tell me why you've blessed me with your visit today. But let me answer your most recent question. Yes, my mother is my receptionist and it does seem uncouth. But I dare you even to try to get her to leave that desk. I assure you, you'll walk away with one ear pulled from your head."

He took a step forward, and suddenly he was standing so close. Too close. I could see the tiny stripes in his tailored suit jacket, see the shadow of stubble on his chin.

"I came here to talk to you," I said. I must have sounded minuscule, and I needed to find some power to put behind the words I wanted to give him. I didn't want to be how I was with Andy initially: easily bulldozed. After six years, I realized the problem was I'd never really cared enough to fight for anything.

He smiled. "I figured as much. Do you want to sit?"

I shook my head.

"Do you want something to drink?" He walked over to a small bar in the corner and held up a crystal bottle filled with amber liquid. Without thinking, I nodded, and he poured two glasses.

Handing it to me, he whispered, "Just two fingers today, Petal."

I surrendered to my laugh. "Thank you. I'm sorry, this whole situation is just . . . eating at me."

He raised an eyebrow but seemed to rethink lacing further innuendo into the moment. "Likewise."

"I feel a little out of my depth with you," I started.

He laughed, but not rudely. "I can tell."

"See, before what happened in the club? I'd been with the same guy since I was twenty-one."

Max took a sip of his drink and then stared down into the glass, listening. I considered how much I really wanted to tell him about Andy, and me, and who we were together.

"Andy was older. More established, more settled. It was fine," I said. "It was always *fine*. I think a lot of relationships end up that way, just sort of . . . fine. Easy. Whatever. He wasn't my best friend; he wasn't really my lover. We cohabitated. We had a routine."

I was loyal; he banged women all over Chicago.

"So what happened? What detonated?"

I paused, looking at him. Had I used that word with Max? I thought back, and realized no, I hadn't. I'd used that to describe my life when I left, but I'd never shared it with him. I felt goose bumps spread along my arms. A million answers flashed through my head, but the one that I gave him was "I got tired of being so old when I was so young."

"That's it? That's all you're going to tell me? You're a complete puzzle, Sara."

Looking up at him, I said, "For what we've done together, you don't need to know more than that I left a lot of unhappiness in Chicago and am not looking to be involved with anyone."

"But then you found me at the club," he said.

"If I remember correctly," I said, dragging my finger down the front of his shirt, "you found me."

"Right," he said, and smiled, but for the first time I could remember, his eyes didn't do it first. Or even later. "And here we are."

"Here we are," I agreed. "I figured it was my one wild moment." I looked out the window, at the billowing white clouds, looking for all the world so solid, and hearty as if I could leap from this floor and catch one and go somewhere, anywhere, where I would feel sure of what I was about to say. "But I've seen you a few times since then and . . . I like you. I just don't want things to get crazy, or off track."

"I understand you perfectly."

Did he? He couldn't possibly. And in truth, it didn't matter whether he understood that even more important than my life staying on track was my need for it not to be as safe as it had been in Chicago. Safe was a nightmare. Safe was a lie.

"One night a week," I said. "I'll be yours one night a week."

He stared at me with that calm reflective expression and I realized that every time I'd seen him before this, he'd been showing every card he had. His smile was complete honesty. His laughter was him being perfectly real. But this expression was his mask.

My stomach tightened painfully. "If you even want to see me again, that is."

"I absolutely do," he assured me. "I'm just not entirely sure what you're saying."

I stood up and walked over to the window. I felt him move behind me and I said, "I feel like the only way I can handle it right now is to give it a clear boundary. Outside that boundary, I'm here to work, to build a life. But inside that boundary . . ." I trailed off, closing my eyes and just letting the idea take hold. The idea of Max's hands, and his mouth. His sculpted torso and the thick length of him pressing into me again and again. "We can do anything. When I'm with you I don't want to worry about anything else."

He moved to the side, so that I could turn my head just slightly and look right at him, and stared directly into my eyes. He smiled. The mask was gone, the midafternoon sun blazed into the room, and his eyes looked like green caught on fire.

"You're offering only your body to me."

"Yeah." I was the first to look away.

"You'll truly only give me one night a week?"

I winced. "Yes."

"So you want to have . . . what? Some sort of committed fling?"

I laughed and said, "I certainly don't like the idea of you whoring your way across the boroughs. So, yes, that's part of the deal. If you even do that."

He scratched his jaw, not answering my implied question. "What night? The same night all the time?"

I hadn't really thought this part through, but I nodded, winging it. "Fridays."

"If I'm not to see other women, what if I have a work function, or an event on a Thursday or a Saturday that requires a date?"

My chest twisted with anxiety. "No. No public appearances. I guess you can take your mom."

"You're a demanding little thing." His smile followed his words and grew slowly, like a low-burning fire. "This feels so organized. That hasn't been our modus operandi, to date, little Petal."

"I know," I allowed. "But this is the only way that felt sane to me. I don't want to be in the papers with you."

His eyebrows pulled together. "Why that specifically?"

Shaking my head, I realized I'd said too much. I murmured, "I just don't."

"Do I get any say in how this goes?" he asked. "Do we just meet at your flat and fuck all night?"

I ran my index finger down his chest again, venturing lower, to his belt buckle. Here was the part I hoped he was up for and the part that scared me most. After the club, the restaurant, the fund-raiser, I was starting to feel like an adrenaline junkie. I didn't want to give that up, either.

"I think we've done pretty well so far. I don't want to go to my apartment. Or yours, for that matter. Text me where I should be, and generally what to expect so I know what to wear. I don't care about the rest."

I lifted myself on my toes, kissed him. It started out teasing, but then turned deep enough to make me want to take back everything I'd said and give myself to him every night of the week. But he pulled away first, breathing heavily.

"I can avoid photographers, but I've become obsessed with taking pictures of you. That's my only condition. No faces, but photos are allowed."

A shiver moved up my spine and I stared up at him. The thought of having proof of him touching my bare skin, of him looking at pictures of us together and getting hard, made a hot flush spread up my chest to my cheeks. He noticed, smiling and running the backs of his fingers along my jaw.

"When this ends, you delete them," I said.

He nodded immediately. "Of course."

"I'll see you Friday then." I reached inside his jacket, taking a moment to run my hand over the hard lines of his chest before pulling his phone from his inside pocket and dialing my cell number. It rang in my purse. I could sense his amused smile without even looking up at his face. I slipped his phone back in his pocket, turned, and walked away, knowing if I looked over my shoulder at him, I'd walk back.

I waved goodbye to his mother and took the long elevator ride back to the lobby, thinking about that cell camera of his all the way down.

Two blocks away my phone buzzed in my purse.

Meet me Friday at 11th and Kent in Brooklyn. 6:00. Have a cab bring you and stay in it until I've opened the door. You may come straight from work.

Six

Back when I was young and naïve, Demitri Gerard had been the second client I ever took on. He'd had a small but profitable antiques business in North London. On paper, Demitri's business was nothing special: he paid his bills on time, had a steady client list, and made more money a year than what he put out on expenditures. But what was truly exceptional about Demitri was his uncanny ability to sniff out rare finds that few people knew existed. Pieces that, in the right hands, sold for small fortunes to collectors around the globe.

He'd needed capital to expand and, I'd later learned, to bankroll a long list of informants who kept him apprised of what was to be found and where. Informants who made him a very, very rich man. Legally, of course.

In fact, Demitri Gerard had become so successful he currently owned twelve warehouses in New York City alone, the largest of which stood at Eleventh and Kent.

Pulling the paper from my pocket, I entered the code Demitri had given me on the phone this morning. The alarm beeped twice before the door buzzed, the lock disengaging with a loud, metallic click. With a quick wave to my driver, I opened the heavy steel door, hearing my car pull away from the curb as I stepped inside.

A freight elevator took me to the fifth floor and I slipped off my jacket, rolling up my sleeves as I looked around. Clean, cement walls and floors, bay lighting suspended from a beamed ceiling. Demitri used these buildings to house collections that would later be sold at auction or moved to various dealers. Thank fuck this collection had yet to sell.

Sunlight still poured through the dingy and cracked windows that lined two walls of the warehouse, and row after row of draped mirrors filled the space. I crossed the room, stirring up small plumes of dust with my footsteps, and lifted the plastic covering from the only piece of furniture in the entire warehouse: a red velvet chaise I'd had delivered earlier that day. I smiled, running my hands along the curved back, and imagining how gorgeous Sara would look later, naked and begging on top of it.

Perfect.

I spent the next hour carefully uncovering each of the mirrors and arranging them around the space, angling each one toward the chaise I'd placed in the center. Some were ornate, with wide gilded frames and glass that had become speckled and hazy around the edges with time. Others were more delicate, simple filigree or rich, gleaming wood.

The sun had ducked behind the surrounding buildings

by the time I'd finished, but still shone bright enough that I wouldn't need to turn on any of the fluorescent lamps overhead. Soft light filtered though the warped glass and I checked my watch, noting that Sara would be here any moment.

For the first time since I'd devised this little plan, I considered the possibility that she might not show up at all, and how disappointing that would be. Which was strange. Most women were easy to read, wanting me for my money or the notoriety that came with being seen on my arm. But not Sara. I'd never had to work even remotely this hard to get a woman's attention before, and I wasn't quite sure how I felt about that. Was I honestly that much of a cliché? Only wanting what I couldn't have? I pacified myself with the fact that we were both adults, we were both getting what we wanted, and would each move on soon enough. No harm done.

Simple.

The fact that she was a stellar shag didn't hurt, either.

My mobile vibrated from across the room, and with a final glance around, I let myself into the lift and traveled the short ride down to the empty lobby.

Her head snapped up at the sound of the door, and my dick got hard at the sight of her standing there expectant, unsure.

Easy, mate. Let's get her inside before we ravage her.

"Hello," I said, bending to kiss her cheek. "You look beautiful." Her scent was already familiar, a little something like summer and citrus. I stepped outside and paid the driver, turning back to her as he drove away.

"That was pretty presumptuous of you," she said, lifting a brow. Her hair was smooth with just the slightest bit of wave in it tonight, the front held in place with a small silver barrette. I imagined what it would look like later, that prim little clip gone, tangled and wild after I'd fucked her. "Especially considering I already paid him."

I looked back in the direction of the cab before shaking my head with a smile. "Let's just say that lack of confidence has never been my hang-up."

"What is your hang-up then?" she asked.

"I don't think I have one, actually. I think that's why you like me."

"*Like* is a pretty strong word," she said, the corner of her mouth curving up into a smirk.

"Touché, devil child." I grinned as I opened the door, indicating that she lead the way.

We were silent as we walked to the elevator and throughout the short ride up, but a new, heavy sense of anticipation seemed to pulse all around us.

The lift opened directly into the warehouse, but instead of moving inside, Sara turned to face me.

"Before we go in there," she said, nodding toward the room, "I need you to tell me that there are no chains or, like, *implements* inside."

I laughed, only now seeing how bad this looked, how

much trust she was placing in me by coming here. I promised myself I'd make it worth it.

"No shackles or whips, I promise." I leaned down, kissed her ear. "There may be a little light spanking, but let's see how the night goes first, shall we?" I swatted her on the behind before I walked past her to lead us inside.

"Wow," she said, a hint of color still blooming across her cheeks as she crossed the threshold.

So many contradictions.

I let myself watch as she took in the room, turning slowly. Burgundy wrap dress, legs that went on for miles and ended in sky-high black heels.

"Wow," she repeated.

"I'm glad you approve."

She ran a finger along the surface of a large silver mirror, her eyes meeting mine in the reflection. "I'm sensing a theme here."

"If by theme you mean that watching you gets me off, then yes." I sat in one of the large window frames, stretching my legs out in front of me. "I love watching you come. But, even more, I love the way *you* get off on being watched."

Her eyes widened as if what I'd said was somehow shocking.

I paused. Had I misread her? To me she was pretty clearly at least a little exhibitionist, and more than a lot fascinated with the thrill of being seen. "You know I enjoy looking at nude photos of you. I know you enjoy public sex. Where have I misunderstood what we're doing here?"

"It's just hearing it out loud that surprised me." Turning away, she walked around the room, looking at each mirror she passed. "I guess I always assumed other people liked this kind of thing, not me. I realize that sounds ridiculous."

"Just because what you had before was different doesn't mean it's what you like."

"I don't think I fully understand *what* I like," she said, turning to face me. "At least, I don't feel like I've done enough in my life to really know."

"Well, here you are in a warehouse, with nothing but a velvet chaise in the middle of the room and mirrors all around. I'm happy to help you try to figure that out."

She laughed, walking back over to me. "This building isn't yours."

"More checking up on me, I see."

She set her bag against the wall and took a seat on the chaise, crossing her legs. "I needed to know something outside of the gossip columns. Make sure we wouldn't be re-creating a scene from *Leatherface*."

I shook my head, laughing, surprised at how relieved I was she hadn't just shown up blindly. "It belongs to a client of mine."

"A client with a fetish for mirrors?"

"I don't know how much you found in your digging," I said. "But I have two partners, and each of us has his own area of expertise: Will Sumner specializes in biotech, James Marshall in technology. I focus more on the arts: galleries and—"

"Antiques?" she said, motioning around the room.

"Yes."

"Which brings us to why we're here," she said.

"Done with the twenty questions?"

"For now."

"Satisfied?"

"Hmmm, not yet."

I crossed the room, bending to kneel in front of her. "You're okay with this?"

"With you taking me in a warehouse full of mirrors?" She tucked a strand of hair behind her ear and shrugged, in a wildly innocent gesture. "Surprisingly, yes."

I moved my hand to the back of her neck. "I've been thinking about this all day. How you'd look sitting here." Her skin was so soft, and I let my fingers trail down along her throat, along her collarbone. I pressed a kiss over her pulse, feeling the beat of it against my tongue. She whispered my name, her legs falling open as she brought me closer.

"I want you naked," I said, wasting no time and pulling down the front of her dress. "I want you naked and wet and begging for me to fuck you." I moved to her breast, sucking, before I bit down on her nipple through the delicate lace of her bra. "I want you to be so loud that the people at the bus stop across the street know my name."

She gasped and reached for my tie, loosening it and pulling it from my around my neck.

"I could bind you with that," I said. "Spank you. Suck on your pussy until you begged me to stop." I watched as she fumbled with the buttons of my shirt, the hungry look in her eyes as she pushed it down my shoulders.

"Or I could gag you," she teased with a smirk.

"Promises, promises," I whispered, taking her bottom lip into my mouth. I kissed down her chin, sucked on her neck.

She gripped me through my trousers, my body already responding, my cock hard in her palm.

I unfastened her dress and pushed it open, pulling her arms free and tossing it to the side. Her bra followed closely behind.

"Tell me what you want, Sara."

She hesitated, watching me, before whispering, "Touch me."

"Where?" I asked and trailed a finger up her thigh. "Here?"

Her skin was milky white against the red velvet of the chaise—the image better than any I'd conjured up on my own—and I nibbled her hip bone as I slipped the tiny scrap of lace she wore down her legs. Dipping a finger inside, I sucked in a sharp breath at how wet she was already. I circled my thumb over her clit, both of us looking down to where I touched her. I watched the muscles of her stomach quiver, heard the soft sounds as I moved over her wet skin.

Standing, I unfastened my trousers, tossing a condom

to the chaise before pushing my clothes down my hips. She didn't waste any time, sitting up and taking me in her hand, running her tongue along the head of my cock. I watched as she sucked on the tip, her lips warm and wet.

Glancing up, I caught our reflection across the room. She held on to my hips, her pretty caramel-colored hair twisted around my fingers, her head bobbing as she moved over me. I forced myself not to look down, knowing what her long, dark lashes would look like from this angle, resting against her pink cheeks.

Or better, her dark eyes open as she looked up.

I felt the point where each of her fingers gripped me, felt the soft brush of her hair against my stomach, the heat of her mouth and the vibration of each encouraging moan. It felt so fucking good. *Too* good.

"Not yet," I said, gasping but somehow managing to pull away. I ran my fingers along her lips. It was so tempting to just watch her suck me off, to let myself come down her throat. But I had other plans. "Turn around. I want you on your knees."

She did as I asked, glancing over her shoulder at me as I stood behind her.

That look nearly did me in and I had to force myself to think of spreadsheets—or even Will's bad jokes—as I reached for the condom and tore it open, sliding it over my length. I gripped her hip, taking one hand and guiding myself to her entrance, rubbing my tip against her before pressing down and pushing inside.

Her head fell forward, hiding her face from my view. That wouldn't do at all.

I reached out, wrapping my hands in her hair, and pulled, bringing her head back up.

Her breath caught, eyes wide in surprise and hunger. "There you are," I said, drawing back slightly and shifting forward. "Right there." I nodded to the mirror opposite us. "I want you to look right there, yeah?"

She licked her lips, nodding as best she could.

"Do you like that?" I asked, tightening my hold.

She stuttered out a "Yes-s."

I moved faster, watching her with something like awe. It was clear she was letting me lead tonight, take what I wanted. The gears spun in my head, already trying to sort out how I could draw her out, how I could make her as tangled with need as I felt when I was close to her.

"See how much better it makes it?" I asked, following our every movement in the mirror as I continued to push in and out of her tight body. "See how perfect that is?" I circled my hips, sped up my movements. "And over there." I tilted her head to the right, to another mirror angled toward us. "Fuck. Look at the way your tits move as I fuck you. The curve of your back. Your fucking perfect ass."

I brought my hands from her hair to her shoulders, gripping them, using them for leverage. I squeezed the muscle there, my thumbs bracketing the curve of her spine. Her skin was slick with sweat, her hair beginning to cling to her forehead. I bent my knees to change the angle and she arched under my palms, her body rocking back against mine.

She shifted her weight to her elbows and cried out, asking for harder, her fingers twisting into the fabric of the chaise. I gripped her hips in each hand, fucking into her, pulling her back roughly with every thrust.

"Max," she moaned, her cheek turned into the cushion. She looked so wrecked, so overwhelmed and lost to everything but the feeling of where my body fit inside hers.

My legs were starting to burn and pleasure buzzed up and down my spine. Pressure began to build in my stomach and I bent forward, wrapping my arms around her waist to shift our position. She reached back with one hand, holding my hip, pulling me into her.

"That's it," I said through panting breaths, closer and closer, feeling her start to tighten around me, my own pleas muffled against her shoulder. "Can you get there?"

"So close," she said, eyelids fluttering closed, teeth buried in her bottom lip. I reached forward to touch her clit, finding her own slick fingers already there. The chaise creaked beneath us and I briefly considered the possibility that it might collapse. "Max, faster."

I looked around again, seeing us in different mirrors and

from different angles, both of our fingers moving over her while we moved, and knew I'd never seen anything even re-motely like this. I knew this was a game, but fuck if I ever wanted to stop playing.

I shifted my eyes back to her as she said my name over and over, her head thrown back against my shoulder as she came, her body squeezing me tight. Everything felt hot and electric, my heart pounded inside my chest.

"Don't close your eyes, don't you fucking close your eyes. I'm about to come." I followed, my body shaking as I came, filling the condom. I fell forward, hand clutching at her waist and fingers tightening there, feeling the hot flush of blood pump through my veins.

"Holy . . . ," she breathed, looking back at me with a small smile.

"Indeed." I managed to pull myself up and dispose of the condom, and arrange us both on the settee. Sara was pliant, boneless, and smiled sleepily as she lay back on the cushion with a small sigh.

"I'm not sure I can walk," she said, reaching up to push the sweaty hair from her forehead.

"You're welcome."

She blinked over to me. "Always so cocky."

I grinned, closing my eyes while I tried to catch my breath. At least until I could feel my legs again.

Several moments of silence stretched on. Car horns blared on the streets below, a helicopter sounded somewhere in the distance. The room had grown darker when I felt the cushion shift, and I looked up, seeing Sara stand and begin gathering her clothes.

"What plans do you have for the rest of the evening?" I asked, rolling to my side and watching her slip back into her dress.

"Going home."

"We've both got to eat." I reached out, running my hand along her smooth thigh. "Certainly worked up an appetite."

She gently brushed me away, kneeling on the floor to find her other shoe. I didn't even remember taking them off. "That's not what this is."

I frowned. I suppose I should have felt some sort of relief knowing that she wasn't moving this into needlessly emotional territory. But she was such a mystery to me. Obviously inexperienced, obviously naïve. But she'd come here, quite recklessly in fact, and was putting her trust in me.

Why?

Everyone plays a game. What's hers?

She slipped into her shoes, straightened, pulled a brush from her purse to smooth through her hair. Her eyes were bright, her face a bit more flushed than usual, but other than that Sara looked perfectly presentable.

I'd have to try harder next time.

Seven

Maybe this was how Andy got so much done every single day. Nothing cleared the head better than a screaming orgasm with a gorgeous stranger who didn't expect me to go pick up his dry cleaning afterward. Monday morning, I felt energized and completely engaged in the nine o'clock department meeting.

The other executives and their assistants had finally arrived to the new office, and because some things Bennett had been working on came through, we were inundated with the prospect of twenty new marketing clients. I was buried. On the upside, I had very little time to fantasize about Andy-shaped voodoo dolls and castration techniques.

But in between the frenzy—walking from one meeting to the next, a trip to the restroom, a quiet lull after a phone call—I remembered my night with Max, his hard, naked body behind me, my limbs heavy with delicious exhaustion and his hands fisted in my hair.

"Don't close your eyes, don't you fucking close your eyes. I'm about to come."

Despite how much fun it had been, I'd felt off for a couple of hours on Saturday morning. Not regretting anything, exactly, but slightly embarrassed that I'd actually done it. It occurred to me that I was giving Max a very bad impression, showing up in some random neighborhood and willing to let him do what he wanted to me in front of hundreds of mirrors where it was very likely no one would be able to hear me if I needed help.

The thing was, even below that thin layer of mortification, I knew I'd never felt more alive. He made me feel safe, as strange as that was, and like I could ask him for anything. Like he saw something in me nobody else did. He didn't seem even the slightest bit surprised or judgmental when I'd laid out my terms in his office. Didn't even blink when I told him we wouldn't be having sex in any bed.

I sat back at my desk in my office, closing my eyes as the memory returned from the last time Andy and I had had sex, more than four months ago. We'd stopped bothering to argue over his schedule, or mine. Instead, the lack of intimacy in our relationship felt like a dark shadow growing to cover the room.

I'd tried to spice things up, showing up at his office late one night in nothing but a long coat and heels. But I'd have been better off showing up wearing a yellow duck suit, for how embarrassed he was to see me. "I can't have sex with you *here*," he'd hissed, looking over my shoulder.

Maybe he said that because he could only have sex with other women in the office. I'd been humiliated.

Without saying anything, I'd turned and left.

Later that night, he came home and made some effort: waking me up, kissing me, trying to take his time and make it good.

It hadn't been.

My eyes blinked open, as the reality of everything seemed to hit me in this one, totally random moment. Max made me feel so good, and Andy had only ever made me feel miserable. It was time for me to woman up, and stop apologizing for taking whatever the hell I wanted.

❧

Although I still craved him uncomfortably much, knowing that I would hear from Max eventually let me shut off wondering how or when it would happen for most of the week. But when lunch rolled around on Friday, and he still hadn't contacted me, it occurred to me that if Max wanted to end things he might just decide to not text me. We had no rules for how to let this go, or how to back away gracefully. In reality, the way I'd set it up meant that the most graceful way to back out would be to simply disappear. There was something comforting about an arrangement that was so tenuous it could just evaporate.

Still, I wanted to see him again.

I put my phone in my desk drawer, determined to not take it with me to the afternoon team meeting. But ten minutes into discussions about a lingerie marketing campaign, and with the memory of Max slipping my skimpy lace panties down my legs still playing on a loop inside my head, I found an excuse to get up and go back to my office to retrieve it.

No message. Damn.

Returning to the conference room, I found Bennett flipping through slides at lightning speed. It was okay for me because I'd seen the deck beforehand, but I could tell the newly arrived junior executives wanted to throw up their lunches.

"Slow down, Bennett," I came up and said to him quietly.

He snapped his attention to me, his temper barely tied down. *"What?"*

I swallowed. Colleagues or not, he still scared the hell out of me. "I think you clicked through the marketing segmentation too fast," I explained. "You just finished it yesterday, when these guys were on a plane. Let them digest it."

He nodded tightly and looked back to the screen.

I could almost feel him counting to ten in his head as he let them read the slide, and I looked across the table at Chloe. She was watching him, biting down on her pen to keep from laughing. I doubted Bennett had any sympathy for the RMG employees who had just uprooted their entire lives and were expected to have memorized seventeen tables of market figures in twenty-four hours.

"Good?" he asked, clicking to the next slide without waiting for an answer.

Catch up or catch the next train. That's what I'd overheard Bennett saying to a new marketing associate named Cole.

My phone vibrated loudly on the table and I picked it up, apologizing under my breath for the interruption. Thank the universe for Bennett Ryan and his endlessly entertaining, impatient perfectionism; for two whole minutes I'd forgotten to wonder if Max was still interested in meeting.

New York Public Library has some fascinating volumes. Schwartzman Building. 6:30. Wear a skirt, your tallest heels and skip the pants.

I grinned down at my phone, thinking Max was a pretty lucky bastard that all I would need to do was remove my panties before meeting him. When I looked up, Chloe still had her pen between her teeth, but this time she was watching me, eyebrows raised.

Looking back to Bennett, I studiously ignored her stare, but I couldn't seem to lose my giddy grin.

∿

There were altogether too many iconic buildings in New York. Every building seemed familiar or laden with history. But few were as immediately recognizable to me as the New York Public Library, with its lion statues and hulking stairs.

I'd seen him four times since the first night we had sex, and even though this was a planned meet-up, I still felt like the breath had been kicked out of me when I spotted my beautiful stranger. He stood far above everyone around him, and as he searched the crowd for me, I took a few seconds to just drink him in.

Black suit, dark gray shirt, no tie. His hair had grown out in the last couple of weeks and although he kept it longer on top, I liked it messy like this, imagined tugging on it with his head between my legs.

He cut quite a shadow on the steps, as people parted around him. *I want to see you naked in daylight,* I thought. *I want to see pictures of you with me in full sun.*

Max found me then, and I was totally busted for ogling him. A knowing smile spread across his face and he hooked a finger at me, beckoning.

When I drew closer, he teased, "You were staring."

I laughed, looking away. "Was not."

"For someone who so enjoys being stared at in her most intimate moments, you're awfully shy about being caught playing the voyeur."

I felt my smile shrink a little as something ached beneath my ribs. I spoke before even really planning to. "I'm just really happy to see you."

This clearly caught him off guard. He recovered with a bright smile. "Ready to play?"

I nodded, oddly nervous despite the rush of heat that spread across my skin. We'd had an audience of a hundred mirrors last week, but had otherwise been entirely alone. Here, even at six thirty on a Friday night, the library was bustling.

"This looks interesting," I mumbled, turning to lead us inside when he pressed two subtle fingers to the small of my back.

"Trust me," he said, leaning forward to whisper, "this is right up your alley."

Once inside, he moved in front of me, walking ahead as if we were simply two strangers passing through the library entryway and headed in the same direction. As I followed his lead, I noticed a few people watching him; a couple pointed and nodded to each other. Only in midtown Manhattan would an investment whiz playboy be immediately recognizable.

I followed him, admittedly paying more attention to the fit of his jacket across his wide shoulders than to where we were headed.

Slowing, Max asked, "How much do you know about the New York Public Library, Sara? This branch specifically?"

I searched my memory for details I would have picked up from movies or TV. "Other than the opening scene in *Ghostbusters*? Not much," I admitted.

Max laughed. "This library is different from most in that it relies heavily on private philanthropy. Donors— such as myself," he added with a wink, "take a special interest in certain collections and give generously—very generously in some cases—and are sometimes granted small perks in return. Quietly, of course."

"Of course," I repeated.

He stopped, turning to smile at me. "This is the room most people would recognize, the Rose Main Reading Room."

I looked around. It was warm and inviting, filled with hushed voices and the muted sounds of footsteps and the turning of pages. My eyes moved to the ornate ceiling painted to resemble the sky, the arched windows and glowing chandeliers overhead, and for a beat wondered if Max planned on taking me on one of the large wooden tables lining the cavernous and *very busy* room.

I must have looked unsure, because Max laughed

softly beside me. "Relax," he said, placing a hand on my elbow. "Even I'm not that bold."

He asked me to wait while he crossed the room to speak with an older gentleman, who I got the impression knew exactly who Max was. The man glanced at me over Max's shoulder and I felt myself blush, quickly looking away and back up toward the painted ceiling. Only a few moments later, I was following Max down a narrow flight of stairs and into a small room filled with row after row of books.

Max knew exactly where to go, and I couldn't help but wonder if he came here a lot, or if he'd scouted the location sometime during the week. I liked both ideas, actually: the Max who was as intimate with the library as someone who worked here, and the Max who had been thinking about this as much as I had.

He stopped in a quiet corner, in a narrow, crowded row of books. It felt like the stacks pressed in on us from both sides; the tight quarters gave me the strange illusion of the walls closing in. I heard a cough and realized that there was at least one other person in the room with us.

Anticipation thrummed low in my belly.

Max lifted a book from a shelf without even really looking. "Do you read smut, Sara?"

I knew when he laughed a little at my reaction that my eyes must have nearly popped out of my head. I wasn't a prude, and I wasn't closed to the idea of erotica; I'd simply never gone looking for it. "Not much."

"Not much? Or not any?"

"I've read some romance novels . . ."

He was already shaking his head. "I'm not talking about soft-focus covers with sweaty bare-chested men. I mean books that tell you how the woman feels when the man penetrates her. How she aches when he slips his tongue inside her. How he describes her flavor when she asks him to. I mean books that describe the *fucking*."

My heart began to drill beneath my sternum at how casually he talked about things that made me want to close my eyes and squirm. "Then no. I haven't read anything like that."

"Well, then," he said, handing me the book, "I'm happy to be here for this momentous occasion."

I glanced down at the cover. Anaïs Nin. *Delta of Venus*. I knew the name and, like everyone, I knew the reputation, too.

"Great, let's check this one out." I flipped it over, looking for some kind of bar code or number. But the volume was leather, with heavy gilded pages. Obviously a rare edition. "Take it with us . . . ?"

"Oh no, no, no, no. One can't actually check out the books at this library," he began. "And, besides, where would the fun be in that anyway? The acoustics in here are so lovely, with the wood, and ceilings and whatnot . . ."

"What? Here?" My heart drooped a little. As much as I loved the idea of reading something racy with Max nearby, I loved the idea of being completely wild with him tonight even more.

He nodded. "And you're reading to me."

"I'm reading you erotica in *here*?"

"Yes. And I'll probably feel the need to fuck you in here, too. You got to be loud last week. But this week"—he brushed some hair off the side of my face, lips pursed—"not so much."

I swallowed heavily, unsure whether this was exactly what I wanted to hear or whether it terrified me. His hand spreading across the back of my neck was soothing. His palm was warm; his fingers were long enough to wrap almost to my windpipe.

"You did only give me Fridays, and no beds," he said. "Circumstances being what they are, I want to do something with you I know with absolute certainty you've never experienced before."

"And you?" I reconsidered why he knew this room so well.

He shook his head. "Most people aren't allowed down here at all. And I can assure you, I've never fucked a girl in the library before. For as much of an expert at this as you think I am, most of my adventures are in a limo on the way to drop someone off somewhere. I'm more of an arse than a slut, if I'm being introspective about it."

There was freedom in his determined bachelorhood;

I didn't have to pretend that this meant any more than it did. And even though it was only sex, and even though he was the first man I'd been with whom I really didn't need to *know* at all, I had craved his touch all week long.

I reached up and pulled his face close to mine. "Fine with me. I don't need you to be a nice guy."

He laughed into a kiss. "I'll be quite nice to you, I promise. You've so far refused the back of my limo or a quick shag at my place. You're making me break all of my habits."

We were invisible from across the room, thanks to the books surrounding us, but if anyone walked down to our dark little corner, we'd be exposed. Something inside me began to ache in that heavy, sweet way that caused my spine to arch and my heart to pound wildly.

Max stepped forward and bent to kiss me, starting with the corner of my mouth, humming at the contact and smiling.

"I'm following your rules, but it does mean I'm hard all the time. I deleted the video, but I'll admit I regret it. You'll let me take some more pictures tonight?"

It took so little from him to make me feel like I was no longer solid, but turning into a warm, honeyed ooze. "Yes."

He gave me a smile that made me fear for a beat that I'd handed a slice of my soul to the devil. But then he kissed my jaw, whispering, "You know I'd never show anyone. I despise the idea of another man seeing you like this. When you leave me, the next poor bastard will need to figure out all on his own how to please you."

"When *I* leave *you*?"

He shrugged, eyes wide and clear. "Or end this. However you choose to describe it."

"I half wondered this Friday if you'd simply not text. If that's how it would end."

"I think that'd be pretty shite," he said, frowning thoughtfully. "If either of us wants to end things, let's have the courtesy to say it, right?"

I nodded, surprisingly relieved. I suspected that even though I'd made the deal with myself to keep this about sex, if it ended I would still miss it—miss him. Not only was Max an amazing lover, he was also *fun*.

But he was a player, and took this just as seriously as I did . . . which is to say not at all.

"Now that that's settled . . ." He turned me to face the stacks. Reaching around me, he opened the book, flipping to a specific passage, and then moved my hand to hold it open. With him pressed behind me and a shelf in front, I felt completely hidden, like I was buried in this hulking man. Or maybe sheltered.

"Read," he whispered, his breath hot against my ear. "Start there."

He indicated with his fingertip that I begin at a paragraph partway into a chapter. I didn't know what was happening, who was narrating. But I understood it didn't matter.

Wetting my lips, I read, "'When he and Louise met, they immediately went off together. Antonio was powerfully fascinated by the whiteness of her skin, the abundance of her breasts, her slender waist. . . . '"

Max's hands ran up beneath my dress, over my hips, across my stomach, up to where he cupped my breasts.

"Fuck, you're soft."

One of his hands smoothed down my side and between my legs, teasing at my wetness.

It was work to focus on the plain English in front of me, but I kept reading. Max moved his hands away, clearing my head for only a beat, because behind me, I could feel him shifting, could hear the click of his belt as he unlatched it. I barely processed the words as I said them, instead listening to the sounds of *him* behind me.

Could I do this? This wasn't a wild dance floor, with strobing lights and writhing bodies; this wasn't an empty restaurant and his hand under the table. This was the most famous public library, full of rare volumes, marble flooring . . . *literary history.* Since entering the building we hadn't even spoken at full volume. And we were going to have sex? It was one thing to imagine it, another to be standing here about to actually do it.

I was nervous.

Hell, I was terrified. But I was also buzzing, every

neuron firing, my blood pumping wildly in my veins. My words faltered as I read.

"Focus, Sara."

I blinked down at the book, struggling to push my attention to the words on the page.

"'Everything made him laugh. He gave one the feeling that the whole world was now shut out and only this sensual feast existed, that there would be no tomorrow, no meetings with anyone else—that there was only this room, this afternoon, this bed.'"

"Read that again," he growled and then lifted my skirt. "This room, this afternoon, this bed."

Just as I was about to speak, and without any warning, he slid right inside me, so wet was I that he hadn't even really had to tease, stroke, or pet me. He just had to give me a book, the briefest teasing touches, and the sounds of him undressing. I groaned, wishing he could find a way to push all of him entirely inside me. I was convinced that being ripped in two by him would be the best pleasure I'd ever known.

"Quiet," he reminded me, moving back and then into me slowly. He was so hard, so long. I remembered the sharp sting when he'd taken me roughly on all fours last week in front of the mirrors. I remembered how I dreaded and welcomed every brutal thrust. When he caught my face in my orgasm on a hundred different mirrors, he'd completely come undone. More than anything, seeing him like that had been the climax of my night.

We were at the end of a darkened row, but I could hear the faint sounds of someone else a few stacks down. I bit my lip as Max slid his hand around my hip and between my legs, teasing my clit.

"Keep reading."

I felt my eyes go wide. Was he serious? If I gave my throat permission to make any sound, I couldn't be held responsible for what came out. "I can't," I squeaked.

"Sure you can," he said, as if he'd suggested I simply take a deep breath. His fingers swept across my clit again, teasing. "Or we can stop."

I threw him a dark look over my shoulder and ignored his silent laugh. I had no idea where I'd left off, or what was happening in the story other than Antonio ripping off Louise's dress but leaving on some giant, heavy belt. I could barely find my breath, but I began reading again in a tight, stuttering cadence that seemed to make Max crazy. His fingers dug into my hips and he swelled inside me.

"Please . . . ," I begged.

"Christ," he gasped. "Keep going."

Somehow, I strung the words together, and the passage grew heated and wild. So descriptive. Her wetness was "honey." The man sucked and tasted every single place on this woman's body, probing into her and teasing until I started to feel heavy with her want and mine. To my horror, I could feel my own wetness going down my thighs, sliding between us with the force of his movement.

Max shuddered behind me, losing both patience and rhythm. He seemed unable to move his hand from where it gripped my hip, and I suspected the other held his phone, taking pictures.

"Sara. *Fuck*. Touch yourself."

I carefully pinned the book open with one forearm and reached between my legs, rubbing. I'd been so swollen, so heavy with the weight of my orgasm pressing down on me that I began to come within only a few seconds. The last of my words came out broken.

"' . . . thought she . . . would go in-sane . . . with a hatred and a j-oy . . . '"

When my muscles stopped trembling, he thrust hard into me a few more times and then stilled, stifling his groan with his mouth pressed to my neck.

The room was completely silent, and I realized I had no sense of how loud we'd actually been. I'd whispered every word I read, I knew. But when I came, had I made some other loud noise? I lost myself so completely with him.

He pulled out of me, releasing a quiet grunt, and a whispered, "Be right back."

I stood, hearing him disappearing behind me while

I fixed my clothes. He returned, kissing the back of my neck. "Mmm. Lovely."

I turned to face him.

"And per your rules," he said, looking down at me as he buttoned his suit jacket, "I suppose this is where we part."

I straightened my already straightened dress. This was our arrangement—*I'd* been the one to demand it—but it felt . . . odd. He continued to watch me with a twinkle in his eye, almost as if to say, *I just gave you an insane orgasm and you look a little dazed, but hey! Here's your dumbass rule!*

I was tempted to agree.

"Right. Perfect. I'm glad we're on the same page," I said instead.

He laughed as he slid the book back onto the shelf. "And thank God that page isn't Page Six, right? A brilliant shag and no one's the wiser. We are most definitely in agreement."

"Do you ever get tired of it?" I asked. "People watching you?" I remembered how much I hated the unsolicited opinions about my hair or what I wore when I was with Andy, the speculation on whether I'd gained or lost a few pounds or who I was seen with. I wondered if it was the same for him.

"It's not like being a true celebrity. People here just like to know what I'm up to. I think most people reading that rubbish just want to think I'm having fun."

That seemed so optimistic. "Seriously? I think they all want to catch you with your pants down."

"Wait, isn't that what you're after?" He laughed at my eye roll, and continued: "The slut image is convenient for them. I'm not fucking a different girl every night."

Stretching to kiss him, I added, "Well, at least not lately."

Something passed across his eyes, a tiny flicker of confusion before it cleared. "Too right." He leaned forward and kissed me sweetly, his hand cupping my face. "Let's go, shall we?"

I nodded, a little dazed. Max motioned for me to lead the way and we climbed the stairs, stepping back onto the main floor of the library. Nothing had changed: the sound of whispers and pages turning still filled the air and nobody even glanced in our direction. There was a thrill in what we had done, and the fact that nobody seemed the wiser.

We were nearing the exit when Max reached for my arm and pulled me into a darkened corner. "Just one more," he said, right before he brought his lips to mine. It was soft and sweet and his lips lingered there, as if he didn't want to be the one to pull away.

I swallowed when I met his eyes again.

"Till next week, Petal."

And then he was gone. I watched as he crossed the floor and headed out into the fading sunshine, and wondered how much I would regret this when it was over.

EIGHT

Monday afternoon I was in a crap mood. It was hotter than balls outside, my oldest sister was making noises about convincing Mum to move back to Leeds, and Will's office had a better view.

"You're a fucking tosser," I muttered, stabbing at my chicken.

Will laughed and shoved an enormous bite of his lunch into his mouth. "Is this about my view again?"

"Fucking gross." I pointed my chopsticks at his face, barely able to understand him around all the spicy eggplant. "Remind me again how you ended up with this office?"

"You were late to the walk-through. I put my name plate on the door. Boom."

Right. It had been the first time since moving to New York that I shagged a woman at her place and, just as I expected, I got trapped. Normally I preferred sex at my place, where I could always make an excuse that my mother was dropping by or I had somewhere to be. At her place, a woman would want to offer tea, ask me to sleep over.

I wasn't a complete prick. I had always been as open to a relationship as anyone. I just hadn't yet met a woman who made me want to skip a night in my own bed. The women I'd met all introduced themselves to me, knew who I was, knew who it was they thought they wanted. For such a big city, New York often felt minuscule.

I looked out the window, at the fantastic view—fuck Will—and thought about Sara. She was my default distraction lately. She was a mystery, that one. If a woman wanted a man to think of her constantly, she should tell him he can only have her once a week and *bam*—concentration blown.

So here I was wondering, if she asked me to stay over at her place some night, what would I say?

You know the answer to that, you twat. You'd say yes.

I'd had sex with a few dozen women since moving to the States, but lately I'd had a hard time remembering details. Every memory of sex made me think of being with Sara. She was sweet and wild. She hid so much of herself, and yet she let me do fucking *anything*. I had never met a woman I found so paradoxically secretive and open.

"I met a woman, mate."

Will shoved his chopsticks back into the takeout container and slid it across the desk. "So you're going to talk about it now?"

"Oi. Maybe."

"You've been seeing her for a while now, haven't you?"

"Few weeks, yeah."

"Just her?"

I nodded. "She's a fucking stellar lay, and it's good because she told me she doesn't want me sleeping with other women."

Will gave me the *holy shit* face. I ignored it.

"But she's different. There's something about her . . ." I rubbed my mouth, stared out the window. *What the fuck is wrong with me today?* "I can't get her out of my head."

"Do I know her?"

"Don't think so." I thought back, trying to remember if Will had actually met Sara at the fund-raiser. I was with him most of the night after I left her to straighten her dress and freshen up, and I don't think I ever saw them speak.

"So you won't tell me who she is." Will laughed, leaning back in his chair. "Has she captured your soul, young lover?"

"Fuck off." I grabbed the plastic bag and shoved the mostly empty containers inside. "I just like her. But it's just sex right now. By mutual agreement."

"Which is good," he said, carefully. "She's not a digger then."

"Am I a wanker for thinking that's weird? She doesn't *want* more. Even if I did, I think that would just make her run off. She's terrified of being seen in public with me. Do you think I like her so much because she's so bloody uninterested in anything but my dick?"

And like I always did when I thought of Sara, I began to make guesses about her endgame.

Will whistled quietly. "She sounds fantastic. But I can't imagine why she'd be interested in *your* dick. With that tiny thing you'll never be half the man your mother is."

"You just insulted Brigid? You're an arsehole."

He shrugged, cracked open a fortune cookie.

"You put the seat down to piss, don't you?" I asked, grinning.

"Nah. Don't like getting my dick wet."

"Will. The only way you could give a woman pleasure is by handing over your credit card, mate."

And somehow, in the flurry of insults that followed, Will made me forget to act like a pathetic arse about the whole thing and I stopped worrying about whether Sara was fucking with my head.

After lunch, I left the office, hailing a cab almost immediately for a quick jaunt to see a new art installation being set up in Chelsea. I'd helped an old client find and open a gallery, and he was showing a set of rare E. J. Bellocq photos for only a few weeks. All it took was a one-line email from him—*They're here*—and the rest of my day was shot. I was mad to see the never-before-shown reconstructed pieces from the damaged negatives of Bellocq's "Storyville" collection. Although I had come to his work rather late in my education, his had been the art that triggered my fascination with photographs of the body, of its angles, its simplicity, its everyday vulnerability.

Though, until Sara, I'd never taken a picture of myself with a lover.

And there was the real rub. My shots of Sara and me together in no way mimicked Bellocq's art, but still it reminded me of her. Her thin waist, soft stomach, and the gentle curve of her hips.

Glancing down at my phone, I wished for the thousandth time that I had one single picture of her eyes when we were making love.

Fuck.

Having sex. When we were having sex.

It was warm, without being unbearably thick outside, and after viewing the photos, I wanted to walk off my excitement for a bit. Chelsea to midtown wasn't awful, but around Times Square I realized a man with a camera was following me.

I always assumed that the paps would learn I wasn't nearly as interesting as they suspected, but that hadn't yet happened. They stalked my weekend activities, my fund-raisers, every work function. It had been almost four years since anything of interest had happened to me—other than a date with the occasional semifamous woman—but at least half of the time that I dared to walk Manhattan alone, someone found me.

And suddenly my light mood vanished; I was ready for home, for a mindless viewing of *Python* and a few pints. It was fucking Tuesday and I wanted Sara.

"Piss off," I called over my shoulder.

"Just one shot, Max. A shot and a comment on the rumor of you and Keira."

Fuck. This rubbish again? I'd met her once, a month ago at a concert. "Yes. I'm totally fucking Keira Knightley. You really think I'm the person you should ask for confirmation?"

A cab screeched to the curb, scaring the ever-loving shit out of me as the back door flew open. A smooth, bare arm reached out, the hand frantically waving me in before Sara leaned forward, grinning. "Get in already!"

It took several seconds for my brain to connect to my mouth, and my legs. "Shit. Yeah. Brilliant."

Ducking in the cab, I shoved my briefcase on the floor and looked over at her.

"Hey, Max. You looked a little . . . stalked."

"You spotted that pretty well," I said, eyeing her.

She shrugged, giving me her strange, elusive smile.

"Fucking paps," I grumbled.

Sara crossed her legs and gave me a tiny shrug. "Poor baby. Need a cuddle?"

She had a fire in her eyes I hadn't seen since the night at the club when she dragged me down the hall.

You're in trouble, mate.

She wore a short red wrap dress and it had come undone a bit at the top. I understood the feeling. I gazed down at her left breast, the black lace of her bra peeking out.

"Nice to see you," I told her cleavage. "I've had a day. Can I bury my face in you?"

"No sex in my cab!" the cabbie barked. "Where are we going now?"

I looked to Sara for guidance but she only raised her eyebrows and smiled.

"Up toward the park," I muttered. "Not sure yet."

He shrugged, turning the wheel away from traffic and muttering something under his breath.

"You look beautiful," I told Sara, leaning to kiss her.

"You always say that."

I shrugged, and licked her neck. *Fuck.* She tasted like sweet tea and oranges. "Come home with me."

She shook her head, laughing. "No. I have tickets to a show at eight."

"With whom?"

"Myself," she said, straightening and looking out the window. I reached for her hand, slipped my fingers between hers.

"It'll play another night. Which means you should come home with me and ride my cock instead."

Sara's eyes widened as she glanced at the cabbie. He glared at us in the rearview but said nothing.

"No," she whispered, eyes searching mine. She tried to pull her hand out of mine, but I didn't let her. "But can I ask you something?"

With her hair tucked behind her ears and looking so small on the seat beside me, I felt a completely foreign panic: was this all wrong for her? In her bare, unguarded moments she looked so naïve.

"Anything," I told her.

"I've been thinking about it. Why *are* you so famous around here? Yes, you're gorgeous and successful. But New York breeds gorgeous and successful. Why do photographers stalk you on a random Tuesday?"

Ah. I smiled, realizing that although she had looked me up online, she hadn't looked very far back. "I thought you did your homework."

"I got bored after going through three pages of pictures of you in a tux with your arm around all of the women."

I laughed. "I assure you, that isn't why they follow me." Pausing, I wondered why I was talking about this now, after being so tight-lipped about it for so long.

"I moved here a little over six years ago," I began. She nodded, clearly familiar with that part. "And about a month after I arrived, I met a woman named Cecily Abel."

Her brow furrowed. "I know that name . . . Do I know who that is?"

I shrugged. "You may know her, but I wouldn't be surprised if you didn't. She was very big on Broadway but, as is often the case in the New York theater world, her fame didn't extend very far into middle America."

"What do you mean she 'was' big on Broadway?"

I looked at her fingers woven between mine. "I believe Cecily—and her dramatic departure from the theater scene—is the reason I'm noticed at all. She left New York quite abruptly, after mailing a letter she wrote that was printed in the *Post*. It detailed all of her gripes with this city, including," I quoted, "'directors who couldn't keep their hands to themselves, whoring politicians, and investment hounds who didn't know a good thing when they had it.'"

"She loved you?"

"Yes. And, as is often the case in life, it was unrequited."

Sara's eyes grew a bit dark, her red mouth curved into a frown. "That sounds pretty flippant."

"Believe me, I am anything but flippant about Cecily. She's fine now. Happily married in California. But for a time, she was under a doctor's care." Before she could say more, I added, "She was a good friend, and her decision to leave everything here showed me she wasn't very . . . stable. Really there were many reasons she left the city and I was just the most recent disappointment. I simply didn't love her the way she loved me."

Sara blinked up at the ceiling and seemed to consider this. "It's better you were honest with her."

"Of course," I assured her. "Her mental state was, ultimately, not about whether or not I loved her. She was troubled regardless . . . but that doesn't make very good newspaper copy, now does it?"

Sara looked back at me and her eyes softened, her

smile returned. "So people became interested in who this man was, the man who broke the local star's heart and drove her mad."

"And thus I was made into a mystery. The press loves a good roguish playboy, and her letter was quite dramatic. Their portrayal is true, and it's also not. I do love women, and I do love sex. But my life's rarely as interesting as the tabloids hope. I've learned to not care much one way or another what people are saying."

Our cabbie swerved to miss hitting a kid on a bike, and laid heavily on the horn. In the jostling, Sara's breast pressed against my arm and I pressed back, grinning, as her eyebrow rose in mock exasperation. "There are a *lot* of pictures of you online."

"Some of those women were lovers, some weren't." I ran my thumb across the swell of her breast, and she looked down to watch, eyes hooded. "I'm not abnormally averse to commitment; I just haven't made one in a very long time."

Her head snapped up and I could see with perfect clarity how her pupils dilated, her lips twitched in a smile.

"Yes," I admitted, laughing. "I suppose our arrangement is a commitment of sorts. It just doesn't count when you refuse to ever go on an actual date with me."

The smile shrank slightly. "I don't think either of us is good at anything more."

"Well," I admitted, "we certainly are good at what we do. Speaking of which, I discussed you with Will," I told her, letting the vibrating heat of her irritation focus on the side of my face for just a moment. She was fun to rile, this one. "Without names, Petal. Settle down."

I waited for her to ask what I said.

And waited.

Finally, I looked over at her to find her still watching me carefully. We were stopped at a red light and everything in the cab felt completely still.

"So?" she said, giving me a slow, wicked smile when we accelerated forward. "You told Will you found a woman who likes to have sex in public?"

"Not in my cab!" the cabbie yelled so loud we both jumped and then broke into laughter. He pumped the brakes, jolting us. "Not in my cab!"

"Don't worry, mate," I told him. I turned to her and murmured, "She doesn't let me fuck her in cars. Or on Tuesdays."

"She doesn't," she whispered, though she did let me kiss her again.

"Shame," I said into her mouth. "I'm good in cars. And especially good on Tuesdays."

"So this conversation with Will," she said, reaching across and shoving her hand beneath the suit jacket I'd laid across my lap. "If you didn't tell him my name, what *did* you tell him?" She pressed her palm against my cock, squeezing.

Was she going to give me a wank in the cab?

Fucking brilliant.

"Sixty-fifth and Madison," I told the driver. "Take the long way round."

He shot me a look, most likely at the prospect of driving through Columbus Circle at rush hour, but nodded, taking Fifty-seventh toward Broadway.

"No sex in cab," he said, quieter this time.

I turned to Sara. "I mentioned I'd met a woman, whom I was fucking quite happily. I may have also mentioned this woman was unlike other women I know."

Sara tugged at my zipper, deftly pulled my cock out, and gave me a rough squeeze. A strange warmth spread up my spine as I registered at the same time as I hardened that she was learning how to touch me quite familiarly.

"How am I different?" Leaning into me, she sucked on my ear and then whispered, "Other women don't get you off in cabs?"

I stared at her, wondering who this woman really was; this fresh, innocent, and highly fuckable woman who barely needed anything from me other than a good shag. Was she playing me? Was this real?

Or would she break after a few orgasms, admit she didn't like the arrangement anymore, tell me she wanted more?

Most likely. But as I looked at her—at her red pout and giant brown eyes so playful and filthy—no way was I going to give her up before she made me.

"I didn't tell him much actually. Serious conversations with Will always devolve into insults about penis size."

"Well, then I'm sure you went easy on him. 'I refuse to enter a battle of wits with an unarmed man,'" she said, giggling into my neck and beginning to stroke me.

"Truly," I whispered, turning to kiss her. "Though I'll be honest: I have no idea how big his dick really is."

"Well, if you want to know, I'm happy to find out and tell you all about it."

I laughed, growling into her mouth, "It's refreshing to have a chat with a woman who doesn't feel the need to show off her intelligence all the time."

"No sex," the cabbie growled, glaring at us in the rearview mirror.

I raised my hands and grinned at him. "I'm not touching her, mate."

He seemed to decide to ignore us, turning up the talk radio and rolling down the window to let in the late afternoon breeze and the incessant city noises. Sara's hand began to slowly stroke up, twisting at the top, and back down.

"I'd suck you off if I didn't think he'd notice," she whispered. "I mean, you deserve the best. At least you're beautiful on the *inside,* Max. Right where it counts."

I burst into laughter, pressing my face into her neck to stifle the groan that followed when she focused her efforts on my tip. "Fuck, that feels good. A little faster, love. Can you?"

She faltered at the term of endearment, and then turned her face to suck on my jaw, her fist tight and fast over my cock. She glanced at the cabdriver but he was absorbed in the radio program and yelling at the traffic in front of us.

"Yeah? Like that?" she asked.

I nodded, smiling against her cheek. "I never would have guessed you'd be so good at this."

Her laughter vibrated along my neck and beneath my skin. I'd never heard her make such a goofy, indelicate sound. Another one of her walls I'd penetrated. Victory surged warm and sharp in my chest, and for a brief pulse I wanted to yell out the window that she was letting me in.

She licked up the side of my neck, nibbled my lower lip. "You have the most perfect cock," she told me. "You're making me want you on a Tuesday."

"Fuck," I groaned. And as I came, jaw clenched, fists tight at my sides, I realized that Sara, too, had made me forget to act like a bloody arse about the whole thing and stop worrying about whether she was fucking with my head.

Sara reached into her bag, fished out a tissue, and wiped off her hand while it was still inside her purse, giving me a goofy grin and hiding the evidence from our cabbie. And then she leaned forward, and kissed me so sweetly it made me want to throw her down on the car seat and make her come against my tongue just to hear her little hoarse cries.

"Feeling better?" she asked quietly, eyes searching.

I learned something else about Sara in that expression:

her first instinct—and the one she continually battled—was to please me.

But then we pulled up a block away from my apartment and she sat back, smiling pleasantly. "Is this where you're getting out?"

I hesitated, wondering if she'd want to come with me. "I suppose, unless you'd like—"

Her voice was quiet, which I realized was her attempt at easing the harshness of her words: "I'll see you Friday, Max."

We were done. I was excused.

Nine

"Are we going to talk about it today?"

I turned from where I stood on the ladder and looked at Chloe. She held a paintbrush at her hip, and leveled her stare at me.

"About . . . ?"

She narrowed her eyes. "About the breakup. About your sudden move. About Andy and this mystery man you're now fucking, and about how different your life is now from how it was only two months ago?"

I plastered a smile on my face. "Oh, that? What's there to say?"

She laughed, but then wiped a delicate wrist across her forehead, leaving a faint smudge of paint. Bennett was out of town on business and Chloe was determined to get the entire interior of their massive apartment painted while he was unable to micromanage the operation. She looked exhausted.

"Why didn't you just hire someone to do all of this?" I asked, looking around. "Lord knows you can afford it."

"Because I'm a control freak," she said. "And stop trying to change the subject. Look, I know how that relationship slowly dragged you down, but I feel weird that I don't know more about the real *him*. Bennett knew Andy through city events, but I never knew him that well, and—"

"Because," I said, interrupting her, "you would have seen right through him. Just like Bennett did." The familiar pang ricocheted through my stomach at the mere thought of Andy.

Chloe started to say something but I held up my hand.

"Come on. I know Bennett was wary of Andy from day one, even if he didn't think it was his place to interfere. And I think by the time I met you, even I suspected Andy was cheating. I didn't want him to be around you, where you'd be able to see what I'd sunk to so blatantly."

Her eyes turned down at the corners, and I realized before she even said it what she was going to say. "Sweetie, I didn't need to know him personally to know he was a cheating dirtbag. No one did. The only thing that helped him look decent was you."

I swallowed a few times, willing the tears back. "Do you think it says something about me, like I'm stupid or blind to have spent so many years with him?"

I thought back to our first anniversary dinner at Everest, and how he arrived a half hour late and smelled strongly of perfume. Such a cliché. When I'd asked him if he'd been with someone else he'd said, "Baby, when I'm not with you, I'm always with someone else. It's just how my life is. But I'm here now."

I'd assumed he meant he was always working when he was away from me. But in truth, it was probably the only time he'd been honest with me about other women.

"No," Chloe said, shaking her head. "You were young; he must have seemed unreal to you when you met. He's charming as hell, Sara, that was for sure. But it's not healthy to change everything so fast and not talk about it. Are you really okay?"

I nodded. "I actually am."

"Does Andy call?"

I stared at the paintbrush in my hand and then dropped it back in the can. "No."

"Does that bother you?"

"Maybe a little. I wish I'd left and he'd realized how he messed up. It would be nice to hear him grovel. But the truth is, I probably wouldn't answer, anyway. I would never go back to him."

"What did he do when you told him you were leaving?"

"Yelled. Threatened." I looked out the window and remembered Andy's face contorted in rage. His anger used to make me calmer, but that last time it made something in me snap. "He threw my clothes onto the street. Pushed me out the door."

Chloe surprised me by dropping her paintbrush on

the plastic tarp without even bothering to look where it landed. She walked over and wrapped me in a tight hug. "You could ruin him."

"I suspect he'll do that himself eventually. I just wanted out." I smiled against her shoulder. "And I had the family attorney evict him. I think the papers liked that one. It was my damn house, remember?"

∾

It had been good to get it all out. Chloe wasn't a stranger to heartbreak, and the entire time we talked about Andy, I remembered how a little over a year ago, when she'd abruptly left Ryan Media, she'd sequestered herself in her apartment and hadn't been in contact for a week. When she finally called, she told me everything that happened between her and Bennett—how they'd started off their secret fling, and how she'd decided that she needed to leave him.

It had been a revelatory moment for me, but in the completely wrong way. Her decision to leave her job and potentially sacrifice her relationship only strengthened my resolve to see things through with Andy. I'd wanted to work hard enough on it for both of us. The thing is, Bennett was the right guy for Chloe to work things out with. Andy would never have been that for me, not really.

Thinking about my ex always left me with a hangover, but talking about him coiled a lead ball in my gut that wouldn't seem to disappear no matter how many rooms I helped Chloe paint or how many miles I ran along the river later that day.

For a brief moment I considered calling Max, but the answer to one man problem was never to create another. He might have wanted dinner the other night, but it wasn't because he wanted depth. He wasn't going to be that guy, either.

Monday and Tuesday flew by. Wednesday was a wall of meetings with new clients, and it felt like every minute ticked by in the span of a year. Thursday was worse in a completely opposite way: Chloe and Bennett left to take a long weekend over the Fourth of July holiday, and George went home to Chicago. The offices grew silent, and although we were a booming business, my entire team had been strangely *too* efficient. I had nothing to do and all around me the halls echoed.

Why am I here, I texted Chloe, not even expecting an answer.

I asked you the same thing before I left yesterday.

My footsteps echo in the hallway when I get more coffee. I've had enough coffee now to stay awake for a month.

So text your beautiful stranger. Booty call. Use that energy for something useful.

It doesn't work that way.

My phone buzzed immediately.

What does that mean? How does it work??

I slipped my phone back in my purse and sighed, staring out the window. I hadn't told Chloe anything else about the arrangement with my stranger, but I could see her patience wearing thin. Thankfully she wasn't in town; I could put my phone away and keep the secret all mine, at least for a few more days.

❦

New York weather in June was beautiful, but the moment July arrived it was unbearable. I began to feel like I never got away from the mazes of high-rises and more than a little like I was being baked in a brick oven. For the first time since I'd moved, I missed home. I missed the wind off the lake, tunnels of air so strong they would push you backward as you walked. I missed the green sky of summer storms and outlasting them at my parents' house, hunkered down in the basement for hours playing pinball with my dad.

The best part of being in Manhattan, however, was how I could just walk aimlessly for a while and randomly stumble upon something interesting. This city had everything: yakisoba delivered at three in the morning, men who found warehouses full of mirrors for sexual escapades, and pinball in a bar in walking distance from my corporate office. When I saw the hint of the machine's lights through the window, I faltered, feeling like the city had given me precisely what I needed.

Maybe more times than I really gave it credit for.

I ducked into the dark building, inhaling the familiar smell of popcorn and old beer. In the middle of a sunny Thursday, the bar was dark enough to make me feel like it was midnight outside, that everyone else was sleeping or in here, drinking and playing pool. The machine up front that I'd seen was a newer one, with polished levers and emo punk music I had no interest in. But in the back corner stood an older model with KISS in all of their painted-faces glory, and Gene Simmons's mouth open, tongue darted down.

I made change for several dollars at the bar, ordered a beer, and made my way through the small crowd of people to the game in the back.

My father had been a collector. When I was five and wanted a puppy, he got me a Dalmatian, and then another, and then somehow we ended up with a huge house full of deaf dogs barking at each other.

Then there were classic Corvairs, mostly bent-up frames. Dad rented a garage for those.

Next came old trumpets. Art from a local sculptor. And, finally, pinball machines.

Dad had about seventy of the machines in storage and another seven or eight in the game room at home. In fact, it was during a tour of the game room that Dad and Andy had first bonded. Although Dad had no way of knowing that Andy had never played pinball in his life, Andy had acted like Dad's collection was the most amazing thing he'd ever seen and managed to sound like he'd been playing since he could reach the levers. Dad had been smitten, and at the time I'd been thrilled. I was only twenty-one and wasn't sure how my parents would feel about a boyfriend who was almost ten years older than me. But Dad immediately did everything he could—with his time and his checkbook—to support our relationship and Andy's ambitions. My father was always easy to win over and, once won, his esteem was almost impossible to lose.

Unless, of course, he ran into you while you were out at a romantic dinner with a woman who wasn't his daughter. Despite what my father told me and how much he urged me to see Andy for who he was and not the public image he strove to portray, I chose to believe Andy's side of the story: the woman was a hardworking staff member, depressed over a breakup, and needed someone to listen, that's all.

What a caring boss.

Two months later he was caught in the local paper cheating on me with yet someone else.

I fed a quarter into the game and braced my hands on the side, watching the shiny silver balls rack into place. Presumably the music and whistles and bells had been disconnected because the game remained eerily quiet as I shot a ball up and over the field, flipped the levers, and nudged the machine with my hips. I was rusty, and playing like crap, but didn't care.

I'd had a few of these quiet, crystallizing moments in the past few weeks. Moments where I simultaneously registered how much I'd grown up and how little I really knew about life and relationships. Some of these moments happened when I was watching Bennett and Chloe, and the quiet way they picked on and adored each other in equal measure. Another moment was here, playing a game by myself, feeling more content than I had in a very long time.

A man or two came and talked to me; I was accustomed to the way guys seemed unable to resist a woman playing pinball by herself. But after four games, I felt someone watching me.

It was as if the skin on the back of my neck was being pressed only with the pressure of an exhale. Draining my beer I turned, and saw Max standing across the room.

He was with another guy, someone I didn't recognize but who was also in formal business attire and who stood out in the bar just as clearly as I must have in my slim gray dress and red heels. Max watched me over the top of his beer, and when I located him, smiled and raised his glass slightly in salute.

I finished my game after another twenty minutes or so, and walked over to where they stood, trying to keep my face from breaking into a goofy grin. I was in the mood to see him and hadn't even realized it.

"Hey," I said, letting loose a tiny smile.

"Hey yourself."

I looked to the friend at his side, an older man, with a long face and kind, brown eyes.

"Sara Dillon, this is James Marshall, a colleague and good mate of mine."

I reached out, shook his hand. "Nice to meet you, James."

"Likewise."

Max took a sip of his beer and then pointed to me with his glass. "Sara's the new head of moneys over at RMG."

James's eyes widened and he nodded, impressed. "Ah, I see."

"What are you doing here?" I asked, looking around. "This doesn't seem like a place for business in the middle of the day."

"Fucked off work early, just like everyone in this

town. And what about you, little miss? Trying to hide?" Max asked with a wicked gleam in his eyes.

"No," I answered, my smile growing. "Never."

His eyes widened slightly, and then he blinked to the bar, nodding at the bartender. "I come here because it's filthy and usually empty and they have Guinness on tap."

"And I come here because they have pool and I like to pretend that I can kick Max's ass," James said, and then finished his beer in a long drink. "So let's play."

I took this as my cue, and secured my purse over my shoulder, smiling a little at Max. "Have fun with that. I'll see you."

"Let me walk you out," he said, and turned to James. "Get me another pint and I'll meet you at the back table."

With Max's hand pressed to the small of my back, we walked out of the bar and into the blinding afternoon sun.

"Aw fuck," he groaned with the heat, covering his eyes. "It's better inside. Come back in and play with us."

I shook my head. "I think I'm going to head home and do some laundry."

"I'm flattered."

I laughed but then looked around anxiously when he lifted a hand and touched the side of my face. He dropped it quickly, mumbling, "Right, right."

"Does James know about me?" I asked quietly.

157

He looked at me, slightly wounded. "No. My friends know there's someone, but not who."

A thick awkwardness settled between us for a beat, and I didn't know what protocol was here. It was exactly why the Friday-only arrangement was ideal: it required no thought, no negotiation of friends, feelings, or boundaries.

"Do you ever think about how weird it is that we run into each other all the time?" he asked, eyes unreadable.

"No," I admitted. "Isn't that the way the world works? In a city of millions you'll always see the same person."

"But how often is it the person you *most* want to see?"

I blinked away, feeling a bubbling mixture of unease and thrill drill up from my belly.

He ignored my awkward silence and pushed on. "We're still on for tomorrow, yeah?"

"Why wouldn't we be?"

He laughed, dropping his gaze to my lips. "Because it's a holiday, Petal. I wasn't sure I had holiday privileges."

"It's not a holiday for you."

"Sure it is," he said. "It's the day we got rid of you whinging Americans."

"Ha, ha."

"Lucky for me there are no other holidays on Fridays this year, so I don't have to worry about missing my new favorite day of the week."

"Have you looked that far ahead at the calendar?" I felt myself moving a little closer to him, close enough to feel the warmth of his body even in this over-ninety-degree heat.

"No, I'm just a bit of a savant."

"Idiot savant?"

He laughed, clucking his tongue playfully. "Something like that."

"So where am I meeting you tomorrow?"

He lifted his hand again, and ran his index finger across my bottom lip. "I'll text."

And he did. Almost as soon as I turned the corner and reached the subway, my phone buzzed in my pocket with the words 11th Ave and W 24th St. There's a high-rise across from the park. 7:00.

No indication of what building, what floor, even what to wear.

When I got there, it was clear there was really only one building he could mean. It was modern stone and glass, and overlooked the Chelsea Waterside Park. It also had a ridiculous view of the Hudson. The lobby was empty but for a security guard behind a desk, and after I fidgeted for about a minute, he asked me if I was Mr. Stella's friend.

I paused, wary. "Yes."

"Oh, good. I should have asked sooner!" He stood, almost as big around as he was tall, and waved me over to the elevators. "I'm supposed to send you up."

I stared for a beat before snapping into action and walking into the elevator beside him. The guard stuck a key in a slot and then hit the R key.

Roof.

We were going to the *roof*?

With a friendly wave, he stepped out. "Have a nice Fourth," he said just as the doors closed.

There were twenty-seven floors in the building, but the elevator was clearly new, and very fast, and I barely had time to think about what could be awaiting me before it let out a quiet ding and the doors opened.

I was in a small hallway, facing a short flight of stairs that led only to a door marked, ROOF ACCESS. NOT FOR PUBLIC USE.

What else could I do but assume that, today, the sign didn't apply to me? This was Max, after all. I had the sense that he respected rules just long enough to learn how to properly bend them.

The door opened with a shrill metallic creak and slammed heavily behind me. I turned and tried opening it back up, to no avail. The day was hot, windy, and I was stuck on the roof of a building.

Holy crap. Max had better be up here or I am going to flip out.

"Over here!" Max called from somewhere to my right.

I blew out a relieved breath and walked around a large electrical box. Max stood, alone, with a blanket, pillows, and a giant spread of food and beer at his feet.

"Happy Independence Day, Petal. Ready to be fucked outside?"

He looked unbelievable, dressed casually in jeans and a blue T-shirt, tanned, muscular arms, and all six foot five of him moving toward me. His physical presence, out in the sun and with the wind whipping his shirt all over his chest . . . holy hell. Let's just say it did things to me.

"I *asked* if you were ready to be fucked outside," he said quietly, bending to kiss me. He tasted like beer, and apples, and something inherently Max-like. Warmth, sex, comfort . . . *he* was my comfort food, the thing you indulge in every now and then, without guilt, knowing that it grounds you even as it's probably not all that good for you.

"Yes," I said. "So you're not worried about helicopters or cameras or"—I looked past him, pointing to the people on a roof in the distance—"the people over there with binoculars."

"Nope."

I narrowed my eyes, ran my hands up his chest to his neck. "Why don't you ever worry about being seen?"

"Because it would change me to worry about it. It would keep me indoors, or make me paranoid, or stop me from fucking you on the roof. Consider what a tragedy that would be."

"A big one." It occurred to me that he was just as indifferent to being seen as not. He didn't seek it; he didn't avoid it. He just lived around the reality of it. It was such a different way of interacting with the press and the public that it threw me a little. It seemed so simple.

He grinned, and kissed the tip of my nose. "Let's eat."

He'd brought baguettes, cheese, sausage, and fruit. Little cookies with jam thumbprints, and perfect, tiny macarons. On a small tray were bowls of olives, cornichons, and almonds. In a metal bucket were several bottles of dark beer.

"Quite the spread," I said.

He laughed. "I'll say." He ran a hand up my side, across my stomach, and to my breast. "I plan to get my fill."

He pulled me down onto the blanket, opened a beer, and poured it into two glasses.

"Do you live in this building?" I asked, taking a bite of apple. The idea that we were this close to his apartment made me feel faintly queasy.

"I live at the building where you dropped me after the handy the other day. I own the apartment here but Mum lives there." He held up his hand just as I opened my mouth to protest. "She's visiting my sister in Leeds for a couple of weeks. She won't be coming up to the roof."

"Will *anyone* be coming up here?"

He shrugged, popping an olive into his mouth. "I don't think so. Not sure, though." Chewing, he regarded me for a minute, eyes smiling. "How do you feel about that?"

Apprehension warmed my belly, and I looked back to the locked door, wondering how it would feel to be spread on the blanket beneath Max, feel him pounding into me, and then suddenly hearing the sound of the door opening and slamming shut.

"Okay," I said, smiling.

"It has the best view for fireworks," he explained. "They set off four simultaneous shows you can see over the river. I figured it was something you'd like to see."

I pulled him closer to me and kissed his jaw. "I'm actually most excited to see you totally naked."

With a little growl, Max pushed some pillows to the side and laid me down on the thick blanket. He smiled, closed his eyes, and kissed me.

Damn, why did he have to feel so good? It would be easier to be casual—though certainly so much less satisfying—if Max were a mediocre lover, or treated me primarily as a convenient way to get off every week. But he was tender, attentive, and so sure of himself in this respect that it took very little for him to make me bow beneath him, ache for him, beg him quietly.

He loved the begging. He'd tease me to get more of it. I'd beg him to tease me longer.

In times like this, when he was kissing me, running his hands over my skin and pinching me in sensitive, hungry places, I struggled to not compare this lover to the only other I'd ever had. Andy was quick and rough. After about a year of playful sex, our contact never really was about exploration or sharing something. It had been in our bed, sometimes on the couch. Once or twice in the kitchen.

But here, Max slid a strawberry over my chin, sucked off the juices. He murmured about tasting me, licking my juices, fucking me until I screamed and it echoed across the street.

He took pictures of me as I peeled off my shirt and then his, as I licked my way down his stomach, unbuttoned his jeans, and took his hard length in my mouth. I hoped he would let me keep going this time.

He whispered, "Keep your eyes open. Look at me." And then he took a picture. I was lost enough in the feel of him that, for the moment, I didn't care.

Eventually, his phone fell to the blanket and his hands went into my hair, guiding me, keeping me slow. My mouth was moving so slow across him I couldn't imagine he would come like this, long pulls back and then slowly taking him in again. But he didn't let me speed up, and his eyes grew darker, and hungrier, and finally he swelled in me.

"All right?" he asked, voice tight. "I'm coming."

I hummed, watching his face flush and his mouth open a little as he stared at my mouth on him. The sounds he made when he came were deep, and hoarse, and mixed nonsense with the filthiest words I'd ever heard. I swallowed quickly, focusing on the dazed expression on his face.

"Fuck," he groaned, smiling. He reached down, pulled me up to his chest.

The sky above had started to darken. It turned pink, and then lavender, and we stared up at the lacy layer of clouds. His skin was warm, and smooth, and I turned my face into it, inhaling.

"I like the deodorant you use."

He laughed. "Why, thank you."

I kissed his shoulder, and hesitated, afraid to ruin the moment. But I had to. "You took a picture of my face."

I felt more than heard his laugh. "I know. I'll delete it now. I just want to look at it a couple of times." He dropped a heavy arm to the blanket and blindly searched for his phone beside him. It was under my hip, and I pulled it up, handing it to him.

Together we flipped through the pictures. My hands on my shirt, on his chest. My breasts, my neck. We paused at the picture of my hands unbuttoning his jeans, pulling him out. When we got to one of my thumb sweeping over the head of his cock, he rolled over onto me, hard again.

"No, wait," I said, the words dying inside his mouth as he kissed me. "Delete the face ones, Max."

With a groan, he rolled back over and showed them to me. I couldn't deny they were some of the most sensual things I'd seen: my teeth bared against his hip, my tongue touching the tip of his cock, and, finally, my mouth spread around him while I stared directly into the camera. My eyes had grown so dark it was clear I would suck him as long as I could. With a photo like that, I would remain in that position forever.

He clicked the delete button, confirmed the request, and then it was gone.

"That was the hottest thing I'd ever seen," he said, rolling over onto me again and kissing my neck. "I really despise that no-faces rule."

I didn't say anything. Instead, I pushed his pants the rest of the way down his legs, then he shoved my shorts off and pulled my legs around his hips.

"Get a condom," I mumbled into his neck.

"Actually," he started, pulling back just enough to look me in the eye, "I was hoping we could move past the condom rule."

"Max . . ."

"I have this." He pulled a paper out from under the blanket. *Ah, the ever-romantic test results.* "I haven't gone bare since high school," he explained. "I'm not fucking anyone else and I want to be bare with you."

"How do you know I'm on birth control?"

"Because I saw the pills in your purse at the library." He shifted back, positioning himself to press against me, and rocked his hips. "Is this okay?"

I nodded, but asked, "Aren't you worried about *my* history?"

He smiled, kissed along my shoulder, and ran a hand up and over my breast. "Tell me."

I swallowed, breaking eye contact and looking to the side. He put a finger on my chin, turning my face back to his. "I've had one other lover," I admitted.

Max's eyes stopped smiling. "You've been with one other person?"

"But he fucked everyone else in Chicago while we were together."

He let out a quiet curse. "Sara . . ."

"So, if you consider that I've been with everyone he was with, then I've been with far more than one." I tried to smile to take the sharpness out of my words.

"Have you been tested since?"

"Yes." I shifted my hips up against his, wanting this more than I realized. Andy had started using condoms halfway through our relationship; that alone should have clued me in somehow. At the time it felt depressingly distancing, although he told me it was to be sure we didn't have kids before we were ready. Now I realized he afforded me at least that one courtesy.

But Max was doing it all backward. Distance at first, and then careening headlong into this strange monogamy we had.

Crap, Sara. That's how most *people do it.*

I tugged at his hips, lifted to suck at his neck.

"Okay then." Max moved back, reached between us, and slid inside with a low groan. Slowly, slowly, slowly he filled me. And then he covered my body with his, kissed his way up my neck, and pressed his lips against mine.

"Fucking brilliant," he whispered. "Christ, there's nothing like this."

A strange desperation took over me. I had never felt his weight on me so fully, felt every bit of his bare skin, and it was a completely different type of possession. His shoulders were so broad, every muscle bunched and defined under my hands. Inside and over me, Max felt like his own planet.

He continued to kiss me as he moved, starting so slow, letting me feel every inch. "Someone could look over here. See you beneath me, thighs spread, your bare feet on my legs." He lifted himself on his elbows, looked down at my breasts. "Think they'd like to see these."

I closed my eyes and arched my back so he could get a better look. God, there was such a strange safety with Max. He never made it seem weird, or wrong that I liked the idea of people watching us. It was as if he loved it just as much as I did, wanted to get caught, too.

"Think you want someone to watch you get fucked sometime?" he asked, speeding up a little.

My honesty tumbled forward, breathless: "I like the idea of people seeing *you* like this with me."

"Yeah?"

"I don't know that I wanted this before I met you."

He fell over me, heavy and warm. "I'd give you anything you wanted. I love how you transform when I'm fucking you and watching. When I'm taking pictures, you lose your mysterious little shield and open up, like you're finally breathing."

I stretched under him, pulling him as close as I could, and looked up at the dark sky just as the first firework shot out over the river. The sound followed the light, and a deep boom shook the roof below my back.

More fireworks exploded in a flurry—stars and flames and lights so brilliant and close that it felt like the sky was on fire. The building under me vibrated, shaking my bones and ripping through my chest.

"Holy fuck," he said laughing, and moved harder, jerking roughly, growing close. I knew his tells already so well. He was barely hanging on. The sound was almost deafening so near to the river, and the air grew heavy with sulfur, smoke, and light. He reached near my head, raised himself up on his knees, and pounded into me, snapping a picture of where we came together as the lights shone red and blue and green on my skin.

I took a deep breath and fell to pieces, crying out sharply, but my sound was lost in the thundering all around us.

∼❦∽

Max drew a blanket from a pile and wrapped it around us both, perhaps less because it was cold and more because we were no longer performing for our imagined audience. We were simply sipping beer, holding hands, watching the fireworks.

"You said you haven't made a commitment in a while, but is it weird to be monogamous with a sex buddy?" I asked, turning to watch his face.

He laughed and tilted his beer bottle to his lips. "No. I'm not such a wanker that I can't be with one person if that's what she wants."

"'What *she* wants'? You'd be okay if I was with other men?"

He shook his head and looked back to the river, where the smoke was just now starting to clear. "Don't think so, actually." He lifted his beer again, emptied it. "We didn't use a condom tonight, if you recall. Couldn't do that if you were with other men."

He reached over to grab another beer and the blanket fell off his shoulders, revealing his bare back, each muscle tightly defined. I leaned forward and kissed my way up from the middle of his spine to his neck. "When was the last time you had a girlfriend? Was Cecily a girlfriend?"

"Not really." He moved back beside me and cuddled under the blanket. "I've dated a couple of women exclusively since I moved here. But it's been forever since I loved someone, if that's what you mean."

I nodded. "I guess that's what I mean."

"I had a serious girlfriend at uni for a bit. She went off with a mate of mine. Married him, actually. I was right pissed off at women for a bit after that. Now I just realize relationships are a lot of work, and energy, and time." He took a sip, swallowed. "And I haven't had a lot of that, trying to get the company up and running. I'm not opposed to the idea of having someone, but it's hard to find a good fit in this city, strange as that sounds in a place with like eight million people."

I felt absolutely nothing when he said this, no pang of hope that it would be me, no worry that Max was hoping to find someone else. For someone like me, who had, if anything, always felt more rather than less, it was jarring. The eeriest hollow sensation bloomed in my chest.

"I should probably go," I said, stretching and letting the blanket fall away.

Max looked over my naked body before meeting my eyes. "Why're you always in such a hurry to leave?"

"We don't do overnights," I reminded him.

"Not even on holidays? I could use a morning shag. We can use Mum's guest room."

"So call Will. He's cute."

"I would but he always insists on being big spoon. It's awkward." He paused. "Wait. You think Will is cute?"

I laughed, taking a final sip of beer and reaching for my clothes. "Yes, but you're more my type."

"Posh? Gifted in the penis department? Godlike?"

I looked over at him and laughed. "I was going to say you have the perfectly filthy mouth."

His eyes darkened and he leaned to kiss me. "Stay over. Please, Petal. I want to fuck you in the morning when you're all sleep-rumpled and drowsy."

"I can't, Max."

He stared at me for a long beat and then looked away, raising his bottle to his lips, mumbling, "He really did a number on you," around it.

I felt my smile fade. "It's better when you don't try to find meaning in a woman who wants sex to just be sex. Yes, Andy did a number on me but that isn't why I don't want to stay over."

I looked at him for a moment before remembering to pull my smile back in place. "I can't wait to see what you come up with next week."

⤸

By the time I made it home, the high of being with Max had fizzled into a strange ache beneath my ribs. I tossed my keys and bag to the table in the hall and leaned back against the wall, looking into the inky darkness of my living room. My place was small but in the few short months I'd been in New York it had come to feel more like home to me than had the palatial home I'd shared with Andy for almost five years.

But tonight, with the echo of music and sparklers bouncing off the buildings, and the sound of laughter and celebrations shouted from the sidewalks outside, my tiny space felt lonely for the first time since I'd arrived.

Without turning on any lights, I stripped as I made my way to the bathroom and stepped into the cramped shower. I stood under the hot spray and closed my eyes, hoping the sound of water would drown out the noise in my head.

It didn't work. My muscles were tense and sore and the subtle ache between my legs made it almost impossible for my thoughts to not continually circle back to Max.

I'd never been the type of girl to obsess over a man before, but that was definitely what seemed to be happening. Max wasn't only gorgeous, he was *nice*. And I knew it was the sex that made us truly compatible. I was still having a hard time wrapping my head around my newfound obsession with being watched by him— maybe even also by others—but that need pushed up like steam beneath my skin: warm, and exciting, and impossible to ignore.

And Max seemed to accept it, embrace it even, as easily as he did everything else.

Where my relationship with Andy had been only for public display, Max seemed to have tapped into my unfamiliar desire to be watched while respecting my need for privacy. For as much as Max was the playboy and seemed to be wrong for me in every possible way, he was letting me experience something I never would have felt safe enough to try with Andy. Was it really that simple? Was I keeping Max at arm's length because it was the opposite of everything I had with Andy? My relationship with Andy had false depth and lacked any spark. My relationship with Max was intentionally simple, and even seeing him from a distance made it feel like a torch ignited in my chest.

I turned off the water, suddenly too warm. For a beat, I regretted not still being with Max. I'd squandered the chance to touch his skin, taste his sounds, and feel his weight over me all night long.

But when I walked into my bedroom and studied my reflection in the mirror on my closet door, I looked suddenly unfamiliar to myself. I stood straighter, blinked less, watched more. Even I could see there was some wisdom in my eyes that hadn't been there before.

TEN

"I still don't understand why you're coming with me today."

I bit back a smile as I met Will's annoyed expression in the mirrored doors of the elevator, ignoring the curious glances we'd earned from some of the other passengers around us. He hit the button for the eighteenth floor.

My attention lingered on the label beside it: RYAN MEDIA GROUP. "You know how much I enjoy seeing you in action. Fish in a barrel or whatever it is you Americans say."

"First of all," he said, quieter now, "you're using that wrong, and nobody says that anymore. And second, you're full of shit. You have a hundred other meetings this week; I know you're swamped. Why on earth are you coming to this? It's not anything I need you for."

"You're right, technically I don't need to be here, but I've seen you in these kinds of meetings before, mate. Someone starts talking about neurotransmitter somethings or chemical scaffolds and it's like you've smoked a blunt. Just here to make sure you don't geek out on us all and agree to some ridiculous budget."

"I do not geek out."

"No, of course you don't," I said. "And weren't you the one going on about great contacts? I'll spend some time chatting up Bennett while we're here and kill two birds with one stone, yeah?"

I couldn't even swallow my own excuse; I wasn't used to feeling this out of my depth with women. I certainly wasn't used to sneaking around like a bloody teenager in order to catch a few minutes alone with one. This thing with Sara was engineered to be simple, but right now it felt anything but. A few hours ago I'd thought I had it all figured out: tag along to the meeting at RMG, use Bennett as an excuse should Will question, and if luck was on my side, run into Sara on a Monday rather than having to wait all the way until Friday. Spending time with her outside of our arrangement had spoiled me. Getting a wank in the back of a cab hadn't hurt, either. But now I felt conflicted, wondering if I was asking for trouble by blurring the lines like this.

The doors opened and Will turned to me. "As long as you understand that this is my show. You just sit there and look smart."

"Mr. Sumner, Mr. Stella," the receptionist greeted us. "Nice to see you again." She led us down the hall to the large conference room lined with windows, New York poised like a postcard on the other side. "Mr. Ryan is on his way down."

"Seems like a shame to spend your free afternoon here

when you could be visiting your mysterious little sex kitten," Will said when we were alone again.

I walked over to the window and looked down at the traffic on the street below. "What makes you think she's free in the afternoon?"

Will began going through his papers and I took a seat at the long table, letting my mind wander to the last time I'd been in this building. I'd been chasing after her that day, too, though admittedly not that much had changed. Sure, I'd spent time with her, fucked her and tasted her and touched practically every inch of her body, but I was no closer to understanding what was going on in that pretty little head now than I was then.

The sound of voices carried down the hall and I looked up just as Bennett walked inside.

"Will," he said, reaching out to shake his hand. "Thanks for coming down." He gave me a curious smile. "Max. Wasn't expecting to see you today. You joining in on our discussion of B&T Biotech?"

It was impossible to miss the smug look of satisfaction on Will's face. Both he and Bennett knew I'd only scraped my way through biochemistry by flirting with the professor, Dr. William Haverston. They loved to reminisce about the "boyfriend I almost had."

"He's just full of surprises," Will said.

"He certainly is," Bennett agreed. I hadn't really considered the Bennett angle. It had been a few weeks since the fund-raiser, but I couldn't help but wonder whether he knew I was here more for Sara and less for discussion of the latest in proteomics.

"I think you're both a couple of tossers," I mumbled.

There was a flurry of activity as the others filed in; unfortunately for my attempt at maintaining a cool front, Sara was the last through the door. She looked amazing, and as Bennett made the introductions, I let my gaze travel up the length of her body. Navy skirt, cute little pink sweater over the gentle swell of her breasts, and a neck I wanted to suck on for hours.

"This is Sara Dillon, head of our finance department," Bennett said to Will.

Will stepped forward. "Yes, we've been exchanging emails. So nice to finally meet you, Sara. We missed each other at the fund-raiser last month, I think."

They spoke for a moment before she glanced my way, her eyes going wide for the briefest moment. She walked over, hand outstretched, and did not look entirely pleased to see me.

"I believe we met at the fund-raiser," she said, tight smile in place. "Max Stella, was it?"

I took her hand, letting my thumb graze the inside of her wrist. "I'm flattered you remember, Sara."

She pulled her hand back, smiling blandly at me and moving to her seat.

I moved on to Chloe, making small talk and accepting a vague invitation for dinner sometime in the next few weeks. It was pretty clear why Bennett was so taken with her: she was beautiful and obviously sharp. I didn't miss the way her eyes flickered to Bennett's and then back to me, as if they were having some sort of silent conversation. At one point he rolled his eyes, face stretching into a smile unlike anything I'd ever seen on him before. The poor bastard was whipped.

As the meeting started, I took the only seat available, right next to Sara. Judging by her expression, I wasn't entirely convinced this was a good thing.

The minutes seemed to drag by and, Jesus Christ, this really was the most boring thing I'd ever sat through, science and strategies about science. At one point I could have sworn I saw Will's eyes roll closed in ecstasy.

Sara was still silently fuming beside me. What happened that had her so tense? I could feel every bit of space that separated her body from mine. I had to consciously work to keep my hands in my lap. I was aware of every movement she made, every time she shifted in her chair or reached for her bottle of water. I could smell her. I hadn't realized how hard it would be to be this close and not be able to run my hands along her skin, to do something as simple as tuck her hair behind her ear.

Why the fuck did I suddenly want to tuck her hair behind her ear? This plan had officially gone to shite.

Immediately after Will's portfolio presentation, Sara excused herself and left before I could talk to her any more. When I finally disentangled myself from a conversation about the best way to highlight the firm's proteomic technology in the marketing strat plan, I practically sprinted to her office.

"Hello," her assistant said, looking me up and down from behind his monitor.

"I'm here to see Miss Dillon," I said, continuing on to her office.

"Good luck, because she's not in there," he called over my shoulder. I turned to find that he'd gone back to his spreadsheets.

"Any idea where she might be?"

Without looking up he answered, "Probably out for a walk. She just stormed through here like someone had set her shoes on fire." He blinked over to me. "She usually goes to the park when she wants to stab someone."

Oh, for fuck's sake.

I ran to the elevator, ignoring the looks I got along the way, and watched the floors count down. What the hell had gone wrong? I'd barely said two words to her in there. The heat of the afternoon hit me like a wall as I stepped outside, even in the suffocating shadows of the buildings overhead. I looked up and down the street, turning on foot in the direction of the park. The sidewalks were crowded with dog walkers and tourists, but hopefully her shoes would slow her down enough that I'd be able to catch up.

It was the strangest feeling to move from the city and into the park, where the smells of asphalt and exhaust were replaced with trees and leaves, damp dirt and water.

I saw a flash of pink at the end of the trail and I sped up, calling out to her. "Sara!"

She stopped on a paved trail and whipped around to face me. "Holy hell, Max. What were you thinking?"

I pulled up short. "What?"

"Back there!" she said, short of breath. "I didn't know you guys funded B&T! They don't need to disclose that at this stage. Hello, conflict of interest!"

I scrubbed my face, wishing this simple arrangement would stop feeling so fucking complicated. "I didn't think it would be a problem."

"Let me lay it out for you," she said. "The head of finance of B&T's marketing firm is sleeping with the head of the venture capitalist firm that pays said marketing firm. Think you maybe have a conflict? Do you think maybe you'd like your new sex buddy to have some business? Or maybe you'd like to ensure your new venture gets the best possible price on premium marketing strategy?"

Was she kidding with this bollocks? I felt my face grow hot with indignation. "*Christ,* Sara! I'm not bringing you business because I worry about you, or shagging you to ensure you do your job well!"

She sighed, holding her hands up. "I don't actually think that. But that's how it could look. How long have you been doing this? Don't you know how these things get spun? This is a new position for me. This is your *business* and people are hungry for every detail about you. Look how much the press follows you, even five years after Cecily left town."

She was hypersensitive about publicity, and *spin,* and it was bewildering. This was all a load of bullshit, and I could tell she knew that. She looked away, arms crossed over her midsection, shoulders slumped. The truth was, I didn't care who saw me with Sara. Five years out from the Cecily drama and I realized you couldn't help what anyone said anymore. No way could Sara understand that.

I walked over to a willow tree several feet away, ducking under the curtain of leaves, and sat down with my back to the trunk. "I don't think this is as big an issue as you're making it out to be."

She stepped closer but remained standing. "My point is that there needs to be some level of discretion. With or without a potential conflict, I don't want Bennett to think I sleep with clients as a point of habit."

"Fair enough, but I don't think Bennett has a lot of room to criticize."

I watched her legs move closer, bend, and then she was sitting next to me on the warm grass. "There wasn't any reason for you to be there. I wasn't expecting to see you and it threw me."

"Bloody hell, Sara. I wasn't going to try to finger you beneath the table, I just wanted to come along and get a chance to see you, say hello. You could be more adaptable, you know."

She laughed a little, and then stopped. But then a few seconds passed and I realized she'd started to laugh again: silent at first, and then she was holding her stomach, bent in half, practically howling with laughter.

"You think?" she managed.

I had no idea what I had said that triggered her reaction, so I just sat still, imagining that less was probably more when sitting beside a woman who might or might not really be losing her kit.

She calmed, wiping her eyes and sighing. "Yes, I could be more adaptable. Having sex with a guy in a club, in a banquet hall, a warehouse, a library—"

"Oi, Sara. I didn't mean—"

She held up her hand. "No, it's just a good lesson to me. Stretching myself is a constant process. As soon as I stop and consider how well I'm handling one thing, I see how rigid I am about something else."

I pulled up a long blade of grass, considering this. "I should have texted."

"Probably."

"But you know, I would have been thrilled to see you randomly show up at a meeting at Stella & Sumner."

"You also want to go out to dinner with me, and have me sleep in your mother's guest room, and probably even make cookies with me or something."

"Because I don't care if we're seen together," I said, growing frustrated. "Why do you?"

"Because people will get invested," she said, turning to look at me. "People will discuss it, make a narrative out of it. They'll speculate, look into who we are, what we both want. Relationships in the public eye don't do well and it will follow you forever if you admit you care."

"Right," I said, nodding once.

I listened to the wind blowing past us, muted by the curtain of leaves. I liked being in this little cave of quiet, hidden from foot traffic, birds, anything else that might want to witness our conversation and my silent meltdown. Too many things were bubbling up inside me: the realization that I wanted Sara, that I'd always wanted Sara—from the first day I saw her. I also accepted the truth that I'd expected Sara to eventually hope for more, and that I would be the one setting limits, not her.

"Max, I'm kind of a mess," she said quietly.

"Will you at least tell me why?"

"Not today," she said, looking up at the branches overhead.

"I'm happy with what we're doing, but it's not always easy to be kept at such arm's length."

She laughed a little, humorlessly. "I know." And then she leaned over, and pressed her mouth against mine.

I expected a tiny peck, a discreet public kiss to wipe the slate clean after I'd admitted I should have given her a heads-up and she admitted she'd overreacted. But it turned into something wholly deeper: her hands on either side of my face, mouth open and hungry for more, and finally her climbing over me, straddling my thighs.

"Why are you so nice?" she whispered, and then kissed me, muting any possible reply.

But this one stuck. It felt too big to disregard and pave over with my hand in her underwear or a grind under a tree. I pulled back. "I'm nice because I'm genuinely fond of you."

"Do you ever lie?" she asked, eyes searching mine.

"Of course I do. But why would I want to be dishonest with *you*?"

Her face straightened and she nodded thoughtfully. After a long pause, she whispered, "I should get back."

My mood shifted immediately from warm and intimate to re-signed business-as-usual. The girl was a boomerang. "Okay."

She stood, wiping the grass from her knees and skirt. "We probably shouldn't walk back together."

I could only nod, for fear I'd let loose a litany of frus-tration over her publicity rules, particularly after she'd just climbed into my lap beneath a tree.

After a lingering look, she stretched and kissed my jaw once, carefully. "I'm fond of you, too."

I watched her walk away, head straight and shoulders back. Looking to all the world as if she were returning from nothing but a brisk walk through the park.

I looked around me as if it were possible to collect to-gether the heart I'd nearly spilled all over the grass.

Eleven

To say my interaction with Max at the park had been odd would be an understatement. I knew I'd overreacted, but honestly? So had he. Worrying about my reaction in the conference room? Chasing me down? What were we *doing*?

Monday night I came home and spent two hours making æbelskivers for dinner. Puffed balls of dough, fried and powdered in sugar, traditionally served for breakfast, but screw it. I needed something elaborate. It was my grandmother's recipe from Denmark, and focusing on making them perfect gave me time to think.

I hadn't spent much time thinking at all lately.

But cooking something so associated with my family also made me miss home, miss my parents, miss the safety of a predictable life, no matter how depressing or untrue.

I reached for my phone, not caring how messy my hands were. Mom picked up on the seventh ring. So typical.

"Hi, pumpkin!" I heard something crash in the background and she swore, "Fucksticks!"

"You okay?" I asked, smiling into the call. It was amazing how three words could make me feel grounded.

"Fine, just dropped my iPad. You okay, honey?" And when she asked this I remembered I'd called her that morning on my walk to the subway.

"Just wanted to hear your voice."

She paused. "Feeling homesick?"

"A little."

"Tell me," she said, and I immediately remembered the hundreds of times she'd said exactly this, urging me to let it all out.

"I met a man."

"Today?"

I winced. I'd spoken to my parents a few times a week since I'd moved and had never mentioned Max. What was there to mention? They didn't want to know about my sex life any more than I wanted to share it.

"No. A few weeks ago."

I could practically hear her strategizing her best response. Supportive, but protective. How one reacts the first time their daughter starts dating after a horrible, public breakup.

"Who is he?"

"A finance guy here. Local. But not," I said, shaking my head and wishing I could start over. "He's British."

"Ooh, a foreigner, how fabulous!" she said laughing, putting on her thick southern drawl. And then she paused. "Are you telling me this because it's serious?"

"I'm telling you this because I have no idea."

I loved my mother's laugh. I missed its frequency. "That's the best stage."

"Is it?"

"For sure. Don't you dare squander it. Don't let that jerk of an ex-boyfriend keep you from having fun."

I sighed. "But it feels so uncharted. I always knew what to expect with Andy." As soon as I said it, I regretted it, and her answering silence felt thundering.

"Did you?"

She knew me so well. I could practically see her arms crossed, her I'm-gonna-kick-some-ass face. "No. I didn't."

"Do you feel like you know this guy?"

"That's the weird thing. I kind of feel like I do."

❧

No matter how much I thought about it, or how little sleep I got that night, it'd be fair to say I had no idea where Max's head was after what happened Monday. The dynamics were backward: *He* was supposed to know how to do this casual thing. *I* was supposed to know how to do commitment.

And neither of us was supposed to want anything but sex. But somehow, it had never been like that. The niggling desire to know each other had started pushing its way in from day one, and I knew that as much as I wanted to be a person who could compartmentalize my relationship into Just Sex, I never really would be.

I remembered the panic on his face when he chased me down, and felt a stab of guilt.

Sara, you are complete fail at Booty Call for Beginners.

On Wednesday he texted me a picture from our night at the library. It was of the hem of my dress, pushed up against my lower back. A simple shot, but he'd stylized it into black-and-white, and the original was blurry enough for me to know he'd taken it toward the end, when I'd dissolved into inarticulate recitation and he'd followed me into orgasm with a groan muffled against my neck.

On Thursday, it was a picture I remembered seeing as we flipped through his phone on the Fourth of July. It was a photo of my hands unbuttoning his jeans. I'd pulled the denim away from his skin just enough to see the faint shape of his cock straining against his gray boxer briefs.

Both pictures were sent around lunchtime, and I received them while I worked on finalizing two major contracts. I tried to convince myself that I felt giddy from getting a few contracts done rather than from the prospect of seeing him.

I was a giant lying liar.

"Question," George said, walking into my office without knocking first. "Are we entirely sure Max Stella is straight? I've been thinking about this since he was here on Monday."

I blinked, trying to figure out if I'd just said his name out loud or if George was just doing what Chloe had been doing since the Stella & Sumner meeting: making constant, casual references to their firm, and then watching me for any reaction.

"Pretty sure."

"Maybe he's bi?"

I looked up at him and dropped my red pen onto the thick contract in front of me. "Honestly? I really doubt it."

George lifted two curious eyebrows. "You know *personally*?"

I gave him my most intimidating glare, which, to be fair, was . . . not very intimidating. No way was George going to play this game today. "Did you get signatures from Miller and Cortez on the Agent Provocateur campaign?"

My assistant narrowed his eyes at me. "Fine. I won't ask more. But just know that I'm suspicious, ma'am. *Very* suspicious. You looked like your underpants were on fire when you saw him on Monday. And yes, I got the signatures."

"Good." Just as I spoke, my phone buzzed on my desk and I quickly flipped it over, reminding myself for the millionth time that I needed to change my preview settings in case Max was texting me another picture.

George's face was priceless: his restraint appeared to cause him physical pain.

"You're adorable, but go," I said.

"Who's texting you?"

"Until you marry me and pay all my bills, that will never be an appropriate question. Even then, you're unlikely to get an answer."

"Fine." With a long middle finger raised, he swept from my office and back to his desk.

I glanced down at my screen, holding my breath. It *was* a text from Max, and my pulse exploded into a gallop.

Office being painted and recarpeted over the weekend. Must pack it up Friday after work, so I'm stuck in I'm afraid.

Quickly, I typed, So I won't see you until next week? As soon as I hit send, I realized just how desperate I sounded.

Hello, Sara. You sound desperate because you are.

Within a couple of minutes, he replied, I presume you remember where my office is? I'll see you at six, Petal.

∾

Like many of the floors in our building, the Stella & Sumner offices were nearly deserted by six on Friday night. Max's mother wasn't at the front desk, and only a couple of people remained in cubicles as I walked through the halls to his office.

I knocked on his door quietly, and heard his deep voice tell me to come in.

I have it bad for this man, I realized when I saw him, sitting behind his desk with his sleeves rolled up and wearing thick-rimmed glasses. He wore an expression of such acute concentration it nearly stole my breath.

It turned out Max's focused-at-work face closely mirrored his concentrating-on-giving-Sara-an-orgasm face.

"Lock the door behind you, if you would," he murmured, without looking away from his computer monitor.

I turned, clicked the lock, and then glanced around his office again. How long were we going to be here? And when would he look up and tell me I looked beautiful? Our habits were already so heavily ingrained.

His office didn't look at all like it was on the verge of being painted. He'd barely started putting things away:

books and piles of papers lined one wall, and at least twenty empty boxes were stacked in a corner, waiting to be filled.

"I'm sure it will be boring for you to be here with me, and I'm a selfish prick for asking you to do this, but go ahead and take off your clothes."

I felt my mouth fall open, eyes go wide. "What?"

"Clothes. Off," he said, and pulled his glasses down his nose as he finally looked over at me. "You expected to remain clothed?" Shaking his head, he pushed the frames back up and returned his attention to his computer. "I fucking hate packing. Seeing you naked will be the only good thing about this night."

"Um," I said, trying to form a response. The truth was that old Sara would never have even entertained the idea of just casually sitting naked in front of someone. Which was exactly why I wanted do it. I walked toward the couch and pulled my short-sleeved cashmere sweater over my head. I slipped out of my blue ballet flats with the British flag embroidered on top, and then wiggled out of my dark skinny jeans, mumbling, "You didn't even notice my shoes."

"Like hell I didn't. God save the Queen," he said dryly, winking at me. "I notice every single thing about you, Sara."

"You do?"

"Try me."

"Where's my birthmark?"

"On your right side, just beneath your smallest rib."

"Do you have a favorite freckle?"

Tricky question, I thought. I don't have many freckles.

"The one on your wrist." I glanced down to the freckle in question, impressed.

"What do I say when I'm about to come?"

"When you're coming, you just make unintelligible sounds. But when you're close, you just whisper 'please' over and over, as if I'd ever deny you."

"What does my pussy taste like?" I asked, and his eyes shot away from the screen and to me. I bit back a grin as I pushed my underwear down my legs and stepped out of them.

"Some pussy just tastes like pussy. Yours tastes like *good* pussy." He stood, walking over to me. "Lie down on the couch with your head here." He positioned the back of my head on the arm of the leather couch. It was surprisingly comfortable for such firm leather.

"And knees up, legs spread."

My eyes widened slightly but I did what he told me to, smiling when he brushed the hair from my forehead, and adjusted my posture as if I were a piece of art he was hanging on a wall.

"Draw me like one of your French girls, Jack," I said, looking up at him.

He reached down and pinched my ass. "Cheeky."

To test him, I closed my legs a little as he started to walk away.

"Wide," he called over his shoulder.

I laughed, and moved back to how he'd positioned me.

Max returned with a book and handed it over. "This is to entertain you while I work."

"You're not going to be naked, too?"

"Are you mad?" he asked, grinning. "I have to pack."

I glanced down at the book in my hands. It had a bare-chested man on the cover with a cat and a half-naked woman at his feet. *Cat's Claws.*

"This looks . . . interesting," I said, flipping it over to read the summary. "The guy has two partners. One is the human named Cat, and then she has a Werecat." I glanced up at him. "As a *pet*. A pet they both have sex with."

"It sounded rather cerebral."

"You got this off the dollar table, didn't you?"

"I did. It looks smashingly crude, though, so I knew you'd love it." He turned and started moving things around on his desk. "Now, quiet, Petal. I'm very busy."

At first it felt almost impossible to focus on the book in my hands, but as the minutes ticked by, and Max apparently grew absorbed in the process of packing up his desk, I started to forget that I was sitting on his couch. Alone.

Totally naked.

The book he'd given me was ridiculously filthy, not to mention wordy as hell; the writing was horrible but I suspected that wasn't really the point. There were multiple men, multiple women; too many appendages to keep straight but again—it didn't matter. The point was the sex happening, and how descriptive it was. Everyone had some body part that was hard or dripping. Or both. People screamed and—sometimes literally—clawed at things.

And in the corner, the hero sat simply watching.

"You're blushing." He put a stack of books down and leaned against his desk watching me. "You've been reading that for fifteen minutes and something you've just read made you flush scarlet."

I looked up at him and winced. "It's the c-word. It just surprised me, that's all."

"Cunt?"

I nodded, surprisingly aroused by the bluntness of the word in his accent. It lacked the t. Somehow, that softened it. Made it into something far sexier.

"I bloody love that word. Such an ugly one. *Cunt.* Sounds so depraved, doesn't it?" He scratched his jaw, considering me. "Read me the line."

"I don't . . ."

"Sara."

If possible, I felt my face heat further. "He gripped

her thighs, forced them apart, and stared at her wet, flushed . . . cunt."

"Wow," he said, laughing. "That's something all right." He moved back to his desk and started sorting through a stack of papers. "You can tell me all about your favorite parts over dinner." I started to protest, but he lifted a finger to his lips and hushed me. "Read."

I stared at the page as the words swam together. What kind of a woman makes a big deal over *dinner*?

The kind of woman, Sara, I thought, *who recognizes that dinner leads to sleeping over, which leads to staying together every night.* And that leads to keys, and then moving in. And then come excuses, and quiet sex, and then no sex and no conversation, and hoping that there is some public engagement that invites us as a couple so that I'll have time with him.

Then again, I'd regretted not sleeping over with Max on the Fourth. And I was starting to miss him during the week.

Damn.

I coughed, squeezing my eyes shut.

"All right?" Max murmured from across the room.

"Fine."

After another twenty minutes passed and I'd read about seventeen more sex scenes, Max walked over, ran a hand from my collarbone to my knee, and whispered, "Close your eyes. Don't open them until I say."

"You're awfully bossy today," I said, even as I dropped the book to the floor and did what he'd asked. Almost immediately, my sense of hearing seemed to become so acute the room almost vibrated. I heard the sound of his belt, his zipper, and a quiet sigh.

Is he . . . ?

I could hear the soft brushing sound of his hand moving, how his rhythm started slow and then grew faster, firmer. The way his breath came out in short, tight gasps.

"Let me watch," I whispered.

"No." His voice was tight. "I'm watching *you*."

I'd never listened to a person masturbate before, and it was torture to keep my eyes shut. The sounds were teasing, his quiet grunts and instructions to spread my legs wider, touch my breast.

"The book made you wet," he remarked, and then I heard his hand speed up against his cock. "How wet?"

I reached down, eyes still closed, and touched myself to find out. I didn't even have to say anything; he just groaned, and then swore in a familiarly deep voice as he came.

I wanted to watch his face, but I kept my eyes closed, my heart pounding.

The room went suddenly silent except for the heavy rhythm of his breathing and my own. I became aware of the air-conditioning vent overhead, the cool air as it poured over my too-hot skin.

Finally, he zipped up his pants, fastened his belt. "I'll be right back. Going to clean up."

His footsteps retreated, and at the sound of the door opening, he laughed quietly. "You can open your eyes now," he said, just as he stepped out.

It felt like the room had grown darker in just the past ten minutes. My hand was still between my legs, and the sounds of his orgasm lingered in my ears. I gave myself an experimental stroke and realized how quickly I could come. Maybe in less than a minute. Certainly before he would return.

Without any more hesitation, I arched into my palm, remembering the sound of his hand, the speed of his movements, his little grunts and instructions, how easily he told me exactly what he needed.

We had such an easy understanding, such a perfect balance.

It was so *easy*.

With that thought, my orgasm climbed up my thighs and burst forward, pressing starbursts of light into the back of my eyes and leaving me gasping.

The door opened, and my hand flew to my neck, where my pulse hammered wildly. I swallowed down a gasp and tried in vain to slow my breaths. I don't know why, after what he'd just done, I felt like I'd been caught with my hand in the cookie jar, but I did.

Max smiled, walked over to me, and sat on the couch near my waist. I shifted over to make room and he leaned a hand on the back of the couch as he bent over and pulled my fingers into his mouth. "Have a nice rub, Petal?"

"I guess if you'd stuck around to see you wouldn't have to ask," I said, fighting the heat as it crawled up my neck.

"No matter," he murmured into my throat, sucking gently. "I'll just watch the video later." He stood, walked over to an open cabinet, and pushed a button on a camera I hadn't even noticed, balanced on the top shelf.

"You . . . *what?*"

He turned, a wicked smile pulling at his mouth.

"You got video of that?" I asked. I had never felt so conflicted. Be discovered—*terrifying*. Be watched—*thrilling*.

"I did."

"Max, my face . . ."

His brows pulled together. "I trained the camera lower and put you exactly where I needed you. I wouldn't record your face." He walked over to me and kneeled beside the couch. "Which is a shame, actually, because I love watching you when you fall."

He ran a fingertip down my cheek, studying my face before blinking and seeming to pull back into the present. "Now, for dinner I was thinking Thai but you're allergic to peanuts, and my favorite place has peanuts in *everything*. How about Ethiopian? Do you mind eating with your hands?" He grinned. "I swear no one there will know who the hell I am."

I gaped at him, completely forgetting that I was going to argue over going out for dinner. "How did you know I'm allergic to peanuts?"

"You wear an allergy bracelet."

"You read it?"

He looked genuinely confused. "You wear it so that people *won't* read it?"

Shaking my head, I sat up, running my hands through my hair. The man I'd loved had barely noticed me. The man I just wanted to have sex with noticed everything about me.

To my surprise, I whispered, "Ethiopian sounds perfect."

❧

Max led us out the back of the building and to a black car waiting in an alley.

"Really?" I asked as he opened the door. "Paparazzi follow you home?"

He laughed and gently ushered me into the backseat. "No, Petal. I'm not nearly that famous—they only hit me up at events or on the street sometimes. The secrecy is for your paranoia, not mine."

"Queen of Sheba. Hell's Kitchen," he told the driver, and then turned to me. "Thanks for keeping me company while I packed. You made an otherwise boring task quite enjoyable."

"You didn't get much done. Really wasn't the most efficient evening for you, was it?" I leaned forward, giving him my best skeptical eyebrow raise.

He smiled, stared at my mouth. "You've caught me. I wanted you to come over tonight so I could remember how you looked naked on my couch. I've hired someone to pack up my office tomorrow morning before the painters arrive." He closed the distance between us and kissed me once, sweetly. "Sometimes at work I wish I saw you more. I liked seeing you there."

I shifted in my seat, feeling a little like the world had been tipped on its end. "I didn't really think there were men like you," I said, without thinking. "Honest. Easy to be around." I looked over at him.

"I already told you. I *like* you."

He reached for me, slid me closer, and had his lips to mine for the rest of the drive. It could have been a minute, an hour, or a week. I had no idea. But when we arrived in Hell's Kitchen I didn't want to get out, and I most certainly didn't care that I was half hoping Max would ask me to stay the night with him.

The waitress put down a large platter in front of us, with wedges of assorted vegetarian dishes fanning across the plate.

"Take the injera bread and scoop the food," Max said, tearing a piece and demonstrating.

I watched him lick his fingers, chew, and then smile at me.

"What?" he asked.

"Um . . . ," I stammered, pointing. "Your mouth."

"You like my mouth?" His tongue slipped out again, sweeping across the corner of his lips, and then he lifted his glass and took a deep drink of wine.

He made me feel more than drunk. He made me feel disoriented, reckless. I curled my hands into fists beneath the table, running through the fantasy of asking him to leave here, take me home, and touch me.

Other than the kissing in the car, he'd barely touched me all night. Was that intentional? Was he trying to drive me crazy? Because seriously, mission accomplished.

I blinked, looking down at the platter, and then did

what he'd done: ripped off some bread, grabbed some lentils, and took a bite. The food was peppery, warm, and delicious. I closed my eyes and hummed. "So good."

I could feel him watching me, and when I looked up, he smiled.

"What?" I asked.

"You know what I do at work, that my mum works for the company, that I have at least one sister. You know about Cecily. All I really know about you—other than you're a fantastic shag—is that you moved here from Chicago a bit over a month ago, left a real twat back there, and work with Ben and his fiancée."

Uneasiness nipped at my stomach, and I forced down the bite of food. "I don't know, you seemed to know a bit more than that earlier."

"Oh, I have a library of *observations*. I'm talking about knowing you."

"You know where I live. Where I work and that I'm allergic to peanuts."

"It's been a few weeks, Sara. It's weird that you still hold me at arm's length." He blinked away. "I'm not sure I can forever be strangers."

"But we're so good at being strangers," I joked, and when his face fell, I relented. "What do you want to know?"

He looked back at me, thick, dark lashes pressing to his cheeks as he closed his eyes, thinking. He was so gorgeous; my pulse took over my entire head, hammering inside my cranium like a drill.

Opening his eyes, he asked, "Have you ever had a dog?"

A laugh burst from my lips. "Yes. My father always had Dalmatians, but my mom is currently obsessed with labradoodles."

"I beg your pardon?"

"Labrador retriever and poodle mix."

He shook his head, grinning. "You Americans always messing with our canonical breeds." I lifted my wine to my lips and took a sip just as he asked, "Why are you so scared of being with someone?"

I stammered out a few unintelligible noises before he laughed, waving me off. "Just checking to see how far I could go. Do you have siblings?"

I shook my head, relieved. "Only child. Crazy parents, so thank God they only had me. Another would have killed them."

"Why?"

"My parents are . . . eccentric," I explained, smiling as I thought about them.

Eccentric almost didn't cover it. I imagined Mom with her feather-wigs and jewelry. Dad with his thick glasses, short-sleeved dress shirts, and bow ties. They were from another time—almost another planet—but their eccentricities only made them easier to love.

"My dad's always worked a lot but when he's not at work, he becomes obsessed with one thing or another. Mom likes to be busy but Dad never wanted her to work outside the house. She grew up in Texas and met Dad in college. She was a math major, but once they got married, she sold cosmetics from home, and then sold some crazy no-wrinkle cotton clothes. And most recently, skin stuff."

"What exactly does your dad do?"

I hesitated, wondering, *How can he ask this? Does he really not know anything about me?*

"So, my last name is Dillon, right?"

He nodded, interested.

Max is British. He's probably never heard of Dillons.

Telling him this felt like lifting a heavy iron chain. It was nice to think about being unburdened, but almost easier to leave it alone than try to lift it. My entire life people had looked at me differently after learning who my family was; I wondered if Max would be any different.

I took a deep breath and looked at him. "My family owns a chain of department stores. They're regional, like, in the Midwest? But they're big there."

He paused, eyes narrowed. "Wait. *Dillons?* As in 'You Should Love to Live,' Dillons?"

I nodded.

"Oh. Wow. Your family owns Dillons. Okay then."

Max ran a hand over his face and laughed to himself, shaking his head. "Shit, Sara. I . . . I had no idea. I feel like a wanker."

"I like that you didn't know who I was." I felt my stomach drop, realizing that now that he knew I was *someone,* he probably would look me up. He'd learn about Andy, and realize what a fool I was to not know what an entire city had known all along.

Max would know I'd been someone else's doormat before I'd ever been his mystery.

I looked away, feeling a little deflated. I didn't want to talk about lives or histories or family. I searched wildly for a new topic.

But he spoke before I could come up with anything. "You know what fascinates me about you?" he asked, pouring me another glass of honey wine.

"What?"

"The first night we met, and then our first night in the warehouse in Brooklyn: the things you let me do. And then tonight, you flush at the word *cunt.*"

"I know!" I laughed, taking a sip of wine.

"I like that about you. I like your internal conflict, your sweetness. I like that you have this insanely wealthy family but I've seen you wear the same dress a few times." He licked his lips and gave me a predatory smile. "Mostly, I like that you're so clearly good and yet have let me do such bad things to you."

"I don't think they're bad."

"Ah, but that's the point. Most people would think you were mad to meet me at that warehouse. You're an American heiress and you let some whorish Brit take pictures of you naked. Take video of you masturbating in my office tonight just for the thrill of knowing I'll watch it. But it's what *you've* asked me for."

He leaned back in his chair, watched me. He looked so serious, almost perplexed. "I'm a fucking bloke; I'm not going to say no to that. But I didn't think women like you existed. So naïve in all these really obvious ways, yet so fucking sexual that a friendly, gentle little shag on a mattress would never be enough."

I lifted my glass, took a sip while he watched my mouth. Licking my lips, I smiled at him. "I think you'll find most women aren't always satisfied by a friendly, gentle little shag on a mattress."

Max laughed, murmuring, "Touché."

"And *that's* why the cameras and the women chase you," I said, looking at him from over the top of my glass. "It's more than the history with Cecily. If it were just that, they would have lost interest within a few weeks. But you're the man from the paper with a different woman all the time. The one nobody can seem to catch. The man who obviously knows his way around a pussy."

Max's eyes widened a little, pupils dilating like a

drop of ink into the dusk sky. "I'm not with a different woman every night lately."

Ignoring him, I finished my thought. "Women don't always want to be treated like we're delicate, or rare, or somehow more precious. We want to be *wanted*. We want sex to be just as raw as you do. You're the guy who knows that."

He leaned forward on his elbows, studying me. "But why do I feel like you're the one giving me something special? Something you've never given anyone before?"

"Because I am."

He opened his mouth to say something, but then my phone rang, vibrating where I'd put it on the table. And as both Max and I looked down at it, I knew we saw the name at exactly the same time.

ANDY CELL.

TWELVE

I put Sara in a cab and watched as the taillights disappeared into the darkness.

Fuck.

She'd ignored the call at dinner, glancing at the screen before silencing it to vibrate against the table, but not before I saw who it was, and definitely not before I saw her try to hide her reaction.

ANDY CELL.

I'd never seen anyone shut down like that before; it was like someone flipped a switch and the light slowly drained from her face. She'd begun picking at her food and stopped talking, withdrawing into herself and answering in single-word sentences for the remainder of the meal. I'd tried to lighten the mood, told a few jokes and flirted with her shamelessly, but . . . nothing. After about ten minutes she'd put us both out of our misery, feigning a headache and insisting that she take a cab home. Alone.

Fuck.

I continued to stare off into the empty street as my car pulled up to the curb, idling quietly behind me. I waved off my driver, opening the door myself and climbing inside.

"Where to, Mr. Stella?"

"Let's head home, Scott," I said, slumping back into the seat. We pulled away and I watched the city rush by in a blur, my mood darkening with each block we passed.

Things had been going so well. She'd finally started to open up, to let me into that vault of a mind of hers. I was still reeling from her admission that her parents owned one of the largest luxury department store chains in the country, and then "Andy cell." *Fucking Andy cell.*

Anger flared in my chest and for a brief moment I wondered how often they spoke. Six years was a long time and meant they had a history that would be hard to simply brush under the rug; I don't know why I'd assumed he was completely out of her life. It made sense that she didn't want to be in another relationship, but her forced distance always felt so much larger than that.

Maybe he wanted her back.

I frowned as I let that thought roll around in my head, hating the way it felt.

Of course he wanted her back; how could he not? For the hundredth time I found myself wondering what exactly happened between them and why she was so against telling me.

We drove through midtown and were almost to my building when my mobile vibrated in my pocket.

Home safe. Thanks for dinner. xx

Well, this night certainly went tits up.

I reread her text and considered calling, knowing it'd be a lost cause. She was so fucking stubborn. I typed out at least ten different replies, deleting each one before sending.

The problem was that I wanted to talk about this and she didn't. The problem was also that I'd somehow misplaced my balls and my spine.

"You mind driving around a bit, Scott?" I asked, and he shook his head, turning north past the park. I flipped through my contacts and pressed Will's name. It rang twice before he answered.

"Hey. What's up?"

"You got a few?" I asked, looking out over the passing streets.

"Sure, give me a second." There was some shuffling and the sound of a door closing before he was back. "Everything okay?"

I leaned my head back against the seat, not sure where to start. I just knew I had to unload some confusion with someone, and, unfortunately for him right now, that someone in my life was Will. "I have no idea."

"Well, that was cryptic. I didn't have an email telling me something is on fire, so I'm assuming this isn't about work."

"I wish."

"Okay . . . Hey, didn't you say something about having plans tonight?"

"That's sort of why I'm calling, actually." I scrubbed a hand along my jaw. "Jesus. I can't believe I'm doing this," I said. "I think I just need someone to . . . to listen. Like, if I say it out loud it'll make more sense."

"Well, this should be good," he said, chuckling into the phone. "Let me get comfortable."

"You know the woman I've been seeing."

"Fucking. The woman you've been fucking."

I closed my eyes. "Will."

"Yes, Max. Your amazing shag. The secret sex-only situation with the woman who does not want to be photographed and which will most definitely not go down in flames."

I sighed. "So, about that," I mumbled. "I mean . . . this is just between us, yeah?"

"Of course," he said, sounding a bit offended. "I may be an asshole but I'm a trustworthy asshole. And shouldn't you be over here so we can, like, I don't know, do each other's nails while we talk about our feelings?"

"It's Sara Dillon."

Silence. *Well, that shut him up.*

"Will?"

"Holy shit."

"Yeah," I said, rubbing my temples.

"Sara Dillon. Sara Dillon of Ryan Media Group."

"The very one. It started before I even knew she worked with Ben."

"Wow. I mean, she's gorgeous, don't get me wrong, but, she seems really . . . reserved? Who would've thought she had it in her. Nice."

And because it felt so good to just say it, I barreled on. "It started out as just a hookup. I could tell she was using me to play around, explore things."

"Things?"

I scratched my jaw and winced as I admitted, "She likes to have sex in public."

"Uh?" he said, laughing. "That doesn't sound like the Sara Dillon I've met."

"And she lets me take pictures of her."

"Wait—what?"

"Photographs, sometimes more. Of us."

"Of you . . ."

"Fucking."

The silence stretched for a few moments and I swear I could hear his rapid-fire blinking. He cleared his throat. "Okay, the sex in public is pretty awesome, but every guy I know has taken pictures while he's fucking a girl."

"What's your point, tosser?"

"That you're behind the trend, *dick*."

"Will, I'm being fucking serious here."

"Okay. So what's the problem?"

"The problem is tonight was the first night I managed to get her to go to a restaurant. I find out her parents own fucking *Dillons*, Will. The department store? These are things I didn't even know before yesterday."

He was quiet for a beat and then laughed quietly. "Yeah."

"So, like this, we're actually talking for once, and then her twat of an ex calls."

"Yeah."

"And it's obvious he did a right number on her but she just shut down and couldn't get away fast enough after that. She'll have sex with me until she can barely walk, but she won't tell me why it took her over a month to agree to actually have a meal with me."

"Uh huh."

"So her parents own a store and she grew up in Chicago. That's it? I know nothing about her, really."

"Yeah."

"Will, are you even listening to me?"

"Of course I'm listening. You know nothing."

"Right."

"So . . . have you googled her?" he asked.

"Of course not," I said.

"Why?"

I groaned. "I thought we had this conversation after the Cecily debacle. Nothing good comes from personal Google searches."

215

"But *professionally,* if you're working with someone new, you look them up, right?"

"Of course."

"Well, *I* googled Sara as soon as I knew she'd be one of my contacts at RMG. It sure was informative."

My throat grew tight, and I tugged uselessly at my collar. "Tell me what you saw."

He laughed. "Not a chance. Find some balls and strap them on while your laptop boots. And on that note, this little chat's been great but I gotta go. Company."

I directed Scotty back to my building. Once upstairs, I made it all of five minutes before I was at the computer and typing the name "Sara Dillon" into the search engine.

Holy shit.

There wasn't just the odd mention here and there; there were pages and pages of results, possibly more than I'd find on myself. I took a deep breath and went to the images first, scrolling through photos of her that had to span at least the last ten years of her life. She was so young in some of them, her butterscotch hair styled in a sleek pixie in some, a messy shag in others. In all of them, her smile was unguarded and naïve.

And these weren't just a collection of family snapshots or selfies; they were high-definition paparazzi photos taken with expensive zoom lenses, bought and sold to newspapers and magazines with exclamation-point-heavy titles, even video and archived news footage. There were parties and weddings, charity events and vacations, and almost always with the same man at her side.

He was only a few inches taller than she was, with black hair and sharp, Roman features. His bright, toothy smile looked about as sincere as I imagined it would, which is to say not sincere in the slightest.

So this was Andy. Known to the world as Andrew Morton. Democratic congressman, serving the seventh district of Illinois.

Suddenly, a lot of things were falling into place.

With a resigned sigh, I clicked on what seemed to be a fairly recent picture; her hair was about the same as it was now and there was a Christmas tree in the background. The caption below the photo read:

Sara Dillon and Andrew Morton at the annual Chicago Sun-Times Holiday Bash, where Congressman Morton announced his plans to run for the United States Senate next fall.

I clicked the link and read the entire article, confirming that this story was written only last winter, and that meant the congressman was probably already on the Illinois campaign trail. I routed back to the main image page and scrolled back to the top where, beside several similar shots, there was a picture of Sara running through a tangle of paparazzi, covering her face with her coat. I'd ignored these at first because her face hadn't been visible. I clicked the link to the story associated with the photo, dated only a few weeks before I met her, and an article from the *Chicago Tribune* came up.

Democratic congressman Andrew Morton was spotted last night in an intimate tête-à-tête with a woman other than his fiancée, Sara Dillon. The brunette, identified as Melissa Marino, is a junior aide in his Chicago-based offices.

In the middle of the article was the photo in question, of a man—obviously Andy—passionately kissing a woman—obviously not Sara.

Dillon and Morton have been linked since 2007, and the pair, the darlings of the Chicago social scene ever since, were engaged last December shortly after Morton announced his intention to run for the U.S. Senate. Sara Dillon, head of finance for the commercial firm Nieman & Shimazawa, is the only child of Roger and Samantha Dillon, founders of the well-known department store chain found across seventeen states and hefty financial backers of the Morton campaign.

The Dillon family spokesperson couldn't be reached for comment, but a spokesperson for the

Morton reelection campaign responded to the Tribune inquiry with only, "Mr. Morton's private life has never been a subject for public consumption."

Unfortunately, the widely rumored playboy legislator may have finally broken strategy and brought his extracurricular activities front and center.

Widely rumored playboy. Motherfucker.

I sat back in my chair as I looked at Sara and Andy together, a hot curl of anger sparking in my chest. She was the kind of woman men hoped they'd get to drink in for days, to know better than any other man has, to protect somehow, to take a punch for or to sweep away from an oncoming bus. I looked at every image I could find. She'd smiled so brightly in every photo prior to the ones dated last April. She'd been a natural in front of the camera, the brightness of her smile changing very little over the years.

And this twat had cheated on her—multiple times, if the article was to be believed.

He was a good enough looking bloke, I supposed, though obviously older than her. I clicked through to another article, one that listed his age at thirty-seven, ten years her senior.

According to one story published only two months ago, it was the world's worst-kept secret that Andy had cheated on Sara several times in the past year, and a growing perception was that he was using her for her family's name and their money, exploiting the press's love for their local-celebrity romance whenever his reputation was in need of a little public relations boost.

I glanced through a few more photos before I pushed back from my desk, disgusted. That arsehole had used her. He'd asked her to marry him and then proceeded to fuck everything in a skirt. Christ, no wonder she had issues. And no wonder, too, that she was so mistrustful of paparazzi.

My flat had grown dark by the time I powered off the computer and left the den. I made my way to the wet bar, switching on a few lamps as I went, and poured myself a scotch. The drink burned on its way down, immediately spreading warmth throughout my veins.

It didn't help, but I finished it anyway.

I poured myself another drink and wondered what she was doing. Was she home? Had she called the cheating bastard back? After looking at those hundreds of pictures, I could just imagine the history they had. What if he called to apologize? What if she was on a plane, headed back to Chicago right now? Would she even tell me? I checked the time and let myself imagine tracking her down, throwing her over my shoulder and bringing her back here. Fucking her into the mattress until I was the only man she remembered.

Clearly, I needed a distraction, and drinking wasn't the answer.

It took me less than five minutes to change out of my suit and into a pair of shorts and trainers. I took the elevator to the gym on the twentieth floor and took to the running track. As usual this time of day, it was blissfully empty.

I ran until my lungs were on fire and my legs numb. I ran until practically every thought had been wiped from my mind, except one: it would break me if she went back to him.

I went to the locker room, stripped off my sweaty clothes, and then collapsed on the bench, dropping my head into my hands. The silence was broken by the sound of my mobile ringing inside my locker. My head snapped up; I was surprised that anyone would be calling at this hour. I crossed the room and froze when I saw Sara's picture—a photo I'd snapped of her hand at her throat, the brush of caramel hair against creamy skin—light up the screen.

"Sara?"

"Hey."

"You all right?" I asked.

A horn honked somewhere in the background and she cleared her throat. "Yeah, I'm good. Look, are you busy? I could—"

"No, no. Was just finishing a run. Where are you?"

"Actually," she said, laughing softly, "I'm outside your building."

I blinked. "You're what?"

"Yeah. Could I come up?"

"Of course. Give me a few minutes and I'll meet you—"

"No. Can I just meet you up there? I just . . . I'm afraid I'll lose my nerve if I wait."

Well, that was cryptic. My stomach dropped. "Yeah, of course, Petal. Let me ring the front desk."

A few minutes later, Sara was walking through the door of the locker room to find me wearing nothing but a towel around my waist.

She looked tired, with red-rimmed eyes and her bottom lip chapped and swollen. It was a softer, younger-looking version of Sara, one I had only seen today in photos. She smiled weakly, giving a small wave as the door closed behind her.

"Hey," I said, crossing the room. I bent at the knees to bring my eyes level with hers. "You okay? What happened?"

She sighed, shook her head, and something snapped back in place in her expression. "I wanted to see you."

I knew she was avoiding my question but felt the smile pull at the corners of my mouth before I could stop it. I couldn't keep my hands to myself and I placed them on either side of her face, brushing my thumbs along her cheeks. "Well, that definitely warrants a trip to the men's locker room."

"We're alone, right?"

"Completely."

"We didn't get to finish earlier," she said, pushing me back toward the showers.

I felt my heart speed up at the feel of her in my arms again, the buzz of static in my ears. She stood on her toes to kiss me, her hands moving to the towel at my hips.

"Hmm," I said, humming against her mouth. I felt her

reach behind me and heard the water start, felt it run warm down my back. "You want to do this here?"

She answered wordlessly, pulling her shirt over her head and shimmying out of her jeans.

I guess that's a yes, then.

"My apartment is just downstairs . . . ," I said, trying to slow her down. I could already imagine what it would be like to fuck her right here, to hear her screams as they echoed off the tile, but for once I wanted nothing but her naked body on my bed, top sheet and blankets in a pile on the floor. Maybe her hands tied over her head and strapped to the rails of my headboard.

She ignored me, wrapping her fingers around my cock and leaning in to bite my shoulder. I tried to clear my head, remembering her expression as she'd walked through the door. It wasn't unlike her to avoid answering my questions, but tonight she didn't look hard and feisty; she looked wild for the wrong reasons. Her eyes were too bare, her face drawn. She'd only come for distraction.

My throat was suddenly dry and I ran my tongue over my lips, tasting the cherry lip gloss she wore.

I was a bit surprised by the Sara catalog I'd managed to compile without even realizing it. I knew what her face looked like when she came, the way her nipples hardened, and how her eyelids fluttered closed only at the very last second, like she wanted to watch every moment until it was suddenly too much.

I knew what her hand felt like curved around my waist, her nails digging into my back and scratching up and down my sides.

I knew the sounds she made and the way her breath caught when I moved my fingers just the way she liked.

And there were things that were new, things I found myself noticing and wanting to see again and again. The little smile she made when she knew she had just said something funny and was waiting for me to catch up. It was the subtlest thing, just a slight tilt to the edges of her lips and eyes. A challenge.

The way she gently pinched her lower lip when she was reading.

There was the way she kissed me that day on the roof, slow and lazy and like there was nowhere else, nowhere at all to be.

But I didn't know this Sara. I'd always suspected that the feistiness I enjoyed so much about her was a form of self-preservation. But I never anticipated the way it would feel to see it gone like this; it was like a punch in the gut that took the breath straight from my lungs.

I gathered her hands in mine and took a step back. "What's going on?" I asked, gauging her expression. "Talk to me."

She leaned into me again. "Don't want to talk."

"Sara, I don't mind being your distraction but at least be honest with me about it. Something's wrong."

"I'm fine." But she wasn't fine. She wouldn't have come here if she were.

"Bullshit. You're breaking your own rules by even being here. This is better—this is *real*—but it's also different and I want to know why."

She pulled back, looking up at me. "Andy called."

"I know," I said, my jaw clenched tight.

She smiled apologetically. "He said he wanted me back. Said all the things I once wanted him to say, about how he's different now and he messed up and could never hurt me again."

I watched her, waiting. She pressed her face to my wet neck, getting courage. "He's just worried about his campaign. Our entire relationship was a lie."

"I'm so sorry, Sara."

"I looked up Cecily."

I blinked, confused. "Okay?"

"Something about her name stuck with me, and after you told me about her, I wanted to know what she looked like." She pulled back, looking at me. "She was familiar, but it didn't sink in until tonight. I'd met a lot of people with Andy and usually I'd forget their faces two seconds after I shook their hands . . . but I remembered her."

I nodded, my stomach warming, but let her keep talking.

"So I went home and I looked her up again before I called him back." She paused, her voice shaking slightly. "He went on and on for a half hour about how sorry he was, how it was just the one time and he'd never be able to forgive himself. So I asked him about Cecily. And do you know what he said?"

"Cecily . . . what?"

"He said, 'Fuck, Sare. Do we have to do this now? That's ancient history.' He fucked her, Max. Andy was the politician she talked about in her letter. Andrew Morton, whoring congressman from Illinois and fucking his way through the Seventh District. They slept together the night I met her, at a campaign event for Schumer."

I groaned. I'd been at that fund-raiser, but not as her date. Cecily had been upset with me all night, and left angry, but I never knew why.

She flinched in my arms. "I remember catching him walking out of a bathroom, and we started talking and he was trying to get me to move, but I told him to wait, that I had to use the restroom. And then she stepped out of the men's room, and looked at him, and then me, and it was really awkward and I had no idea why she stormed off. But she'd been in there *with him*."

I wrapped my arms around her as the water pounded down around us, insulating us in a soundproof bubble. This was the smallest world; smaller even than I thought it'd been when I saw her playing pinball, or she urged me into the privacy of a cab in the middle of the afternoon. This was a world where, years ago, Cecily had sex with Sara's boyfriend because she was upset with *me*. I didn't regret having Sara in my arms; I didn't regret passing up a relationship with Cecily. But I couldn't help feeling guilty somehow.

"I'm sorry," I whispered again.

"No, you don't understand." She looked up at me, beads of water running over her face and she didn't even care. "We'd only been together for a few months at that point. All along, right up until the end, I'd assumed he wasn't cheating back then. I thought that had only started recently. But he was never faithful—never."

I tightened my hold, whispering into her hair, "You know that had nothing to do with you, yeah? It only tells me what a despicable human he is. Not every man is so horrible."

She straightened, looking up at me, and I could see her biting down a smile. Her eyes were still brimmed with tears but the gratitude in them was real. Something seized in my chest with the way she looked at me, because the dirty sex and no-strings-attached thing we had was great—amazing even—but this, this was something entirely new.

"I was with him for a long time. Part of me wondered if he'd just messed up the one time and I was being unfair. But I'm glad I was right to leave. I'm just . . . ready for better this time," she said.

I swallowed down this new emotion and tried to sort myself out, remembering that feelings and affection weren't supposed to be part of the deal, trying to focus instead on where we were and the fact that her very naked body was still pressed against mine.

"There are plenty of men that would kill for a woman like you," I said, trying to keep my voice steady, completely unprepared for how it felt like I was being hollowed out and filled with ice water to imagine her with someone else. With that sobering realization, I reached behind and turned off the faucet, grabbing a towel that hung nearby. "Let's get you dried off; it's freezing in here."

"But . . . you don't want to—"

"You've had one hell of a day," I said, smoothing her hair. "Let me be the gentleman tonight and I'll defile you next time." I wanted to ask her to stay, but I wasn't sure I could handle it if she said no tonight. "Are you okay?"

She nodded, pressing her face to my chest. "I think I just need some sleep."

"I'll have Scott drive you home."

We dressed in silence, openly watching each other. It was a bit of a reverse seduction seeing her pull her jeans on, fasten her bra, cover her breasts with her sweater. But I didn't think I'd ever wanted her more than in that moment when I was witnessing her put herself back together.

I was falling in love with her. And I was royally fucked.

———

Saturday morning I'd started to dial Sara at least twenty times before hanging up just before it would ring. My head told me to give her some distance. But fuck, I wanted to see her. I was acting like a fucking teenager.

Call her, you git. Ask her to come out today. Don't take no for an answer.

This time I actually walked away, because a man who

says clichéd shit like that doesn't deserve to call any woman.

I made excuses the rest of the morning, telling myself that she was probably busy. Hell, I didn't even know if Sara had friends other than Chloe and Bennett. I couldn't exactly ask her that, could I? Fuck, no. She'd put her shoe in my eye socket. But what exactly did she do when she wasn't at work? I played rugby, drank beer, ran, went to art showings. Everything I knew about her was related either to how she fucked, or to the life she'd left behind. I knew so little about the life she'd started to build here. Maybe she'd love to do something with me after the shitty day she'd had yesterday.

Time to man up, Stella.

Finally, I shoved my spine in my back and let the phone ring.

"Hello?" she answered, sounding confused. *Of course she's confused, you ass. You've never actually called her.*

I took a deep breath and let out the most ungodly ramble of my entire life: "Okay, look, before you say anything, I know we aren't doing the boyfriend-girlfriend thing, and after Congressman Morton's wandering penis I totally get your aversion to relationships, but last night you came over and were a bit out of sorts, and if you wanted something to do today—not that you *need* something to do (and even if you did, not to imply that you don't have other options), but if you'd like you could come to my rugby match." I paused, listening for any sign of life on the other end of the phone.

"Nothing clears the head better than watching a pile of muddy, sweaty Brits trying to break each other's femurs."

She laughed. "What?"

"Rugby. Come watch my match today. Or, if you prefer, meet us all for drinks at Maddie's in Harlem afterward."

For what felt like a week, she remained silent.

"Sara?"

"I'm thinking."

I walked across the room and fidgeted with the blinds at my window overlooking the park. "Think louder."

"I'm seeing a movie with a girlfriend this afternoon," she began, and I felt a small tension unknot in my gut when she mentioned a friend. "But I guess I could be up for drinks later. What time do you think you'll be done?"

Like even worse of a git than before, I made a little fist pump of victory and immediately wanted to smack myself. "Match will probably go until three. You could meet us at Maddie's around four."

"I will," she said. "But Max?"

"Hmm?"

"Do you think your team will win? I don't want to be drinking with a bunch of depressed, muddy Brits."

Laughing, I assured her we were going to crush them.

———

We kicked their asses. I rarely ever felt bad for the other team—most teams we played were American and, although it wasn't their fault they didn't have rugby in their blood, it usually felt great to tromp them. But this may have been an exception. We stopped trying to score about halfway through. I had to attribute my generosity in part to knowing that Sara would meet us after. But only in part. By the end of the match it felt like we were beating up ten-year-olds in the mud, and I felt a twinge of guilt.

We roared into the bar, carrying Robbie on our shoulders and yelling the words to a rather filthy version of "Alouette." The bartender and owner, Madeline, waved when she saw us, lined up twelve pint glasses, and began filling them.

"Oi!" Robbie shouted to his wife. "Whiskey, lass!"

Maddie gave him the V-sign but grabbed a handful of shot glasses anyway, mumbling something about Robbie's drunk, muddy ass sleeping alone.

I scanned the room for Sara and came up empty. Swallowing my disappointment, I turned to the bar and took a deep drink of my beer. Our game had started late; it was already close to five and she wasn't here. Was I really surprised? And then a horrible thought occurred to me: had she been here, waited, and left?

"Fuck," I muttered.

Maddie slid a shot of whiskey to me and I downed it with a wince, cursing again.

"What's wrong?" a familiar husky voice asked from behind me. "Looks to me like you dirty bastards won."

I spun around on my bar stool and broke out into a grin at

the sight of her. She looked like a cake topper, in a pale yellow dress and a tiny green pin in her hair. "You look beautiful." Her eyes closed for a beat, and I murmured, "Sorry we're late."

She weaved a little where she stood, saying, "Gave me time to have a few drinks."

I hadn't seen her drunk since the night at the club, but I recognized a familiar light in her eyes: mischief. The thought of *that* Sara reappearing was fucking fantastic.

"You're pissed?"

Her brows pinched together for a brief pulse and then smoothed as she smiled. "British for drunk? Yeah, I'm tipsy." She stood on her toes then . . . and kissed me.

Holy. Fuck.

Beside me, Richie chimed in. "What the . . . Max. There's a girl on your face."

Sara pulled back and her eyes widened in realization. "Oh, crap."

"Calm down," I told her quietly. "No one here gives a fuck who we are. They hardly remember my name every week."

"Patently untrue," Richie said. "Your name is Twat."

I tilted my head to him, smiling at Sara. "Like I said."

She held out her hand and gave Richie her wide-eyed smile. "I'm Sara."

He took her hand and shook it. I could see the moment he really looked at her and registered how ridiculously pretty she was. He immediately checked out her chest. "'m Richie," he mumbled.

"Nice to meet you, Richie."

He looked at me, eyes narrowed. "How the fuck you land that one?"

"No idea." I pulled her closer, ignoring her mild protest that I was going to get her dress dirty. But then she wiggled free and turned to Derek, on my other side.

"I'm Sara."

Derek put his beer down and wiped a grimy hand across his mouth. "Fuck yeah you are."

"Sara's with me," I muttered.

And like this, Tipsy Sara worked her way down the bar, introducing herself to every single one of my mates. In her, I saw the politician's wife she'd almost been, but even more than that, I saw that Sara was just a really fucking sweet girl.

When she returned to me, she kissed my cheek and whispered, "Your friends are nice. Thanks for inviting me."

"Yeah, sure." I lost my ability to form coherent thoughts. Almost nothing in my life made me feel the way she was making me feel—so bloody good. I wasn't full of self-loathing, but I'd been a bit of a slut, worked in investments that, let's be honest, relied on people losing money as much as others making it, and I'd fostered few deep connections since I'd been stateside. My closest friend was Will and most of the time we just called each other names that were all variations on the word *pussy*.

Tell her, you dick. Pull her to the other side of the room, give her a good snog, and tell her you love her.

"Take this old blues shite off the speaker, Maddie," Derek yelled across the bar.

And just as I was about to touch Sara's elbow, ask her to come talk to me, she straightened. "This isn't blues," she said.

Derek turned around, eyebrows raised.

"It's not. It's Eddie Cochran. It's rockabilly," she said, but under his continued inspection she seemed to shrink a little. "They aren't the same at all."

"You know how to dance to this rubbish?" he asked her, looking her up and down again.

To my surprise, Sara laughed. "Are you asking?"

"Fuck no, I—"

But before he could finish his sentence, she'd jerked him to his feet, and all 115 pounds of her was dragging his enormous frame to the dance floor.

"My mom is from Texas," she said, eyes sparkling. "Try to keep up."

"You're kidding," he said, looking over at us. The entire bar full of Brits had stopped talking and was watching them with interest.

"Go on!" I yelled.

"Don't be a pussy, Der," Maddie yelled, and everyone began clapping. She turned up the music. "Give us a show."

Sara's smile grew, and she placed his hand on her shoulder, shaking her head when he protested. "It's the traditional pose. You put one hand on my back, the other on my shoulder."

And while we watched, Sara showed Big Derek how to do a dance across the floor: two quick steps, two slow steps. She demonstrated how he was to quickly spin her counterclockwise around the room. Within one song, they were moving pretty good, and by the middle of the second, they were both cracking up, dancing together like they'd known each other for years.

Maybe that's what it was about Sara. Anyone who met her wanted to *know* her. She wasn't just appealingly sweet to me, with her innocence pushing through even given her basest fantasies. She was irresistible to everyone.

And in that moment, there was nothing I wanted to do more than punch Andy's smug fucking face. He'd wasted his time with her, wasted *her*.

I stood, moved to the dance floor, and cut in. "My turn."

Those deep brown eyes of hers darkened, and instead of posing my hands like she'd done with Derek, she slipped her arms around my neck, stretched to kiss my jaw, and whispered, "I'm pretty sure it's always your turn."

"I thought there was supposed to be a little more distance between us when we dance to this," I said, smiling as I bent to kiss her.

"Not with you."

"Good."

She broke into a drunken, playful smile. "But I'm starving. I want a burger the size of my head."

A laugh burst from my throat and I bent to kiss her forehead. "There's a place near you that fits the bill. I'll text you an address. Shall I head home to shower and meet you there in an hour?"

"Dinner two nights in a row?" she asked, looking more carefully eager than anything. Where was the cautious, distancing woman I knew only days ago? She'd evaporated. I suspected Distancing Sara had always been a bit of a fantasy.

Hers, not mine.

I nodded, feeling my smile slip away. I was done with the pretense that we had any boundaries left. The single expectant word came out hoarse: "Yeah."

She bit her lip to hold back the smile, but it was impossible to miss.

Thirteen

I'd been in New York for two months and had no real sense of what I was doing when I wasn't at work. I ran. I had a few friends I would meet for shows, or coffee, or drinks. I talked to my parents a couple of times a week. I wasn't lonely; I certainly had a fuller life here than I'd had by the end of my time in Chicago. But most of my life outside of work had become Max.

How in the hell had that happened?

Casual Sex: You're Doing It Wrong.

Then again, for his part, Max never seemed surprised by anything that happened between us. Not when I coerced him into having sex in the club, or when I came to his office offering sex and nothing more, and not even when I sought him out only to break down in his shower, begging him to just take me and make everything else go away.

Even his friends were amazing. Derek was possibly the largest human I had ever met, and though he was not exactly light on his feet, dancing with him had been some of the most fun I'd had in ages . . . other than every time I was with Max.

I waved goodbye to Derek and he winked at me, reminding with a nod to where Max sat at the bar about what he'd said on the dance floor: "He's a prick, that one."

Under the single light of the dance floor, Derek had looked even muddier than he had when I'd introduced myself. I'd glanced down at my dress and noted a few handprints near my shoulder. "He's not so bad."

Laughing, Derek had patted my head. "He's the worst, nice to everyone and never fucks up. Always there for his mates, never comes off like an arsehole." He'd winked. "What a fucking nightmare."

Thanking Maddie as we left, I heard the team's continued drunken singing from behind me in the bar as Max hailed a cab and held the door for me as I climbed in.

"See you in a bit," he said, before closing the door and giving me a small wave through the window as we pulled away from the curb.

I looked out the back window. Max stood still, watching my cab disappear down Lenox.

We'd decided on something simple for dinner: burgers at a small, quiet place in the East Village.

Quiet was good. Quiet would help drown out the mayhem in my brain. My plan to have fun, be wild, and keep things compartmentalized had gone to hell.

I went home and showered off the mud from dancing with Derek and Max, and put on a simple blue jersey halter dress. The songs from the bar echoed in my ear, and I let myself imagine seeing his friends again: curling up with Max on a friend's couch and watching a movie with them, or cupping my hands around a mug of coffee on the sidelines of a rugby match. Each fantasy felt like a given, but I stopped thinking about any of them when the tendrils of my mind began to analyze, worry, play devil's advocate.

I walked out into the hall and locked my apartment, reminding myself, *One thing at a time. No one is making you do any of this.*

Even on this Saturday night, with people out enjoying the lazy evening sunset, it was less hectic in the Village than it ever felt in midtown. When had this place started to feel like home? Max chose a restaurant within walking distance of my building; I no longer needed to read every street sign to find my way there.

Strands of tiny lights glowed yellow and warm above the entrance, and a small bell rang as I opened the door. Max was already there, cleaned up and seated in the back reading the *Times*. I gave myself this stolen moment to take him in: deep red T-shirt, worn jeans with a rip in the thigh. Light brown hair almost gold in the light. Fancy Brit-looking sneakers at the end of his long, stretched-out legs. Sunglasses on the table near his elbow.

Just your average godlike fuck buddy, hanging out at the burger place, waiting for you.

I closed my eyes, took a deep breath, and walked over to him.

The lines had blurred. After today, I couldn't pretend I wanted nothing from him beyond orgasms. I couldn't pretend that my heart didn't twist deliciously when I saw him, or twist with discomfort when I left. I couldn't pretend that I didn't have feelings for him.

I wondered if it was too late to flee.

It was only when I heard his laugh that I realized I'd been staring, my mouth open slightly, and he'd been watching me for . . . I have no idea how long. A smile tilted up half of his mouth.

"You look pretty excited for this beer." He pushed a pint across the table and held up his own. "I took the liberty of ordering you a burger the size of your head, and some chips." He grinned and then clarified, "A.k.a. 'fries.'"

"Perfect. Thanks." I set my purse on an empty chair and sat across from him. His eyes smiled, and then dipped to look at my lips.

"So," I said, sipping my beer and assessing him over the rim.

"So."

He looked positively amused with this turn of events. I wasn't a control freak, but I was used to having a pretty predictable life, and in the past two months, I hadn't been able to anticipate anything that had come my way. "Thanks for inviting me to the bar today."

He nodded, scratching the back of his neck. "Thanks for coming."

"Your friends are nice."

"They're a bunch of arseholes."

I laughed, feeling my shoulders slowly relax. "That's funny. That's what they said about you."

He rested his elbows on the table and leaned forward. "I have a question."

"Yes?"

"Are we on a date?"

I nearly choked on the sip of beer I'd just taken.

"For the love of God, woman, don't have a fit. I just wonder if you'd like to reestablish ground rules. Should we review our previous set?"

I nodded, pressing a napkin to my lips and mumbling, "Sure."

He set his drink down and began ticking my rules off on his long fingers. "One night a week, no other lovers, sex preferably in public—definitely *not* in my bed—pictures are requested, but no faces, no publicity." He lifted his glass, took a deep drink, and then leaned forward again, whispering, "And nothing between us other than sex. Scratching an itch and all that. Did I capture it all?"

"Sounds about right." My heart thundered under my ribs as I realized how far we'd strayed from that in only a day.

A college-age kid brought over two baskets with burgers bigger than any I'd ever seen before and enormous piles of fries.

"Holy crap," I said, staring at my food. "This is . . ."

"Exactly what you wanted?" he asked in return, reaching for a bottle of vinegar.

"Yes, but way more than I can eat."

"Let's make this interesting, shall we?" he said. "Whoever eats more of their burger can set new ground rules."

With a smile, he screwed the cap back on the vinegar and set it down. We both knew he was almost double my weight. No way could I eat more than him.

But was he *hungry?* Maybe he'd had enough beer to fill up and knew that I would eat more than he would? Or did he *want* to make the rules?

"Christ, woman. Stop thinking," he said, lifting his burger and taking a gigantic bite.

"Fine. Deal," I said, suddenly dying to know what Max's rules would be.

❧

I stared at Max as he wiped his hands on a napkin and then balled it up, dropping it into his empty basket.

"That was good," he mumbled, finally looking up at me. He cracked up at the pathetic progress I'd made. I had managed to polish off only about a quarter of my burger, and it looked like I had barely touched my fries.

Dropping the burger back into the basket, I groaned. "I'm so full."

"I won."

"Was there any question?"

"Then why'd you take the deal?" he asked, pushing his chair away from the table. "You could have said no."

I shrugged, then stood, turning to leave before he pressed me to answer. I could be curious about what he wanted between us, but I wasn't sure I was ready to admit it.

My beer buzz from earlier in the day was wearing off, and with the weight of the burger in my stomach I could have curled up on the sidewalk and gone to sleep. But it was only half-past eight, and I wasn't ready for the night to end. The idea of waiting until Friday to see him felt impossible . . . unless he changed that rule.

The East Village was crowded with twenty-somethings

out for Saturday night drinking and music. Max reached for my hand, slipped his fingers in between mine, and squeezed. Out of habit I started to protest that we were *not* going to walk down the street like this, but he surprised me by pulling me into the dimly lit bar next door.

"I know you're full, but sit in here, sip a cocktail, and you'll wake up. I'm not nearly done with you."

God I liked the sound of that.

Squeezed tight together in a booth, we sat in a dark corner, me sipping vodka tonics, Max drinking a few beers and telling me all about growing up in Leeds with Irish Catholic parents, and born smack in the middle of seven sisters and three brothers. They'd lived three kids to a bedroom, and it was so different from my childhood that I barely blinked the entire time he regaled me with stories of the time they decided to form a family brass band, or when, at eighteen, the oldest sister, Lizzy, was caught in the family Volvo having sex with their local priest, *consensual* sex. Max's oldest brother, Daniel, left after high school to go on a Catholic mission to Myanmar, and had come home a Theravada Buddhist. His youngest sister, Rebecca, married right out of college and, at twenty-seven, already had six children. The others had stories just as riveting: the brother born just ten months after Max, Niall, was second in command at the London Underground; one of the middle sisters was a chemistry professor at Cambridge and had five children, all boys.

Max admitted that sometimes he felt mediocre compared to his siblings. "I studied art at uni and then got a business finance degree so I could *sell* art. In my father's eyes, I was a miserable failure, both in my choice of career and in my failure to produce Catholic babies before I hit thirty."

But when he said this, he laughed, as if being an absolute failure wouldn't have really mattered that much to his parents in the end. His father, a lifelong smoker, died of lung cancer the week after Max finished graduate school, and his "mum" had decided she needed a change, so she moved with him to the States.

"Neither of us knew a soul here. I had a couple of indirect connections from uni, and some from my business program—friends of friends on Wall Street—but I knew only that I wanted to be involved in New York art ventures, and wanted to partner with someone who knew science and technology. That's how I met Will."

He sat back and finished his beer. Seriously, the man could drink. I'd lost count of how many beers he'd had and he didn't seem affected at all.

"Well, I met him at a pub, admittedly, but we hit it off and almost the next day we started our little pet project. A couple of years later we brought on James to head up the technology piece, because Will could no longer juggle biotech and IT at the same time."

"How do you not have a giant beer gut?" I asked, laughing. It was unfair. His body was what Julia would call "shredded" and he had muscles on his torso I didn't even know existed.

He looked confused for a beat before glancing down at his empty glass. "Are you taking the piss?"

"Absolutely," I said, feeling the effects of my second vodka tonic. My cheeks were warm and my smile seemed to keep growing. "I am absolutely taking the piss."

"Yeah," he said, shaking his head, "that saying doesn't really work so well in an American accent."

"Do you like American accents, or no? Because the whole British thing you have going on makes me want to do very wicked things to your mouth."

He licked his lips quickly, and actually seemed to blush. "American accents aren't particularly sexy, no. Your little Chicago thing is cute, though. Especially when you're tipsy. It's so flat and like—" He made a horrific whining noise that I had to believe was like no sound I'd ever made.

I cringed and he laughed.

"I absolutely do not sound like that."

"Okay, that might have been a slight exaggeration," he said. "But what I *do* find sexy is your brain, your giant brown eyes, your full lips, your little Sara-is-coming sounds, and your particularly stellar tits and thighs."

I cleared my throat, feeling heat spread along my skin from my chest out to my fingertips. "My *thighs?*"

"Yeah. I believe I've mentioned that your skin is amazing. And on your thighs it's soft as hell. Maybe you haven't heard? I suspect not many people have kissed them as much as I have."

I blinked, stunned. He knew I'd been only with Andy, but he was more right than he knew. Andy barely even kissed me below my chest.

"What are the new rules?" I asked, feeling a little dizzy. Whether it was the drinks, or the man, I wasn't sure.

A wolfish grin pulled at his mouth. "I thought you'd never ask."

"Should I be afraid?"

"Oh, yes."

I shivered, but it was more from the growing heat in my stomach than actual fear. I could always say no to whatever he asked.

But I knew I wouldn't.

"Rule one, we keep Friday nights as a given, but we add more whenever we want. You can say no, but in this scenario I don't have to feel like an arse if I ask. And," he said, reaching to push some hair out of my eyes, "*you* can ask. You can admit you want to see me more, too. You don't have to apologize for coming to see me when you're upset. Sex isn't all there is, you know."

I let out a shaky breath and nodded. "Okay . . ."

"Rule two, you let me be with you *in a bed*. A giant bed with a headboard I can tie you to or bend you over. Maybe even just fuck you into the mattress with a pair of your gorgeous shoes over my shoulders. It doesn't have to be mine, and it doesn't have to be now. I love fucking you in public—which we will return to in a moment—but I want to have you all to myself sometimes. Take me time."

He waited for me to answer, and finally, I nodded again.

"I promise to keep taking pictures of you because we both get off on them. I won't ask you to be seen with me in public until you're ready—that's fine. And if you never want to, that's okay, too. But I'm fascinated by you, Sara, and your need for privacy and your need to be watched. I get it now, I think. And I fucking love it. I want to play with that some more. Explore what we both like."

He spread his hands in front of him and shrugged, before moving in to kiss my lips once, quickly. "All right?"

"That's it?"

Laughing, he asked, "What did you think I was going to say?"

"I don't know." I picked up my glass and finished it in a few, long drinks. The vodka slid into my belly and warmed me further, triggering a quiet hum in my limbs. "But . . . I think I like these rules."

"I suspected you might."

"You're kind of cocky, do you know that?"

"I'm kind of *smart*," he corrected, laughing. "And Sara?"

I looked up from my hands on the table and met his eyes. "What?"

"Thank you for trusting me to be your first crazy decision."

I stared at him, watching his expression morph from playful, to curious, to slightly anxious. And maybe it was that expression, or maybe it was the quiet, pulsing music. Maybe it was that I was seeing Max in such a new way—with depth, and a history full of family and people he loved and kept close in every moment of his day-to-day, but I wanted to be closer to him. Closer not just in proximity.

Putting my hands on his face, I leaned in and told him, "Revision to my previous statement: you're kind of *amazing*."

He smiled, shaking his head a little. "And you're kind of tipsy."

"I may be tipsy, but that doesn't affect your amaz-ingness." I pressed a single kiss to his mouth. "Just makes me more *expressive* about it." I sucked on his lower lip, tasting. And damn, on most days I would rather drink gasoline than beer, but on his lips, it tasted fantastic.

"Sara . . . ," he mumbled around my kiss.

"Say it again. Damn, I love when you say my name. Sahhhrahhhh."

"Sara," he said again, obligingly, before he pulled away. "Darling, you do realize we're somewhere we could be seen."

I waved a floppy hand. "Don't care."

"You might care tomorrow when you're a little less . . . expressive."

"I'm not *that* drunk. And I honestly don't care. I realized last night I was photographed all over the country with a man who didn't give a crap about anything more than my name. And you're here, being all nice and wanting to see more of me and revising my stupid rules—"

"Sara—"

I pressed a finger to his lips. "Don't interrupt me, I'm on a roll."

"I see that." He smiled into my touch.

"So my point is that you're amazing and I want to kiss you in a bar. I don't care if someone sees me and thinks, *Wow! That woman wants to be Mrs. Stella, how pathetic! Does she even know he bangs a different woman every night?*"

"I don't."

"But they don't know that, and the point is"—I took a breath, putting my hand on his chest and staring into his amused eyes—"I don't care what they think right now. I'm tired of caring what people think. I like you."

"I like you, too. Very much. In fact—"

I leaned in and kissed him. It was a mess: hands in hair and practically climbing into his lap right there in that stupid bar but I didn't care. *I didn't care.* His hands moved to my face, and his eyes—when I peeked—were open and pleading and *something* was there. Something I couldn't quite put my finger on.

"Sweet Sara," he murmured around my wild kisses. "Baby steps. Let's get you home."

It was a good thing my head stopped pounding by Monday morning because I had a lot of work to do. First up was the pricing strategy for the new Provocateur line. Second was handing over all of the B&T Biotech workload to Samantha. Most definitely not on my list was obsessing over Max, and how the entire dynamic of our relationship had shifted in the last thirty-six hours.

First: work. There was plenty of time to freak out later.

Or so I thought.

"Saaaaarrrrrraaaaaa," George called, somehow managing to stretch my name into about seventeen syllables. I stopped short just inside my office, dropping my laptop case on a chair and taking in the scene before me: George, in my desk chair, with his feet up and a newspaper spread on his lap.

"Why are you at my desk?"

"Because I figured it was a better place to enjoy Page Six with you than in the break room. Are you ready?"

My stomach dropped to my feet. "Ready for what?" I asked. It was seven thirty on a Monday, for crying out loud. I was barely ready for conscious breathing.

George flipped the paper to face me, and in a giant picture, in black-and-white, was half of Max's face. The other half was covered by my head. Talk about déjà vu.

"What is that?"

"A newspaper, darling," George sang, rattling the paper in his hands, and the word *darling* triggered a tight pull in my abdomen. I'd been rolling that word around in my head for the past day, remembering how it had sounded when Max said it to me. "A picture of Max kissing, ooooh, a 'mystery woman.'" He turned it back around so he could read the caption to the photo. "Millionaire playboy Max Stella spotted out for a drink with a mystery blonde—"

"I am not blond!" I hissed.

George looked up, giddy. "Thanks for confirming! And I agree. More of a sandy brown, really. But let me finish: 'The pair started out the night with quiet smiles and teasing, and ended with some heated action in the corner booth. Looks like the flavor of the week is a *tiger*!'"

George cracked up, extending the page to me, his face growing serious. "You didn't have to lie about you and Max, boss. I'm wounded."

"It's not your business," I said, practically ripping the paper from his hands and looking it over. It was obviously Max in the photo, but with only the back of my head and part of my arm and hand visible, my identity would be almost impossible to discern by anyone who didn't already know me.

"It's your allergy bracelet and your adorable hair," George crowed. "How long?"

"Not your business."

"Is he amazing in bed? He is, isn't he? Oh God, don't tell me yet, let me work up a good mental lather first." He squeezed his eyes shut and hummed.

"*Not* your business," I repeated, a hand to my forehead. *Holy hell.* Bennett and Chloe were going to see this. My coworkers. Someone could send this to my *parents.* "Oh God."

"Are you guys, like, a *thing*?" he asked, exasperated and slapping his hand to my desk.

"Oh my God! Not your business! Get out of my office, Skippy."

He stood, then gave me a dirty look that was about as genuine as a politician's smile. He looked more excited than anything else. Maybe even a little turned on.

"Fine," he grumbled. "But you'd better spill every detail after you've had a chance to calm down."

"Not happening. *Go.*"

"This really is great, by the way," he said, serious now. "You deserve a hot guy."

I stopped freaking out for a beat, looking up at him. *He* wasn't freaking. *He* wasn't assuming the worst. He was being a total pervert and enjoying every minute of my torment, but he was also assuming that I was happy, and having fun, and being a single woman in my twenties, doing what we do. He was mirroring my thoughts on Saturday night—*this man is good for you, Sara*—the same thoughts I'd tried so hard to hold on to.

But somehow, in the light of day on a Monday, it was harder than I expected to be young, and wild, and confident that I wasn't setting myself up for another disaster.

"Thanks, George."

"You're welcome. But Chloe is coming down the hall so get your big-girl panties on."

In fact, she was closer than I expected and shoved

my assistant playfully out of the way before walking into my office and slamming my door in his face.

"*Max?*"

"I know."

"The mystery guy is *Max?*"

"Chloe, I'm sorry I didn't—"

She stopped me, holding up a hand. "I asked you if it was Max. You lied to me, very convincingly, and said no. I'm not sure whether I should be impressed or pissed."

"Impressed?" I offered, giving her a winning smile.

"Oh my God, don't be cute." She walked over to my couch near the window and sat down. "Walk me through it."

I crossed the room and sat with her, taking a deep breath before telling her everything: about meeting Max at the club, how we hooked up. I told her about the Chinese restaurant and how I'd tried to tell him not to come looking for me again but ended up letting him get me off. I admitted he was the man I'd been with at the fund-raiser, and how she was the one who made me realize it could be a good distraction to explore this new adventurous side of myself with a man who was practically a world expert on casual flings.

"But it's more," she said, interrupting. "In the past, what? Two months? It's become more."

"For me it has. I think for him, too. Maybe."

"BB saw the pictures this morning," she said, wincing. "I freaked out, because I tried to hide it, but he saw the *Post* outside the subway station."

"Oh no."

She smiled a little. "Honestly, he seemed more worried about my reaction. But he said he knows Max, and if he's promised he'll be with only you, he will. Good thing, because if he hurts you he'll be one appendage short, if you know what I mean."

"That's not the problem," I said. "Which I realize is ironic because"—I pointed to my chest—"hello, cheated on for six years straight. What bothers me more is that I didn't want to *want* someone. This was supposed to be for me. And what if he likes me because I've been clear about what I *don't* want from him. I've given him a goal: make me want him. I don't think he'd ever admit that, maybe he'd never even realize it, but I worry that he's not used to someone setting limits with him. That might be the lure: the challenge."

She shrugged and spread her hands in front of her. "I'm the first to tell you that there's a first time for everyone, and everything. Have you told him how you feel?"

There was a crash from the outer office, followed by George's frantic shout of "Incoming!"

Max burst through the door, George hot on his heels.

"Does he ever listen?" George asked me.

"Not usually," Max answered, stopping short when he saw the paper already in my hands. "You've seen it."

"Yep," I said, tossing it to the desk.

He crossed the room, his expression grim. "Look, it's not a very good picture, I doubt—"

"It's fine," I said, tucking my hair behind my ear. "I—"

"Well, I wouldn't say *fine*," Chloe interrupted, rounding the desk. She crossed her arms and stood between us. "I'll agree it's not the best picture, but I knew it was you. Bennett, too."

"As did I," George volunteered, hand raised.

"Why are you even still here?" I asked, glaring. "Go to work."

"Touchy," George said, pushing away from the wall.

"Well, well." At the sound, every head in the room turned in the direction of the door. "Glad everyone could make it," Bennett said as he walked in, looking like he'd won the biggest, most ridiculous man-bet of all time. "Nice photo, Stella. A *bar*?"

I felt my eyes go wide. "What, the eighteenth-floor stairwell would be better?"

His head whipped to Chloe. "Seriously, Chlo? You told her that?"

"Of course I did." She waved him off with an impatient hand, and beside her, Max laughed.

"You did that, Ben? Shagged your intern at work?"

"A few times," Chloe said in a stage whisper.

Max rubbed his palms together, obviously delighted by this turn of events. "How very, very interesting," he said, eyeing Bennett. "Funny you didn't mention this when you were basically calling me a whore the other day."

"Oh, that's rich. Pot, meet kettle," Chloe said, motioning between the two men.

"And I'm done here," Bennett grumbled. "Max, stop by my office before you leave." He gave Chloe a quick peck on the lips before walking out of my office.

Chloe turned to Max. "I want to know what it's like to work with your mother when this kind of news hits the papers. Did she freak out?"

Max shrugged. "She pretends I don't have an active libido. It's better that way."

"What are we even talking about?" I groaned. "Chloe, I love you but get out of my office. George!" I yelled.

He poked his head in within a few milliseconds of hearing his name.

"Stop listening in. Take Chloe down to the break room and buy her some chocolate." I finally met Max's eyes. "I need to talk to Max alone."

Chloe and George disappeared down the hall and

Max shut and locked my office door. "Are you livid?" he asked, wincing.

"What? No." I sighed, dropping into my chair. "If I remember correctly, I jumped you. I believe you even warned me not to."

"True," he said, flashing his dimple in a smile as he lifted the photo up. "But I also come out of this looking quite good. I mean, the back of this head can only belong to a ridiculously fit woman."

I tried to bite back my laugh and failed. He bent so that we were eye to eye. "We're together a lot, Sara. It's just a matter of time before we're photographed."

I nodded. "I know."

He straightened, looking out my window with a dramatic sigh. "I suppose we'll have to confine our snogs to bedrooms and limos now."

He said this with a smirk, but something twisted in my belly, and not because I was averse to the idea of Max in a bed. It's just that I wasn't done having Max everywhere else.

I'd wanted to hold on to this New Sara a little longer.

"That doesn't look like a happy face," he noted.

"I like what we do."

His face fell the slightest bit. "The wildness of location?"

I nodded. "Just feeling like I could do anything I wanted with you."

He paused, seemed to be thinking something through. "That doesn't have to change, Sara. Regardless of where I have my wicked way with you."

I smiled. "I know."

"But you realize if we continue that, and I'm not averse, it's possible we'll eventually be caught."

He was right, and the reality of it was enough to make my hopes shut down a little.

"We'll figure it out," I said, but even I heard my lack of conviction.

"Sara, it's possible to have fun even with more standard relationship rules."

I nodded, and gave him as convincing a smile as I could manage. "I know."

But the truth was, I didn't know. I only knew that I didn't want what I had with Max to resemble any bit of the life I had before.

FOURTEEN

At three in the morning, I woke up with such an absurd idea I was immediately positive I should go get a shot of whiskey so I could fall back asleep.

But I didn't get up, and I didn't have a shot, and I most certainly didn't go back to sleep.

I was up half the night, my mind spinning over what to do with Sara's paradoxical need to remain a secret yet still explore her wilder side with me. Admittedly, she'd been more relaxed than I expected about the photos in the *Post,* but we'd been lucky, and they hadn't actually gotten her face or anything too telling. Anything more revealing could turn her skittish, if that hadn't happened already. I could tell she had feelings for me beyond the adventure of public orgasms and our shared exhibitionist fetish, but that was a far cry from anything lasting, and miles away from what I felt about her.

I sat up, lit with an idea and wondering if I'd be mad to try this with her. At the same time, it struck me as the perfect solution. Sara clearly got off on the idea of being seen, on the idea of someone watching her orgasm. I wanted to show her that sex could be fun, and wild, and *alive* even in a relationship that grew into something deeper. And yet she wanted to remain anonymous, and I most certainly didn't want to end up with my trousers down—literally—on the subway, or at the movies, or in a cab. Sara had been quick to brush off the photos this time; my nagging worry was that she wouldn't be so forgiving if it happened again.

I looked at the clock and knew it wasn't too early to call. If I knew him at all, Johnny French hadn't even gone to bed yet.

The phone rang once before his gravel-and-smoke voice answered with a simple "Max."

"Mr. French, I hope it isn't too early."

He let out a rumbling laugh. "Haven't gone to bed yet. What can I do for you?"

I exhaled, relieved with the sudden realization that this might actually be the best solution. "I have a situation that I believe requires your help."

When Sara answered the phone, I could hear the smile in her voice. "It's a Wednesday," she said. "And not even eight in the morning. I think I like these new rules."

"I think we're kidding ourselves if we believe this is a rule-driven arrangement anymore," I said.

It was a long moment before she answered, but finally she murmured, "I suppose you're right."

"You're still okay about the *Post*?"

A small pause before, "Yeah, actually."

"I thought about you all day yesterday."

Again, she fell quiet and I wondered if I'd gone too far. And then she said, "That's kind of been true for me for a while."

I laughed. Too right. "Me, too."

Silence filled the line and I braced myself for the possibility that she would say no to this.

"Sara, I think we should be a little more careful about where we choose to be intimate. Until now, we've been careful but mostly we've been lucky. I care more now that this doesn't become a scandal for us."

"I know. Me, too."

"At the same time . . ."

"I don't want to give it up, either." She laughed.

"Do you trust me?"

"Of course. I've let you take me to a warehouse—"

"I mean *really* trust me, Sara. I'm planning on taking you somewhere very different."

This time, there was no hesitation. "Yes."

I figured a Wednesday was a good day to start. No doubt Johnny had customers every night of the week, but he warned me that Fridays and Saturdays might be overwhelming for both of us, and Wednesdays tended to be the quietest.

I'd texted that I'd pick her up at her apartment after she'd had a chance to change after work, and eat some dinner. Was I being a pussy for not taking her out to eat, for fear she might balk at this plan if she had too much time to think it over?

Absofuckinglutely.

A brunette emerged from Sara's building, head down as she fumbled with something in her small bag. It'd been true for a while that I had eyes only for Sara, but even I was unable to look away. The woman wore a dark blouse, skirt, high heels. Her inky hair was glossy in the streetlight overhead, and cut short—just to her chin. She looked to the right, and I saw a long, delicate neck, smooth skin, and perfect breasts. I knew that neck, knew those curves.

"Sara?" I called. She turned and I felt my jaw drop. *Holy shit.*

She smiled when she saw me leaning against the car. I waved Scotty off when he emerged to open the door for her, and let her in myself.

She placed a shiny, red-tipped finger under my chin and closed my mouth. "I'm assuming you approve," she said, grinning as she took her seat.

"That would be an understatement," I said as I climbed in next to her and reached out, brushing a strand of dark hair away from her face. "You look fucking beautiful."

"It's great, right?" she asked, shaking her head a little. "Figured if we were going to be serious about this cloak-and-dagger stuff, I might as well have a little fun." She slipped off her shoes and tucked her feet under her legs on the backseat. "So, are you going to tell me what's going on?"

As soon as I'd recovered, I leaned in and kissed her red mouth. "We have a little bit of a drive. I'm going to tell you everything."

She trained her patient eyes on me and I had to remind myself not to take her in the car. To work her up a little for this. Dark dance clubs were one thing, and she'd been drunk; this was something entirely different.

"One of my earlier clients was a man named Johnny French. I'm almost positive it's an alias; he strikes me as the kind of guy who has a few different names, if you know what I mean. He came to me for help with opening a night-club in a pretty run-down building. He'd done it before, successfully, but wanted to explore how it would work with a venture capitalist firm attached that had more legitimate connections in the marketing world."

"What was the club called?"

"Silver," I told her. "It's still open, and it does very well. In fact, we've made a good amount of money on the collaboration. Anyway, Johnny keeps his habits pretty tightly buttoned up, but in the process of our due diligence, he explained to us that he needed the larger successful business to support his smaller interests."

Sara shifted a little in her seat, seeming to understand that I was getting to the point of the evening.

"Johnny owns a number of other venues. He owns a cabaret in Brooklyn that's done very well."

"Beat Snap?"

I nodded, a little surprised. "You've heard of it."

"Everyone's heard of it. Dita Von Teese was there last month. We went with Julia."

"Right. And Johnny also has some less-well-known venues. The place we're going tonight is a very secretive and protected club called Red Moon."

She shook her head. Even if Sara had been born a New York native I was fairly sure she wouldn't recognize the name. I reached into my jacket and pulled out a small bag from the inner pocket. Her eyes were trained on my hands as I undid its cord and pulled out a feathered blue mask.

I leaned forward and placed it over her eyes, reaching around to tie it behind her head. And then I looked at her and almost lost my will to hold back from touching her. Her eyes were visible, but her face was covered from eyebrows to cheekbones, and her full red lips curved into a tiny smile under my scrutiny. Tiny rhinestones lined the eyes, and from behind the mask her brown eyes seemed to glow.

"Well, isn't this mysterious," she whispered.

I groaned. "You look like something out of a very wet dream." Her smile widened and I continued. "Red Moon is a sex club."

In the low light I could see a shiver pass through her.

Remembering one of our first nights together, I assured her, "There are no shackles or spreader bars . . . at least, they aren't the primary attraction. The club caters to a very high-end voyeuristic crowd. People who enjoy watching people have sex. I've only been there one time, during this due diligence process, and was sworn to absolute confidentiality. On the main floor, Johnny has some truly stunning dancers who are intimate in beautifully complicated, choreographed ways. The rest of the club has rooms where, through windows or mirrors, you can watch one thing or another."

I cleared my throat and met her eyes. "Johnny has offered to let us play in a room tonight, if you want."

———

To all outward appearances, it was a basic, run-down building housing assorted businesses, including an Italian restaurant, a hair salon, and a boarded-up Asian market. The only other time I'd visited, Johnny took me in through a back entrance. The door he'd told me to use tonight was apparently the main entrance, an unassuming battered steel door off the alley, and required the key he'd had messengered over to my office that afternoon.

"How many people have a key?" I'd asked him on the phone.

"Four," he'd told me. "You're five. It's how we keep track of who comes in. Random Joes can't get there. We have a list for each night. Guests phone Lisbeth at the desk and she sends security up to retrieve them." He paused. "You're lucky you're my favorite, Max, or you'd be waiting months."

"I appreciate it, John. And if it goes well tonight, I'm pretty sure you'll want to let me bring this one back every Wednesday."

Pulling out the key and faced with the reality of what we were doing, I started to grow more and more excited. I led Sara down the alley, her hand clammy in mine.

"We can leave anytime," I reminded her for the tenth time in as many minutes.

"I'm excited-nervous," she assured me. "I'm not scared." Pulling my arm so that I would turn to her, she stretched up and slid her lips across mine, nipping and licking at me. "I'm so excited I almost feel drunk."

I gave her one last kiss and pulled away before I found myself fucking her in the alley—something Johnny promised would get me blacklisted for the rest of my days—and pushed the key into the lock.

"That's the other thing I meant to mention. Drinking. There is a two-drink maximum. They want everything safe, consensual, and calm."

"I'm not sure I can promise the calm part. You have a way of making me a little insane."

I gave her a grin. "I think he means between patrons. I'm pretty sure there are some things happening tonight between the performers that will not be calm."

When the door made a soft click, I pulled it open and

we stepped inside. Per Johnny's instructions, we continued through a second door just ten feet beyond that, then down the long flight of stairs leading to a freight elevator. The doors slid open immediately when we hit the down button, and after I entered the code he gave me into a lit keypad, we descended two more floors, deep into the belly of New York.

I tried to explain to Sara what she would see—tables in a semicircle around an open floor, people socializing just as they do in any bar—but I knew that my explanation wouldn't do it justice. To be honest, I'd been so fascinated with this place when I visited with Johnny that only my ethics as a partner in his other businesses had kept me from exploring it further. As much as I'd wanted to return, I never had.

But with Sara becoming an undeniable part of my life, the possibility of her needing something like this and my new, clawing desire to give her anything she wanted changed my mind about staying away.

The elevator doors parted and we stepped out into a small lobby area. Warm lighting filled the room, and a beautiful redhead sat behind a desk, working on a sleek black computer.

"Mr. Stella," she said, standing to greet us. "Mr. French told me you would be here tonight. My name is Lisbeth." I nodded in greeting, and she waved for us to follow. "Please follow me."

She turned and led us down a short hall, never questioning Sara's mask or asking for her name. At a heavy steel door, she inserted a long skeleton key, swung the door open, and motioned us through with a sweep of her arm. "Please remember, Mr. Stella, we allow two drinks maximum, do not use names, and have security just outside of the role-play rooms if you need any assistance." As if to emphasize her point, a very large man stepped up behind her.

Lisbeth turned to Sara and finally addressed her. "Are you here by choice?"

Sara nodded but then said, "Absolutely," when Lisbeth seemed to want her to respond verbally.

And then Lisbeth winked at us. "Have fun, you two. Johnny said on Wednesday nights Room Six is yours for as long as you want it."

For as long as we want it?

I turned and led Sara into the club, my mind reeling. I'd only seen a couple of the rooms on my last visit. Most of the night I'd been here had been spent in the main bar, enjoying a whiskey and watching two women make love to music on the table next to me while Johnny walked around and greeted his customers. We had gone down the hall to see a couple of rooms, but I'd felt strange viewing those things with a male business client. I'd claimed to be tired, and later had regretted not seeing what every room had to offer.

"What is Room Six?" Sara asked, wrapping both hands around my upper arm as we walked into the bar.

"No idea," I admitted. "But if I remember correctly, I'm

guessing Johnny gave it to us because it's at the end of the hall."

The bar was a large, open room with beautifully simple décor: low, warm light, tables for two, or four, and sofas, ottomans, and chaises tastefully positioned throughout the room. Heavy velvet curtains were draped from the ceiling, and the walls were covered in rich, black wallpaper that exhibited a shimmering, barely perceptible pattern in the winking candlelight.

It was early; a few other patrons sat at tables, speaking in low voices and watching a woman and a man dance in the center of the room. As we walked to the bar, the man pulled her shirt over her head and used it to trap her arm and spin her across the floor. Jewels in her nipple rings glinted in the lights.

Sara watched the pair and then blinked away when I caught her looking. She tucked a lock of dark hair behind her ear in what I'd come to know as a nervous gesture, and I could imagine her blushing behind the mask.

"It's okay to watch here," I reminded her, my voice low. "When things get really interesting, you'll see that no one will be able to look away."

I ordered her a vodka gimlet and got a scotch for myself before leading her to a small table in the corner. I stared at her as she took it all in. She sipped her drink and took time to study everything around her. I wondered if she realized how much attention she'd attracted from the clientele.

In her neck, I could see her pulse thrum. I stared at the pale skin, wanting to lean over and suck a mark into her. Shifting in my seat to adjust my trousers, I imagined what it would be like to make her come with my hand while the entire room watched.

Fuck, Max. You're in deep.

"What are you thinking?" I asked her.

She lifted her chin, indicating the dancers who kissed, moved away, and then joined back together again. "Are they going to have sex out here?"

"Most likely, of one form or another."

"So why do they have the rooms, too?"

"Variety. If I remember correctly, the scenarios in the rooms tend to be wilder. And they're smaller, more intimate."

She nodded, lifting her drink and taking a sip, studying me. "No one here knows who I am, but still I'm the one wearing a wig and a mask."

Smiling, I pointed out, "Historically you have been the one who wants to remain hidden."

"You would do this for me? Let people watch us together?"

"I suspect I would do almost anything for you," I admitted. And then, unable to see in the dark corner how my words affected her, I added, "The thought is probably just as much a rush for me as it seems to be for you."

She slid her hand onto my thigh under the table. "But people here *know* you. They know your face."

"There are people all over this room who are far more famous. That man in the corner is an American football player for some team Will is always going on about. And that woman?" I motioned subtly to a table near the bar. "Television."

Sara's eyes widened slightly as she recognized the Emmy Award–winning actress. "But they aren't considering having sex in Room Six," she noted.

"No, but they're here watching. No one will judge me for being here with you. And more important, everyone knows you don't fuck with Johnny French's confidentiality requirement. He has dirt on everyone here, or can find it."

"Oh."

"It stays in this room, S—" I began, but she pressed a finger to my lips.

"No names, stranger," she reminded me.

I smiled, kissed her fingertip. "Nothing leaves this room, *Petal.* I promise."

"The first rule of fight club?" she asked, grinning.

"Exactly." Lifting my drink to my lips, I took a sip, swallowed. "Tell me what else you're thinking."

She leaned in to kiss me but I pulled away.

"Can I touch you out here?"

I shook my head. "Unfortunately, that's another rule. No sexual contact by anyone but the performers."

"What about in Room Six?"

"Yes. You can there."

"Damn." She shifted in her seat, watching the dancers for a bit. They'd shed their clothes by now, and the man steadied a harness that had been lowered from the ceiling so his partner could step into it. Once inside, her legs were spread wide and an invisible pulley lifted her so her hips were level with her partner's head. He began to spin her in time with the music, walking in wide circles as she whipped around, head thrown back.

"What time is it?" Sara asked after a few minutes, not looking away from where the man had abruptly stopped the woman from spinning, and pressed his open mouth between her legs.

"Nine forty-five."

She sighed, and I couldn't tell if she was as antsy as I was. The torture of the club was knowing that if I wanted to touch her, I could do it only where others could see us. Use us for their need as much as we were using them for ours. I wanted more than anything to do to her what the man on the dance floor had begun doing to his partner: tasting, teasing, fucking her with his fingers.

As the man spun the woman away again, a waiter approached our table.

"Good evening, sir." He poured water from a crystal pitcher, beginning near the glass then raising it above his head without altering the water's flow even a little. "The owner has mentioned you've been here but your guest is new. Would you like me to tell you a bit about what you can expect?"

"That would be smashing," I answered.

He turned to Sara. "The club changes the room décor every couple of weeks. Our goal is to keep things fresh for our clientele. You'll find a variety of scenes going on as you walk down to the rooms."

I glanced to Sara and wondered how, beneath the mask, the sweet midwestern girl was taking all of this in.

The host continued, "Shows begin at ten, and go until midnight. I'm told your room is Six. Given that this is your first event, you should feel welcome to watch the other exhibits for a bit before deciding whether you would like to participate." He smiled. "I'm also told the owner would very much like to add something a bit more intimate and sincere to the regular rotation. We've never had an exhibiting couple who looks at each other the way you do."

I felt my eyes go wide, and beside me Sara shifted closer. I could feel the warmth of her thigh against mine. I was truly on the verge of exploding with my need to feel her.

The waiter bowed slightly. "But please do not feel any pressure."

———

At ten, the lights in the hallway illuminated a warm gold. Other patrons around the main room shifted, finished their drinks, stood slowly. But Sara grabbed my hand and jerked me out of my chair.

The hall was at least twenty feet wide, with seats and tables near the windows looking in on the rooms. In Room One, the first room on the left, a young, muscular man stood in the corner wearing jeans and no shirt. On the floor, on all fours, was another dark-haired man with a horse tail extending from an anal plug. The man standing in the corner lifted a whip and cracked it loudly in the air.

Sara's hand flew to her mouth, as I pulled her farther down the hall, murmuring, "Pony play, darling. Not for everyone."

Room Two had a beautiful woman, alone and naked on the couch, just beginning to masturbate to pornography being projected across the expansive wall opposite her.

Room Three had an enormous, pale man in the tragic Melpomene mask, preparing to take a gagged woman from behind. Beside me, I could sense Sara grow more tense.

"This looks . . ." She gestured vaguely to the strangely fascinating scene.

"Adventurous?" I suggested. "You have to understand that people pay a lot of money to come here. They don't want to see things they can see on the telly."

I put my hand to the small of her back and reminded her, "Another thing you can't see on the telly is real intimacy."

She looked up at me and then her attention dropped to my mouth. "Do you think we're really intimate?"

"Do *you*?"

She nodded. "When did that happen?"

"When has it been anything other than intimate? You just wanted to ignore it."

She blinked away, but leaned into my side and we started walking again.

Room Four had three women, kissing and laughing as they undressed each other on a gigantic white bed.

Room Five had a man binding a woman up with rope, while a bound and gagged cuckolded man watched from the corner.

"We're going to be boring," she whispered, eyes wide.

"You really think so?"

She didn't answer, because we'd arrived at Room Six, which stood empty. Without even looking to me, she slipped around the end of the hall to where we could enter the rooms from the rear.

The door handle to Six turned easily, and Sara stepped inside.

After a few moments, our eyes adjusted, and I could make out a bar in the corner and a huge leather couch with a low coffee table in front. Even in the darkness, the room felt very much like a corner of my own living room, and I suspected with a jolt that it *was* a replica of that space.

Without thinking to ask Sara first, I flipped on the light. I was right. Cream walls with deep walnut trim, a wide black couch, and the same plush area rug I had picked up in

Dubai. Tiffany lamps decorated the two small end tables. The room was far smaller than my living room, which I used for large events, but the similarity was undeniable. The giant window through which people could observe us was framed by drapes, just like those at my flat, but from where we stood, it just looked like a window looking out upon a blank darkness.

Johnny had been to my house only once, but in a single afternoon he'd transformed a room in his club for me, no doubt assuming it would be familiar to us both, maybe put us at ease. He would have no idea that Sara had never actually been to my flat.

"What's wrong?" she asked, walking closer and, realizing she could touch me in here, wrapping her arms around my waist.

"He's made a replica of my living room for us."

"That's . . ." She looked around, eyes wide. "That's crazy."

"What's crazy is that this is the first time you're seeing my house. From inside a sex club."

The absurdity of it all seemed to hit us both at the same time and Sara dissolved into giggles, pressing her face into my chest. "This is the weirdest thing anyone has ever done. Ever."

"We can go . . ."

"No. This is the first place we'll have sex where we're

supposed to," she said, grinning. "You think I'm going to pass that up?"

Fuck. The woman could ask me to kneel and kiss her toes and I would do it.

I almost said it: *I love you*. The words got so close to escaping that I literally turned away from her, and walked over to the bar to fix myself a drink.

But she followed me. "And it's probably late to be asking this, but what are we doing here?"

"I believe we're trying to find a way to enjoy this aspect of our relationship without jeopardizing our careers or getting our faces plastered all over Perez Hilton."

I lifted the bottle of scotch, silently offering. She shook her head, eyes wide beneath her mask as she watched me pour myself a drink.

"Three fingers," she whispered, and I heard her smile in her voice.

"Just one, for now."

She stepped close after I took a sip and stretched to kiss me, sucking on my tongue.

Fuck she tasted good.

The feathers of her mask brushed against my cheek. "Three," she insisted.

As she kissed down my neck and spread her hand over the front of my trousers, palming me, I looked over her shoulder at the dark window. Out there, customers might already be sitting and watching, curious about what would happen. Or maybe we were all alone here at the end of the hall. But the idea that we *weren't,* the sheer possibility that others could see how she touched me . . . for the first time I understood how being out in plain sight with me had allowed Sara to be whoever she wanted to be. She could play. She could be wild and adventurous and take risks.

And so could I. Here, I could be the man who was desperately in love for the first time in my life.

"Do you really want to fool around here?" I asked, wincing internally at my own bluntness.

But she nodded. "I'm just nervous. Which is slightly insane considering our history."

She laughed and reached out to lightly scratch my abdomen. *Fuck.* I'd never felt such a tormenting mix of protectiveness, worship, and a blinding need to completely own someone physically. She was so beautiful, so bloody trusting—all fucking mine.

I bent down, kissed her jaw, and slipped the top few buttons on her shirt free. "What do you imagine when you think we're being watched?"

She hesitated, toying with the hem of my shirt. "I imagine someone seeing your face and how you look at me."

"Yeah?" I sucked on her neck. "What else?"

"I imagine a woman who wants to be with you, seeing you with me. Seeing you wanting me."

I hummed against her skin, pushing her shirt off her shoulders and reaching around to remove her bra. "More."

When I kissed her neck, I could feel her swallow against my lips. Her voice came out quieter when she admitted, "I imagine some faceless person who saw Andy treat me badly. I imagine the woman he was caught with seeing how you look at me."

There it is. "And?"

"And him. I imagine him seeing how happy I am now." She shook her head, digging her fists into my shirt and pulling me close as if I'd pull away. "I don't think I'll always hold on to it, but I hate that I still feel so much anger."

Leaning back, she looked up at me. "But you make me feel amazing, and wanted, and yes, part of me still wishes to rub that in his face."

I couldn't hold back my grin. I fucking loved the idea of that bastard seeing me fuck Sara senseless. Because the biggest mistake of his life—his infidelity—had given me the best part of mine.

"Me, too. I'd love him to see how you look when you're coming. Since I bet he didn't really manage to see that much."

She laughed, licking up my throat. "No."

And fuck, for the first time in my life, I wanted to be someone's *only*.

I led her to the couch, then kneeled on the floor between her legs.

Her hands laced into my hair.

"What do you want me to do?" she whispered, looking down at me, always so willing to give me anything.

What do I want? I struggled to find the right answer, suddenly more than a little overwhelmed with the enormity of that question.

You over me.

You under me.

Your laugh in my ears.

Your voice in my chest.

Your wet on my fingers.

Your taste on my tongue.

I think I want to know you feel the way I do.

"I just want you to enjoy this tonight." I leaned forward, pressing my mouth between her legs. She smelled dizzying, tasted too good, looked too beautiful. Sara's sounds were quiet and aching and seemed to be tailored entirely for my ear. Her fingers ran over my head, scratching my scalp lightly before she let go and pulled her leg higher, spreading wider, giving me better access. She didn't move with exaggerated sexuality; she was slow and calm and easily the most accidentally sensual being in history.

And as I focused on making her feel good, I imagined how she looked from outside this room, with my fingers in her and my mouth devouring her and her back arching up from the couch. I was so used to seeing her with the mask now that it wasn't jarring or distancing; the way she looked at me from behind it made me feel like I'd just been given the entire world. The silky black wig framed her face, made her skin paler, her lips redder. Those same lips parted as she began to beg quietly, instructing me to move faster, to not stop sucking on her, to fuck her harder with my fingers.

As she began to fall, her hand moved up her torso, over her breast and up her neck to her face, where she slipped her mask off, exposing the last bit of her skin that had been covered.

Her huge brown eyes were trained on my face, her lips still parted in a quiet pant.

When she came, she never once looked away, never once even blinked her attention to the windows behind me.

Someone was on the other side of that glass. I could feel it. But I don't think we could have been any more alone in this room even if we really were at my flat. Nothing in this world existed other than the way she pressed into my mouth, crying out when she came.

Then she sighed, tugged on my hair, and laughed. "Holy *shit.*"

So maybe if I ever met this Andy twat I wouldn't actually punch his smug face after all. Maybe I'd shake his hand for messing things up with Sara so epically that she moved to New York and stopped being the woman who did what she was supposed to do, and started to be the woman who did what she bloody well wanted.

I kissed my way up her torso, let her suck her taste from my mouth, my tongue, my jaw. Beneath me she was warm and slow; her arms curled lazily around me, her laugh faded into my neck.

"I think that was the most fun I've ever had," she whispered.

And I suspected I'd do almost anything to spend the rest of my life making this woman happy.

Fifteen

I knew it wouldn't be good to have every night of the week filled with Max, because it would shatter my ability to think about anything else. On my morning run, I thought back on what we'd done together, and came up with some of the wildest fantasies I'd ever had in my life: crawling under Max's desk and sucking him off while he spoke on the phone, or having him in the elevator on the way up to his apartment.

It was fun to finally let myself indulge in these sorts of daydreams, and I was starting not to care that he disrupted so much of my structured life. And after what he did for me at the club, I was beginning to realize I'd walk across flaming coals for the man.

I'd been nervous, no doubt. The club felt darkly indulgent and was supported by patrons who'd been thinking about this kind of sexual fantasy maybe longer than I'd been alive. I wasn't sure if there were unspoken rules I was meant to follow. Don't speak too loudly. Don't cross your legs. Don't look anyone in the eye. Don't drink your cocktail too fast.

My parents were so wholly innocent next to this world. Their idea of a wild night out was seeing *The Vagina Monologues* and dinner at some trendy Asian-fusion restaurant. To this day, my father considered sushi just a little too adventurous for him.

And here I was, walking into a secret sex club, and on my first night there, letting Max go down on me where anyone present could watch.

I had no idea, in the end, if anyone had in fact been watching. We left through the back door to the room, where Max's friend Johnny met us and let us leave through a service entrance. Max watched me carefully the rest of the night, like he was wondering if I was ready to bolt or break down. But in reality, I was shaking so hard because everything about it had felt right. Max had been on his knees, between my legs, and had refused to let me reciprocate. Instead he kissed me for long minutes, helped me dress, and gave me a look so pregnant with meaning that goose bumps spread across my skin.

It was one thing to play in a library, but compared to the club last night, that felt tame. And on the way home after, with Max's hand on my knee and his lips on my neck, my ears, my mouth, and—finally—his body over and inside me, completely wild on the backseat, I realized how crazy my life had become.

Crazy good.

Crazy amazing.

It'd been so long since I'd been infatuated like this that . . . I had forgotten how fun it was.

"You're swooning," George said Thursday morning as I approached his desk. He stuck the end of his pen back between his teeth, murmuring around it. "You're thinking about your Max."

How the hell did he know that? Was I grinning like an idiot? "What?"

"You like him."

I gave up. "I do," I admitted.

"I saw how he looked at you when he came in here Monday. He'd let you carry his balls around in your pocket."

Grimacing, I opened my office door. "I'd rather they stay where they are, but thanks for the idea."

"He was here this morning," George offered, casually.

I froze, halfway into my office, waiting.

"Seemed sad to have missed you, but I told him you're kind of a bear in the morning before you've finished your seventeen cups of coffee and rarely get in before eight."

"Thanks," I grumbled.

"No problem." He sat up and pulled an envelope off his desk. "He left this."

I took the envelope into my office to read. Max's handwriting was tiny, scribbly.

Sara,

I'm leaving Friday morning for San Francisco for a week for a conference. Might I see you tonight?

Max.

Lifting my phone, I swiped my thumb across the screen and pressed his name.

He answered after only half a ring. "Are you still in bear mode?"

I laughed. "No. I'm at cup sixteen."

"Your assistant is a character. We had quite a lovely chat about you. I'm pleased to know he's unlikely to be hitting on you while I'm away."

"I think he's more of a Max fanboy, if you want the truth. If you had any inclinations to play for the other team you might never be able to get rid of him."

"I heard that!" George called from his desk.

"Then stop eavesdropping!" I yelled back, and then smiled into the phone. "And yes, I'm free tonight."

"Where?"

I hesitated only a beat before offering, "My place?"

The line went quiet.

I heard the smile in Max's voice when he finally growled, "For a bed?"

"Yeah." My hands were shaking. Hell, everything had changed last night. The idea of being with Max in a bed felt like the wildest adventure yet. I almost wondered if we would survive it.

"Meet you there at eight? I have a late call with the west coast."

"Perfect."

I changed my outfit three times before eight—casual? sexy? casual? sexy?—before finally changing back into the outfit I'd worn to work. I straightened my bed, dusted my entire apartment, and brushed my teeth twice. I had no idea what I was doing and was pretty sure I hadn't been this nervous on the night I'd actually lost my virginity.

I was still shaking when he knocked at my door. He'd never seen my place, but when he walked in, he barely looked around. His hands went to my face, and he pushed me back against the wall, mouth firm on mine, opening, sucking on my lips and tongue. There was nothing gentle about the way he kissed me. It was hard and desperate, hands gripping shoulders and pulling ineffectually at clothes that just seemed to be in the way, lips that almost felt bruised with how *real* it all was. He had a messenger bag slung across his chest and it slid forward, hitting the wall with a heavy thump.

"I'm losing my fucking mind," he said into my mouth. "Losing my fucking *brain,* Sara. Where's your bedroom?"

I walked backward, pulling him and his wild kisses down the short hall with me. I only had my bedside lamp on, and it cast a small cone of warm yellow light around the space. White walls, big bed, giant windows—all within a minuscule floor plan.

He laughed, looking around and letting his hands drop from my face. "Your flat is tiny."

"I know."

Slipping his bag over his head, he dropped it onto my bed. "Why? You could afford more."

I shrugged, mesmerized by the way his pulse hammered in his throat. Why were we talking about the size of my apartment? I wanted to know what was in the bag. He only ever carried his wallet, phone, and a house key. "I don't need more right now."

His eyes moved to mine and he nodded once, lips tilting in a half smile. "You're a complicated woman, Sara Dillon."

Sometimes after I went for a long run, I was so high afterward that I couldn't do anything but go back out and run some more. I would have so much energy in my blood, I couldn't stand to be still. I felt like that now.

"Max, I'm . . ." I held up my hand to show him how much it was shaking. "I don't know what to do right now."

"Undress for me." He dug into his bag and pulled out a huge, fancy camera. "I want pictures of everything tonight," he said, gazing at me through the lens. The sound of the shutter set my heart racing inside my chest. I felt dizzy, lightheaded.

"Including our faces," I said quietly.

"Yeah," he said, voice hoarse. "Exactly."

I looked down at my clothes: ivory silk shirt with small, pearl buttons, and a straight, black skirt.

Undress for me.

I liked having a task to focus on. The weight of last night still pressed on my heart, and the sight of him in my bedroom almost broke me.

I lifted my hands to the top button of my blouse.

My fingers still shook.

It was different like this, in my apartment with no one but his camera to witness. What was I showing him tonight? My body? Or everything beneath my skin: my heart and fears and wild, thrumming longing for him?

I heard the click of the shutter followed by Max's deep voice. "The way you seem nervous makes me think you don't know that I'm in love with you."

I looked up at him, eyes wide and hands frozen.

Click.

"I love you, Petal. I've known it for a while now, but everything changed for me last night."

I nodded, feeling dizzy. "Okay."

He bit his lip and then released it to give me a wicked grin. *"Okay?"*

"Yeah." I returned to my buttons, slipping each one free at a time. I fought the world's most enormous smile.

Click.

"You have nothing to say but 'okay'?" he asked, looking up from behind the camera. "I tell you I love you, and I don't even get a 'thanks' or 'how lovely'?"

I let the shirt fall to the floor and turned my back to him, reaching behind me to unhook my bra—*click*—and dropping it.

Click. Click.

I unzipped my skirt, and it joined the other items on the floor as I turned back to face him.

"I love you, too." *Click.* "But I'm terrified."

He lowered the camera, eyes on me.

"I didn't want to fall in love with you," I said.

He took a step closer. "If it makes you feel any better, you put up a very impressive fight."

He didn't put the camera down when he stepped forward again to kiss me. He just moved his hand to the side and cupped my face with the other, pressing his mouth to mine.

"I'm scared, too, Sara. I'm scared I'm your rebound. I'm scared we'll cock it up somehow. I'm scared you'll tire of me. But the thing is," he said, smiling, "I don't want anyone else. You've rather ruined me for other women."

He must have taken hundreds of pictures of me as I finished undressing, climbed back on the bed, watched him prowl over me and tell me more of how he felt: distracted, insatiable, like he could thank Andy then kill him, like he was sincerely worried he wouldn't ever be able to get enough of me. Every reaction I had, he captured, obsessed over.

Hovering above me, he trained the camera on my torso, where his body brushed against mine. I closed my eyes, lost in the way he felt and in the soft sounds of the camera clicking. When I opened them again, my eyes met his.

I reached out, angling the camera toward my neck. He took the shot, letting me lead as I positioned it higher, and higher still. He looked at me through the lens.

His hands shook as he adjusted the focus, taking shot after shot of my face, of his fingers tracing my jaw or cupping my cheek, as he held the camera away to capture us kissing.

And then everything in the moment became about the feeling of his mouth on me, and the feeling of his hair in my hands, his tongue moving over me, his lips pressing words into my skin. I felt every breath he took and every small sound he made. I could feel his mouth get hungrier and more urgent as he moved down my body. Slowly, he pressed two fingers inside me and sucked on my clit in earnest, pushing me to come. I stayed quiet. I didn't want to hear my voice in my head. I wanted to only feel him.

"You're beautiful," he whispered when I'd given up and cried out, when I'd finally stilled and he'd crawled over me, kissing me deeply. "It's staggering how it affects me."

I reached up and dragged my nails down his chest, urging him to use my body to get what he needed this time, to feel everything he possibly could. My hands moved on their own accord, roaming and scratching, pulling him closer and pushing him back so I could see him when he reached between us to position himself against me. I tickled down his stomach, feeling his muscles clench underneath my fingertips.

I whispered, "Please."

He groaned, exhaling as he lowered his body over mine and pushed into me fully. The sensation was astounding—everything all at once—the feeling of his chest on mine, of his face against my neck, of my arms around his neck and hands diving into his hair, of his hands pulling my thighs around his waist, of his hips pivoting as he moved in me.

Please don't ever let this end. I don't want this moment to stop.

We were out of words, and covered in sweat, and *this,* I thought, *this is what it's like to make love.*

He rolled me on top of him, watched my face until it was too much, too intense, and I let my eyes close as I came. I heard the click of the camera, and the heavy thud of it as it hit the mattress and Max was over me again, wilder now, my thighs pressed up in his hands and his brows pinched together in concentration.

Images of lights and shadows pounded against my retinas but this time I refused to close my eyes.

He fell over me, heavy; his mouth moved to mine and we held them open against each other, breathing and on the edge together. He moved his parted lips over my mouth as he moved on top of me and we both began to speak silently.

I'm coming, we said together without sound, begging. *I'm coming.*

∿

We'd both skipped dinner, so I watched in rapt attention as Max raided the kitchen.

He wore boxers but nothing else, and I registered that I'd never just *stared* at his body. Obviously Max was long and sculpted, but he was also easy in his own skin. I liked watching him scratch his stomach as he considered the contents of my refrigerator. I got lost in the way his lips would move as he cataloged everything in the produce drawer.

"Women are bloody amazing," he mumbled, rifling

through an assortment of cheeses. "I have mustard in my fridge. Maybe some old potatoes."

"I just went shopping." I'd put on his T-shirt and pulled it up to inhale the smell of him. It smelled like his soap, and his deodorant, and the inherent Max-smell of his skin.

"I suspect I last went in May."

"What are you looking for?"

He shrugged, pulling out a bowl of grapes. "Snacks." He grabbed a six-pack of beer and grinned as he held it up. "Stella. Nice choice."

"I'm partial."

He piled grapes, nuts, and a few slices of cheese on a plate and nodded to the bedroom. "Snacks in bed."

Back on the comforter, he slipped a grape between my lips and then took some for himself, mumbling, "So, I have a thought," around his bite.

"Do tell."

"I'm hosting a fund-raiser at my flat in two weeks. How about we make that our big coming-out night? Max and Sara: blissfully in love." He snacked on a few nuts and studied me before adding, "I'll even make a no-press rule."

"You wouldn't have to do that."

"I wouldn't have to, but I would."

It took a while for me to sort out what I wanted to say, and while I thought it all through, Max snacked patiently. It was such a stark contrast from Andy, who always wanted an answer as soon as he'd asked the question. The truth is, my mind had never worked that way. Politicians pop questions and answers like verbal racquetball. It always took me longer to formulate what I wanted to say. And, in the case of Max, it seemed that it took me a couple of months to sort out what I felt.

"I mean, the reason why I felt weird about pictures for so long was that there are so many of me and Andy together. And they'll always be there, easy to pull up every time anyone wants to. I'll always feel humiliated when I see my ignorant smile and his fake, lying one."

He finished chewing his bite before answering, "I know."

"So I think you're right. Maybe no press this time. Maybe we can just be around some of your guests, and see how it goes."

Max leaned forward and kissed my shoulder. "Works for me."

He fed me another grape and then slid the plate next to a bottle of water on the bedside table before pulling his T-shirt up and over my head.

Our lovemaking was unhurried this time, when the night was at its blackest and the wind roared just outside the open windows. With my legs around his waist and his face buried against my neck we rocked together, him underneath, just feeling and watching.

Nothing had ever been like this.
Nothing.

Max was curled up behind me when the sun barely began to light the sky. He looked amazing. Rumpled hair, and the warmth of his arms and legs wrapped all around me. He was hard and pressing against me; hungry and honest and asking for friction even before his mind was awake.

He didn't say a single word once he realized I was watching him. He just rubbed his face, looked at my lips, and reached for the bottle of water we'd left on the nightstand. He offered it to me and then took some, before putting it aside so he could run his hands up and over my breasts.

And I was immediately lost in the feel of him as he rolled onto me and rocked forward, holding there, kissing my lips good morning. I was sleepy and he was sleepy, moving down my body and sucking at flesh and ribs and hip bones. I slid my arms and legs around him, wanting to be smothered in his inches and inches of smooth skin. I wanted him naked on top, and his face between my legs, and his fingers everywhere.

His hands were calm and deliberate; he teased. What he started to build under my skin was a slow burn. He kissed me everywhere, giving pleasure with his hands and mouth and words; asking me what I liked as if we hadn't done this so many times before. But I understood: it was different here, in my bed. Everything had crashed last night, and I couldn't see anything beyond how it felt to finally open my heart to him.

Sixteen

I looked down at her in the late-morning sun, all sleep-warm and cheek pressed into the pillow, her smooth hair a tangled mess around her head. My eyes moved over her body, along the side of her bare breast and down the curve of her spine, to where the sheet rested just at her hips.

There's a list of things you learn about someone the first time you spend the night together: whether they steal the blankets, whether they snore, if they're a cuddler.

Sara was a sprawler: all limp arms and legs, her whole body draped over me like a starfish.

We'd made love again when the sky started to lighten, soft and pink and blue smudging its edges. She'd collapsed on me, boneless and grinning, and immediately fallen back asleep.

It was half ten now and I trailed my finger down her arm, not wanting to wake her, certainly not wanting to leave. My camera still sat on the nightstand and I reached for it, sitting carefully on the edge of the mattress as I began scrolling through the photos. I'd taken hundreds of her last night, some of her undressing but even more of her desperate and arched below me. The sounds of our bodies moving together and her soft cries broken by the click of the shutter would forever be branded into my brain.

I went back to the pictures of the beginning of the night and stared at the photos of her expression as I'd admitted I loved her. She'd let me take so many pictures of her face last night; I relished the memory of the moment she'd brought it up. Our last rule, broken. Her permission said more than words ever could. As I clicked through the series, she went from desperate at first, to relieved, and then to mischievous in rapid succession.

And the photos from later, on her bed, looked just as intimate and carnal as I'd remembered feeling.

I stood quietly, crossed the room, and retrieved my laptop. It took only a moment to boot up and I removed the SD card from my camera, fitting it into the attachment for my computer. I logged into my favorite photo site, a small, discreet company that specialized in printing professional photos. I uploaded the ones I wanted and then erased the files from my hard drive, removing the card and stowing it safely in my bag.

With everything but my camera packed away, I leaned over her, whispering, "I have to go," against the shell of her ear. Goose bumps broke out along her skin and she stirred. "I've a flight to catch."

She mumbled, then stretched, and I watched as her eyelids slowly fluttered open.

"Don't want you to," she said, rolling to look up at me. Her voice was thick and raspy with sleep, and I immediately thought of a thousand things I wanted her to say.

She was too fucking tempting, eyes still tired and pillow creases lining her face, but it was her naked breasts that had my full attention. I braced my hand on either side of her head and hovered above her.

"You look fucking phenomenal in the morning. Did you know that?" I asked.

I reached down and ran my thumb across her bare breast, and had to take a shaky breath, overwhelmed by the immediate and almost suffocating closeness of her, how she seemed to fill up every space inside my chest.

"Yeah?" She smiled, arching a brow and brushing her thumb across my bottom lip. I wanted to suck on it, bite it. Her expression seemed to sober and she blinked up at me, eyes searching mine. "Did last night really happen?"

"You mean did I fuck you senseless and admit that you basically own me? Yes."

"What does 'I love you' even mean? It's weird how different three words can feel. I mean, I've said it before but it's never felt so . . . *big*, you know? I'm not sure it meant the same thing then. Like, I was too young to get it. Is that insane? You think I'm insane. But I'm not. I'm just . . . new to this, I think. Honestly, I think I'm new to this."

"I know you're saying something profound, but it's hard to focus when your tits are out."

Sara rolled her eyes and tried to push me away, but I wouldn't have it. Instead, I leaned in and kissed her, swallowing her protest as I tried to shape every wild and unhinged feeling I had and fit it into that kiss.

I could hear the sound of a summer rainstorm as water began to pelt the windows and thunder bellowed in the distance. Somewhere in the back of my mind I thought briefly of wet roads and everyone hailing a cab at once, and how much more time it would take to get to the airport. But as she wrapped a leg around the back of my thigh and pulled me fully on top of her, talk of the weather evaporated from my mind.

Her lips moved from my mouth to my ear and I tried to remember why I'd needed to leave in the first place.

"I'm sore in a really good way," she said, rocking her hips against mine. "I want more."

Any blood left in my brain evacuated and headed straight for my dick. "That is probably the best thing anyone has ever said to me."

Sara pushed against my chest and I practically whimpered as she rolled me to my back. "Don't go," she said, moving on top of me. The sheet fell away and I gripped her torso, my thumbs brushing the undersides of her breasts. She reached for my camera and held it up, looking down at me through the viewfinder. "I want to take pictures of your pretty face between my legs."

"Jesus Christ, Sara," I said, my head falling back against

the pillows and my eyes closed tight. "And here I thought you were this little innocent little thing and I was the Great Corruptor."

She burst into giggles and I just stared up at her.

"I love you," I said, gripping the back of her neck and bringing her mouth to mine. My hand trailed down her side, naked and smooth and covered in goose bumps.

"We're really doing this, aren't we?" she asked, pulling back just enough to meet my eyes.

"We're really doing this."

"Officially."

"A hundred percent. Dinners, dates, introducing you as my girlfriend. The whole thing."

"Think I like the sound of that," she said, her cheeks pink. She dragged her nails across my scalp and I melted, turning in to her touch. Not wanting to be anywhere but right here.

But . . .

The time on the clock near the bed reflected back at me. "Fuck. I really do have to go," I said, closing my eyes.

"Okay." I felt the heat of her lips against mine, not moving or doing anything in particular, just there, a chaste kiss made so much hotter by all the decidedly unchaste things we'd done only hours before.

I groaned, tugging my tie from my collar and tossing it somewhere over my shoulder. Pushing up on my knees, I looked down at her as I began to unbutton my shirt.

"But your flight," she said, even as she reached for my belt. An evil grin spread slowly across her face.

"I'll take the next one."

After a mad dash through JFK—totally worth it—and another five hours in the air, I finally touched down in San Francisco. I'd only managed to get an hour or two of sleep the night before, and only a few minutes here and there on the plane, and was really starting to feel it.

I yawned and gathered my bag from the overhead compartment, stepping off the plane and heading out of the terminal and straight for the closest cup of coffee I could find.

It'd been reckless to blow off my flight just to get an extra hour with Sara; I knew that even as I was looking down at her, watching myself move in her. But I'd never felt anything even close to this before, and it was still a bit hard to wrap my head around everything we'd said.

A text from Will popped up as I waited for my caffeine.

Any new sexy pictures, you wild trendsetter?

Fuck off. You'd never have the balls to pull out a camera, I wrote back, then stuffed my phone in my bag. I'd call Will later about the meeting and update him on the Sara situation.

With a smile on my face and my drink finally in hand, I

stepped away from the counter and took off the lid to add cream. I felt a tap on my shoulder and turned around.

"I think you dropped this." A shorter man with thinning blond hair stood behind me, holding out a black leather wallet.

I shook my head. "Not mine, mate. Sorry." I nodded toward security near the escalator to the luggage carousel. "Maybe try one of them." I started to turn and he gripped my arm, stopping me.

"You sure?"

"Pretty sure," I said with a shrug, taking out my own wallet and showing it to him. "Good luck finding the owner, though, yeah? Good man."

He was already taking a step back and I watched as he walked quickly away, headed toward the baggage claim. Having already lost enough time today, I placed the lid back on my cup and bent to reach for my bag near my feet.

My heart stopped.

It was gone.

———

"What kind of bag was it again, sir?" A bored airport employee looked up at me from behind the counter. According to the tag pinned to her too-tight chambray shirt, her name was Elana June. She blew a bubble while she waited for me to respond.

I glanced up at the monitor suspended on the wall behind her, at the image of my own back flickering on the screen, certain I had to be on some sort of hidden camera show.

"Sir?" she said again, sounding, if possible, even more bored than before.

I ran a hand through my hair, reminding myself that reaching out and strangling her would not help the situation. "An Hermès messenger bag. Gray and tan."

"Can you identify all the valuables inside?"

I swallowed down the taste of bile. "My files. My laptop. My phone. Fuck. Everything."

I considered all the client information I'd just lost, all the passwords that would have to be changed immediately. How much time this was all going to take and how many problems this could cause. And I didn't even have my fucking phone to call Will.

She slid a form and a ballpoint pen attached to a chain across the desk. "You look like you need a minute. Just fill this out and check the appropriate boxes."

I picked up the pen and filled in my name and address, checking the spaces for *laptop, mobile phone,* and *personal items*. I looked at the time and wondered if there was a box for sanity, because I was pretty sure I was close to losing that, too. I'd just about finished when I came across a choice that made me feel like I might throw up my spleen.

Camera. I hadn't brought my camera with me, but I *had* packed my SD card, intent on wiping it clean as soon as I had the opportunity.

There just really weren't enough *fucks* in the world for this one.

I looked down at the shitty counter, at the way the laminate was pulling away from the metal edge. There was a crack running along the surface and it seemed like the most ironic metaphor *ever*.

"My SD card," I said to nobody in particular.

"For a camera?" Elana June asked.

I swallowed. Twice. "Yeah. The card, with all the images." I swore and pushed away from the counter, remembering what Sara had let me do last night, how she had trusted me.

Fuck fuck fuck.

An older woman with dark hair pulled back into a bun stepped up to the desk. "Mr. Stella?" she asked.

I took a moment from my breakdown to nod and she continued.

"We looked at the footage. Looks like there were two of them. One distracted you while his partner took the bag. He was down the escalator and almost out of the terminal before you even realized it was missing."

I wondered if it was possible for the floor to open up and swallow me. I kind of hoped it was.

Having done everything I could at the airport, I took a car to the hotel. With no time to replace my phone before the meeting, I called directory assistance and had them ring the office. Will wasn't there, but his assistant assured me she'd change my account passwords herself and explain everything to Will as soon as possible. After promising her a dozen roses and a raise from her boss, I hung up and sat on the bed, glaring at the phone as I tried to decide what I would tell Sara.

Realizing there was no easy way to do this, I dialed directory assistance again and had them ring Sara's office.

George answered and I closed my eyes. I liked the guy well enough, but I was in no mood to deal with him today.

"Sara Dillon's office," he said.

"Miss Dillon, please."

He paused just long enough for it to become awkward before saying, "And good afternoon to you too, Mr. Stella. One moment, please."

I heard the click as I was connected and waited for her to pick up.

Three rings later, she answered. "This is Sara Dillon," she said, and I felt warmth coat the inside of my chest.

"Hey."

"Max? I didn't recognize the number."

"Yeah. I'm calling from my hotel. You all right? Sound a little stressed."

"I could do without the giant stack of pricing research on my desk today. I should have come into work before lunch, but I can't say I regret my lazy morning."

She paused and I closed my eyes, remembering her face when she came for the last time.

"How was your flight?"

"Good. Long," I said, standing and walking as far as the

phone cord would allow. I looked out the window, down to where people scurried about on the sidewalks below, completely lost in their own little worlds. "I miss you."

I heard her stand and a door close before she sat again. "Me, too."

"Did you get any sleep after I left?"

"A little." She laughed. "Someone wore me out."

"Lucky bastard, that one."

She hummed and I tried to picture what she was doing, what she was wearing. I decided she was wearing a skirt, nothing under, and had on her black knee-high boots.

Bad move, Max. You're across the country and ready to go now.

"You're gone for the week?" she asked.

"Yeah. I get back Friday afternoon. Spend the night with me?"

"Absolutely."

I took a deep breath, reminding myself I didn't have any reason to be worried. Most likely the thief would wipe my phone and laptop and just sell them. "So, my bag was stolen at the airport."

"What?" she gasped. "That's awful. Who does that?"

"Arseholes."

"Which bag was it? Your clothes?"

"No, my carry-on." I took a deep breath. "My laptop, my phone. I've already had the passwords changed for anything work related, but Sara . . . the SD card I used last night was in there and I haven't cleared all of it yet. My phone, too."

"Okay," she said on an exhale. "Okay." I heard the sound of leather creaking and could imagine her standing from her desk chair again and pacing the room. "I'm assuming the thief wasn't caught."

"No . . . Just a couple of shithead kids from what I gather."

A few beats of silence filled the line and I remembered why I sucked at phone calls. I wanted to see her, to read her expression and gauge whether she looked worried or relieved.

"Well, odds are that they were just out for a quick buck, right?" she said finally. "They'll probably pawn the laptop and phone and toss the SD drive. For all we know they've cleared the laptop and the card's already sitting in the trash somewhere."

I pressed my forehead to the window and exhaled, my breath forming a cloud of condensation on the glass. "Christ, I love you. I was very fucking stressed-out about how you'd take this news."

"Just come back so we can get some new pictures, okay?"

I smiled into the phone. "Deal."

———

The art show Saturday night and the conference on Sunday were complete insanity. I met several people in person I'd spoken with on the phone for months, and had agreed to a few meetings in New York later on to hammer out possible investments. The pace of the weekend allowed me to keep my mind off the fact that I had no pictures of naked Sara for distraction.

Monday I woke to a sky full of fog and croissant-and-coffee room service. As strange as it was to admit, I quite relished the forced unplugging I had to endure now that I'd lost my bag. I'd be able to pick up a new phone that morning and could make do without a laptop for the rest of the week, but aside from missing my photos, it had been nice to disengage a little from the constant work calls.

And then I noticed that, beside the bed, the light on my room phone was blinking red. Had I missed a call?

Checking the side of it, I realized the ringer had been turned off. I lifted the receiver and hit the voice mail button.

Will's no-nonsense voice snapped through the line: "Max. Check the *Post* then call me ASAP. We have fires to put out back home."

Seventeen

Monday came crashing in with another summer storm and a sky so greenish blue it felt like the ocean was filling up the air. I ran beneath my umbrella to the subway station and barely made my 7:32 train.

For once, there was a seat open and I dropped into it, wrapping up my umbrella and closing my eyes to think about everything I had to get done today. Some pricing research, a wall of meetings before lunch, and then a meeting with my staff.

When I looked up and glanced at the paper the lady next to me was reading, every one of those plans fell away.

Staring at me from the middle of Page Six was a picture of Max next to the headline, MAD MAX'S MANY MISTRESSES.

"*What?*" I shot out involuntarily, leaning forward and not even caring that I was one hundred percent into the personal space of the girl reading the paper.

"Can I see this?" I asked forcefully, and the woman handed the paper over like she thought I might be nuts. I quickly skimmed the story.

Max Stella loves art and beautiful women. It's no surprise to any of us that his (worst-kept) secret is his penchant for combining hobbies: photographing himself with his flavors of the week. Caught only a week ago with a stunning blonde in a bar, new pictures have leaked of Max devouring an equally delicious brunette. While most of the shots were, let's just say, *very* too NSFW to reprint here, one face shot clearly identifies the venture capitalist's "getting the business" partner as the Spanish starlet Maria de la Cruz, only days ago as the time stamp has it.

Come on, Max. Can't we just see a sex tape and get it over with?

As I finished reading the story for probably the tenth time, the train pulled up to a stop and I shot up, stumbling from the subway car and wandering in a daze out to the street.

After walking the last dozen blocks to our building, I wasn't even a little surprised to find Chloe standing inside my office, waiting for me.

With shaking hands, I held up the paper. "I need

you to explain what I'm seeing here. Is this just gossip? Who is this woman?"

She stepped closer, handing me her phone. She had the browser open to Celebritini, which apparently had broken the story. At the top of the page was a picture I'd seen weeks ago, on the rooftop with Max. It was a picture of my hip, with his hand spread across my skin.

Beside the picture of my obviously naked body was a picture of a woman's face. She had dark hair and I would have no way of knowing what color her eyes were because her head was thrown back, eyes closed. At the bottom of the photo was a hint of hair of the man whose face was pressed against her neck.

She was very obviously having an *orgasm*.

"This photo was on his phone." I scanned the story that outlined just how many women Max had pictures of. "Apparently there were a lot of pictures of other women."

Chloe reached for the pair of scissors on my desk. "I'll be back later; seems I have an appendage to re-move."

"He's out of town."

She paused, taking a deep breath. "Well, at least that will save me from prison."

"What did Bennett say?"

Chloe flopped down on my couch. "He said we should try to be circumspect. That we didn't know the entire story. That there is a lot of bullshit in the press. He reminded me I thought he was sleeping with everyone in the office before we hooked up."

I pointed to the picture of his *Spanish Starlet*. "This story says this was the most recent of his photos leaked and that there were many others. And the one of me, the other one, was taken earlier this summer. So he's been with her since then."

She didn't respond. I stared at the wall, considered putting my fist through it, and then almost laughed at the image. Max could put a fist through a wall. I wouldn't even leave a mark, and would probably end up with a broken hand.

"I'm tired of feeling like an idiot."

"So don't be. Kick his ass."

"This is exactly why I didn't want to get involved with anyone. Because I want to see the best in someone, and am totally shattered when I'm wrong."

Chloe still didn't say anything, just watched me from across the room. Max didn't even have a phone or a laptop. I couldn't call to find out anything.

I wasn't sure I wanted to. I picked up my phone and powered it off.

"What do we have on the calendar today?" I hit the spacebar on my computer to wake up the screen, and glanced through my appointments. I looked up at my friend.

She reached over and turned off my monitor. "Nothing pressing. George! Cancel everything and then get your stuff. We're getting day-drunk."

❧

By noon I was hammered, thrilled that the seedy bar we hit up in Queens had a jukebox, and even more thrilled that the proprietor seemed to love eighties hair bands as much as I did. It was my mom's guilty pleasure music and playing Twisted Sister over and over strangely made me feel like I was home.

"He was brilliant in bed," I mumbled into my glass. "Well," I corrected, holding up a heavy hand, "that one night we actually did it in a bed. My bed. And in that bed he was *brilliant*. I think we had sex like seven thousand times that night."

"You only did it in a bed once?" George asked, standing next to the table and leaning on a pool stick for support.

Chloe sighed heavily and ignored him, popping another few highly suspect peanuts into her mouth. "I hate that you feel like you have to give that up. Nothing keeps a relationship together better than amazing sex. Oh, and honesty. I mean, that's important too." She scratched her cheek, adding, "And just, like, having fun together. I mean, sex, honesty, and fun. Secret of success right there."

"We had the sex and the fun."

Chloe looked like she was headed into the nap zone. "BB is fucking stellar in bed, too," she mumbled.

"My complete lack of a sex life is also fantastic," George groaned. "Thanks for asking. Do women really sit around talking about sex all the time?"

Chloe said, "Yes," just as I said, "Not really."

Then I changed my mind and said, "Kind of," right when she said, "I guess not."

We fell into each other giggling, but my laughter quickly dissolved when a tall shadow stepped into the bar. I sat up, heart pounding. He had broad shoulders, the same light brown hair . . .

But it wasn't Max.

My chest felt like it was too small for everything inside it.

"Ouch," I moaned, rubbing over my heart. "Last time I was so far beyond feeling sad I was just mad. This just *hurts*."

Chloe threw an arm around me. "Men suck."

Her phone rang and she answered it after barely one ring. "I'm at a bar." She paused, listening, then said, "Yeah, we're getting day-drunk . . . She's sad and I want to castrate him . . . I know. I will . . . I promise

I won't throw up all over the new carpet, settle down. I'll see you later." She ended the call and gave the phone the finger. "Such a bossy ass."

And then she slumped against me. "You deserve a guy like Bennett."

George bent down, inspecting us and shaking his head. "You two are a mess. Tomorrow night we're doing Buck Up Sara Time the gay way."

❧

Tuesday night, George took us to a gay bar, packed wall-to-wall with people, pounding with music. It was exactly the kind of place I wanted to go with him in happier times, but now it only reminded me of how miserable I was. And the truth was, I didn't really want to go out and party. I didn't want to be in the middle of a fifteen-man grindfest. I wanted to find a way to just skip time, and get to that point where Max didn't matter anymore.

What scared me was that it had taken almost no time to stop *loving* Andy; I'd met Max within a week. I suspected that it would be a lot longer before I'd get over this one.

I finally turned my phone back on Thursday morning to find seventeen missed calls from Max, but he hadn't left a single message. He'd sent me about twenty texts on Monday and Tuesday, as well, and those I read:

Call me.

Sara, I saw the Post. Call me.

More variations on the same thing: call, text, let me know you're getting these. And, just when I was going to call, I saw the last one and it tripped an instinctive wire caging my heart.

Sara, I know it looks really bad. It isn't what you're thinking.

Oh, perfect. How many times had I heard *that* in a past life? The truth is, if you have to say that, it's almost always exactly what you're thinking. It took me forever to learn that lesson, and it wasn't a program I was going to delete very soon.

I turned off my phone again, this time determined to leave it off for good.

❧

Max returned Friday, I knew, but I still hadn't called. He didn't come by my work, and when I turned my phone back on a few days after checking my texts, I realized he'd stopped calling, too.

Which was worse: His clichéd insistence that I misunderstood? Or his silence?

Was I even being fair? I hated the in-between space, where anger met uncertainty. I'd lived in that space for so long with Andy, feeling like something was happening behind my back, but never knowing for sure. I had been caught in a horrible battle between feeling like a guilty nag and being positive he was doing me wrong.

This time my angst was so much worse. Because this time, I'd truly thought Max was a man worth knowing. In comparison, I realized I didn't know that I'd ever felt that about Andy. Maybe I'd just wanted to *make* him into a man worth knowing.

What was the story with the other woman? Was she someone he hooked up with once before we were serious? Could I really hold that against him even though we'd agreed to be monogamous? But when had that picture been taken? Was it really only a few days before he spent the night at my house?

"Sare-bear. I can practically *hear* you thinking in there," George called from his desk. "It is shrill and growing hysterical. Calm your tits. I put a flask in your desk drawer. It's pink and sparkly but don't fall in love; it's mine."

I pulled open the drawer. "What's in it?"

"Scotch."

Slamming the drawer shut, I groaned. "No go. That's a Max Stella staple."

"I know that."

I glared at the wall, hoping he could feel the burn of my eyes on the back of his neck on the other side. "You're an ass."

"You haven't called him, have you?"

"No. Should I?" I pressed a hand to my face. "Don't answer that. He has Spanish flavors of the week. Of course I shouldn't call him."

I stood up and slammed my door closed, but just as I sat back down, three soft taps landed on the other side.

"You can come in, George," I growled, defeated. "But I'm not drinking the scotch."

Bennett walked inside, filling the space as only Bennett Ryan really could fill a space. I sat up straighter, looked down at my desk to instinctively inspect the level of paperwork disorganization.

"Hi, Bennett. I was totally kidding about the scotch. I don't drink at work."

He smiled. "I wouldn't blame you if you did."

"Okay . . . ," I said, wondering what he was doing here. We rarely had cause to interact one-on-one at work. He studied me for a beat before saying, "In Chicago, when I'd hit rock bottom, you came into my office and yelled at me."

"Oh." *Oh shit.*

"You gave me perspective, hinted that my feelings

for Chloe weren't a surprise to anyone. You made it clear that everyone knew I was hard on her because I held her in particularly high regard."

I smiled when I realized he wasn't going to chew me out. "I remember. You were both such sad sacks."

"I'm here to return the favor. I've known Max a long time." He sat down in the chair on the other side of my desk. "He's always been a bit of a playboy. He's never been in love, I don't think. Before you," he added, eyebrow raised.

I knew it wouldn't matter how long I knew Bennett; I would always feel intimidated by him, especially when he pulled the eyebrow move.

"And he hasn't told me what's going on, even though I've broken my own unspoken rules and actually asked, but he did say he hasn't heard from you. And from what I hear from Will, he's not doing well. If you really felt strongly about him, you owe him the chance to explain."

I groaned. "Sometimes I think so, and then I remember that he's a jerk."

"Look, Sara. The way Andrew treated you was unconscionable. We all saw that, and I regret not speaking up on your behalf. But you have the choice to decide how you grow from it. If you're going to think every man is like him, you don't deserve Max. Max isn't that guy."

He watched me for a moment and I had no idea how to respond. But the way my heart squeezed painfully at the thought that I didn't deserve Max told me that Bennett was right.

And that I needed to find a dress for the fund-raiser.

∿

Chloe and Bennett picked me up in a town car and, as I climbed in, I took a second to appreciate Bennett in a tux. Honestly, the man was so pretty it was a little unfair. Beside him, Chloe glowed in a shimmering pearl halter gown. She rolled her eyes at something he whispered in her ear, and she replied, "You're a pig."

He laughed quietly, kissing her neck. "That's why you love me."

I loved seeing them happy, and wasn't cynical enough to think that person didn't exist for me. I just realized, as I stared down at my dress, that I'd spent more than an hour getting ready for this. I had really wanted my person to be Max.

I turned and looked out the window, trying not to remember the last time I'd been to his building, and how safe I'd felt with him in the shower. But to my tangled horror and relief, when we arrived the security guard remembered me, and smiled.

"Good evening, Miss Dillon." He escorted us to the elevator and pressed the button for the penthouse before stepping back to leave us to ourselves. "Enjoy your night."

I thanked him as the doors closed, and I felt like I might fall over.

"I'm legitimately worried I'm going to have a stroke," I hissed. "Remind me why I'm here?"

"Breathe," Chloe whispered to me.

Bennett leaned forward to look at me. "You're here to show him how beautiful you look and that he didn't break you. If that's the only thing that happens tonight, it's fine."

I was swooning so hard at what he'd said that I'd completely forgotten to prepare myself to see Max's living room. When the elevator doors opened, the sight of his place hit me like a wood plank to the chest, and I actually stumbled back a few steps.

The section that had been replicated in Johnny's club was a minuscule portion of the room—a small area set back in a recessed corner and obviously meant for smaller gatherings. But to me it stood out like a beacon. Even with the vast open space and what felt like miles of marble floor between me and that memory, I could barely look away. A couple of men lingered there, sipping drinks and looking out the window. It felt invasive somehow, as if they were on the wrong side of the glass.

Without skipping a beat, Chloe slipped her arm through mine and pulled me forward as a tall, older gentleman led us from the foyer to the main living areas.

"You okay?" Chloe asked.

"I'm not sure this was a good idea."

I heard her inhale a sharp breath and then she said, "Actually, that may be true."

I looked up and followed her attention across the room to where Max had walked in, just behind Will.

He wore a tux, similar to the one he wore at the gala weeks ago. But tonight the vest beneath his jacket was white and his eyes were flat. His mouth smiled in greeting to everyone in the room. But the smile never made it into his eyes.

There were maybe a hundred other people looking at his art, wandering into the kitchen to grab a glass of wine, or standing in the center of the room, talking. But I felt frozen near the wall.

Why had I worn red? I felt like a wannabe siren among the muted creams and blacks. What was I hoping to accomplish? Did I want him to see me?

Whether or not I wanted him to, he didn't. At least, he didn't seem to. Max walked around the room, talking to his guests, thanking them for coming. I tried to pretend I wasn't staring at his every move but it was useless.

I missed him.

I didn't know what he felt, what was real and what wasn't. I didn't know what we had really been.

"Sara."

I turned at the sound of Will's uniquely deep voice.

"Hi, Will." I hated seeing him so serious. I'd rarely seen either Max or Will unsmiling. This looked all wrong.

He studied me for a beat, and then murmured, "Does he know you're here?"

I looked across the room at where Max stood, speaking to two older women. "I don't know."

"Should I tell him?"

I shook my head and he sighed. "He's been such a useless bastard. I'm really glad you came."

Laughing a little, I admitted, "I'm still undecided."

"I'm really sorry," he said quietly.

I met his eyes. "You don't have to apologize for Max's indiscretions."

His brow furrowed and he shook his head once. "He never told you?"

My heart fell and then immediately began thundering. "Told me what?"

But Will took a step back, seeming to reconsider

saying anything else. "Oh, you really haven't talked to him yet."

I shook my head and he looked over my shoulder, to where Max stood. Will put his hand on my arm. "Don't leave without talking to him, okay?"

I nodded and looked back to Max, who was standing with a beautiful brunette. She had her hand on his arm and was laughing at something he said. Laughing too much, trying too hard.

When I turned back around, Will was gone.

Suddenly needing air, I turned and walked down the closest hall. Down here, there were no caterers carting trays of food, no guests mingling. Just a wide hallway lined with closed doors. Between each were beautiful photographs of trees and snow, lips and hands and spines.

Where was I going? Was there more Max to discover here? Would I stumble into a room filled with a woman's things? Was the reason he'd always been so amenable to staying away from his place the fact that it allowed him to have a private space for someone else?

Why was I even here?

Hearing footsteps, I quickly ducked into a room at the end of the hall.

Inside, away from the crowd, it was so quiet I could hear my pulse whooshing in my ears.

And then, I looked around.

I was in an enormous bedroom, with a huge bed in

the middle. On the bedside table, which held the only lit lamp in the room, was a framed photograph of me.

In it, I stood, staring at the camera, with my fingers poised on the button of my shirt, lips parted. I looked at once surprised and relieved.

I remembered that exact moment. He'd just told me he loved me.

Whipping around, I looked at the wall behind me. More photos: My back as I reached behind me to take off my bra. My face as I looked down to unzip my skirt; smiling. My face looking up at him in the morning sun.

I stumbled forward, wanting to escape the realization that I had messed up, hugely. That there was more here for me to understand. But past another door was an expansive dressing room, and if possible, it was worse.

The room was exploding with intimacy. There were probably thirty pictures of us, all black-and-white, all different sizes, artfully tiered and layered across the simple cream paint.

Some were chaste and simply beautiful. A picture I'd taken of his lips pressed against the top of my foot. His thumb sweeping across a small exposed strip of my abdomen as he pushed my shirt up my torso.

Some were erotic but restrained, suggestive of a moment where we were lost in each other, but not showing how. My teeth biting his earlobe, only mouth and jaw visible against his skin but with me clearly gasping, close to climax. Or my torso, beneath him. My fingernails dug into his shoulders and my thighs were pulled up high to my sides.

A few were downright filthy. My hand wrapped around his erection. A blurry shot of him moving in me from behind, in the warehouse.

But the one that stopped me dead in my tracks was the one taken from the side the night at my apartment. I didn't even realize Max had set his camera on a timer but it was an awkward angle, with the camera sitting on my bedside table. In the picture, Max was over me, his hips flexed as he pushed inside. One of my legs wound around his thigh. He was propped above me on his forearms, leaning down over me as we kissed. Our eyes were closed, faces devoid of any tension whatsoever.

It was us, making love, caught in a single perfect image.

And, beside it, a picture of his lips open around my breast, his eyes gazing up at me with naked adoration.

"Oh my God," I whispered.

"No one is meant to be in here."

I jumped, pressing my hand to my chest at the sound of his voice. Closing my eyes, I asked, "Not even me?"

"*Especially* not you."

I turned around to look at him but it was a mistake. I should have taken a bigger breath, prepared myself somehow for how he would look up close: crisp, put-together, unbelievably gorgeous.

But at the edges: broken. Dark lines circled his un-smiling eyes. His lips were tight and pale.

"I was having a hard time out there," I admitted. "The room, the couch . . ."

He looked up at me, eyes hard. "It was like that for me when I came home from San Francisco, you know. I wanted to buy all new furniture."

We drowned in a heavy silence after that until he finally looked away. I didn't know where to start. I had to remember that his phone had pictures of other women on it, ones more recent than those of me. But here in this room, he seemed more hurt than I did.

"I don't understand what's going on right now," I admitted.

"I don't need my humiliation put so plainly before me," he said, motioning to the pictures on the wall. "Believe me, Sara, I feel pathetic enough without you coming in here uninvited." He glanced up at a picture of my lips on his hipbone. "I made a deal with myself. I was going to leave them up for two weeks, and then put them away."

"Max—"

"You told me you *loved* me." His calm exterior cracked slightly; I'd never heard him sound angry before.

I had no idea what to say. He'd phrased it in past

tense. But nothing felt more immediate than my feelings for him, particularly in his room, surrounded by the evidence of what we'd become that night. "You had photos of other wo—"

"But if you loved me how I love you," he said, cutting me off, "you would have given me a chance to explain what you saw in the *Post*."

"By the time explanation is needed, it's usually too late."

"You've made that clear. But why do you assume I've done something wrong? Have I ever lied to you, or kept anything from you? I *trusted* you. You assume I've never been hurt and that trust comes easily to me. You're too busy guarding your own heart to realize that maybe I'm not the arsehole people expect me to be."

Any response dissipated when he'd said this. He was right. After he'd told me about Cecily, and his romantic life after, I'd assumed it *had* been easy for him, and that he had no experience with the harsher side of love.

"You could have let me explain," he said.

"I'm here. Explain now."

His scowl deepened but he blinked away, nodding. "Whoever stole my bag sold the pictures as their own. The good folks at Celebritini found a hundred and ninety-eight pictures of you in my briefcase. On my SD card, my phone, and a thumb drive. Had they been able to decode the password on my laptop, they would have found another couple hundred. And yet, they chose to post a picture of your hip, and the picture of a woman I've never met before."

I felt my brow furrow in confusion; my heart hammered wildly beneath my ribs. "You mean they just put her in there? It wasn't yours?"

"It *was* on my phone," he said, looking back at me. "But I don't know who she is. It was a picture Will had texted me that morning, just before my bag was taken. It was some woman he'd seen a few times a couple of years ago."

I shook my head, not following. "Why would he send you that?"

"I told him about the art I had of you, how it was all new for me. And, as is the way with us, he joked that of course he'd already done that before. Taken photographs of lovers, tasteful ones. It was all a game, *that's old sport,* been there done that. He was taking the piss. He could tell I was sincere and loved you." He stepped back and leaned against the wall. "But we'd been joking about it the day before my trip. He asked me if I'd stocked my phone with Sara porn. He sent just that one because he's a twat and was having a laugh. The timing was just really, really poor."

"The story said you had photos of a lot of women."

"A lie."

"Why didn't you tell me that? Leave a voice mail, or text the truth?"

"Well, one because I thought being adults we'd talk face-to-face. Everything we've done together required a great deal of trust, Sara. I gathered I deserved the benefit of the doubt. But also"—he ran his hand through his hair, cursing—"it would mean admitting that I'd told Will about how you let me photograph you. It would mean admitting I'd betrayed our secret. It would mean revealing that he'd sent me a private picture of a woman who had presumably trusted him. I've had my lawyers handle the containment issue, but honestly, it made us both look like pricks."

"Not as much as seeing her in the paper did."

"Do you not see it's exactly the story they wanted? The story of me and all my many women? They found hundreds of photos of me and you and yet they just post one? There is one image of another woman, and bam—it fits their gossip narrative. I told you I wasn't with anyone else; why wasn't that enough?"

"Because I'm used to men who say one thing and do another."

"But you expected me to be better than that," he said, eyes searching mine. "Otherwise why admit you love me? Why give me a night like that?"

"I guess when the photos came out . . . I didn't think that night meant as much to you."

"That's absolute shite. You were there, too. You're looking at the photos now. You know exactly how much it meant to me."

I reached for him but reconsidered. He looked really pissed, and my frustration with myself and him and all of it just *exploded*. I still remembered the stab I felt in my chest when I saw the picture of the other woman.

"*What was I supposed to think?* It just seemed reasonable that you'd played me. Everything between us always seemed so easy for you."

"It *was* easy. Falling absolutely in love with you was *really fucking easy*. Isn't it supposed to be that way? Just because I haven't been brokenhearted in recent years doesn't mean I'm incapable of it. Fuck, Sara. I've been wrecked for the past two weeks. Positively smashed."

I pressed a hand to my stomach, feeling like I needed to physically hold myself together. "Me, too."

He sighed, stared down at his shoes, and didn't say anything else. In my chest, my heart twisted tightly.

"I want to be with you," I said.

He nodded once, but didn't look back up, didn't even say a word.

I stepped closer, stretched to kiss his cheek, and only made it to his jaw because he wouldn't bend to meet me.

"Max, I miss you," I told him. "I know I jumped to conclusions. I just . . . I thought . . ." I stopped, hating how still he remained.

Without looking back, I walked out of his dressing room, through his bedroom, and back to the party.

❧

"I want to go home," I said to Chloe, once I'd been able to discreetly—semi-discreetly—pull her away from a conversation with Bennett and Will.

The two men watched us in the obvious way men have where they don't even bother trying to hide what they're doing. We all stood in the recessed portion of the living room that looked exactly like the room in the club. The memories sent sharp pangs through my chest. I wanted to get out of this dress, wash my face, and curl up in a tub of cookie dough.

"Give us twenty?" she asked, eyes searching mine. "Or do you need to leave right this second?"

I groaned, looking around the room. Max still hadn't emerged from his bedroom and I wanted to be gone when he did. I certainly didn't want to be standing exactly where I was, remembering exactly how loving he'd been with me in Johnny's club, and every second after. I was mortified, and confused, and most of all, I was wildly in love with him. The memory of the way he'd displayed the beauty in our photographs pulsed like a vivid echo in my mind.

"I just had the world's most awkward conversation with Max. I feel like an asshole and he's being obstinate and has every right to be because I'm an idiot and I just want to leave. I'll get a cab outside."

Will put his hand on my arm. "Don't leave quite yet."

I couldn't help giving him a scolding look. "You're kind of a piglet, Will. I can't believe you did that. I would kill Max if he sent you a picture of me."

He nodded, chastened. "I know."

My attention was drawn up and over his shoulder to the hall to Max's room. He'd come out without me seeing, and stood, leaning against the wall, sipping a scotch. He was staring directly at me. It was the same intense expression he wore the first night we met, as he watched me dance for him.

"I'm sorry," I mouthed to him, eyes welling with tears. "I messed up."

Will was saying something, but I had no idea what. I was too focused on the way Max licked his lips. And then his eyes turned up in the familiar smile and he mouthed the words, "You look beautiful."

Will had asked me a question. *What did he just say?*

I nodded, and mumbled, "Yeah . . ."

But he laughed, shaking his head. "It wasn't a yes-or-no question, lovely Sara."

"I . . ." I tried to focus. But behind him, Max had set his drink down on a table and was headed straight for me. Tugging at my dress, I stood straighter, tried to keep my face impassive. "Could you repeat the question?"

"Max is walking over here, isn't he?" Will asked, watching me with naked amusement.

I nodded again. "Um."

I hadn't realized how close I'd been standing against the wall until I was pressed against it, Max's mouth warm and sliding over mine, whispering my name over and over. I wanted to say something, I wanted to tease him for kissing me like this in the middle of his own party, but I was so wrapped up in the intensity of my own relief that I just closed my eyes, opened my mouth, to let his tongue slide across mine.

He dragged his teeth down my jaw, sucked at my neck. Over his shoulder I saw that the entire room full of people had stopped talking and were watching us, wide-eyed. A few were leaning together, already discussing what they were seeing.

"Max," I whispered, tugging his hair to pull his head back to mine. I couldn't stop smiling; I felt like my face was going to crack in half. He looked at my lips, his eyes hooded as if he was drunk from me. "We have an audience."

"Isn't that your thing?" He leaned forward, kissed me once more.

"I like a little more anonymity."

"Too bad. I thought we agreed this would be our coming-out party."

I pulled away, searching his eyes as they grew more sober. "I'm really sorry."

"I suppose it's obvious that I want to be with you, too. I just . . . needed a moment to collect myself in there," he said quietly.

I nodded. "Totally understandable."

Max grinned and kissed my nose. "At least we got that out of the way. But I've earned the right to a fair trial. No more mistrustful Sara."

"I promise."

Collecting himself, he slipped my arm through his and turned back to his stunned party. Max announced to all near, "Sorry for the interruption, everyone. Haven't seen my girlfriend in a couple of weeks."

People nodded and smiled at us as if we were the most charming thing they'd ever seen. It was a familiar type of attention, the kind I'd received for years. But this time it was *real*. What I'd found with Max wasn't about opinion polls and public perception. For the first time in my life, what happened behind closed doors was ten times better than what others saw from the outside looking in.

And he was mine.

Max was still out saying good night to the last of his guests to leave when I slipped back into his bedroom to look at the photos again. They were so revealing of our emotions, they almost made me feel bare all over.

I heard him come in behind me and quietly shut the door.

"How could you stand it?"

"Stand what?" He stepped behind me and bent to kiss the back of my neck.

"Seeing these pictures every day." I pointed to his wall. "If they'd been on my wall while we were apart it would have hurt so much I would have gone fetal and subsisted entirely on Cap'n Crunch and self-pity."

He laughed and turned me to face him. "I wasn't ready to get over you yet. I was miserable, but would have been more miserable if I'd admitted it was over."

And that's what he gave me, a reminder that the glass wasn't just half full, it was overflowing.

"It'll exhaust you sometimes," I said, "having to be the optimist for both of us."

"Aaah, but eventually I'll bring you over to the light side." He reached behind me, unzipped my dress, and slipped it from my shoulders. It fell in a puddle at my feet and I stepped out of it, feeling the pleasure of his eyes on my skin.

When I glanced up at him, he looked so serious it made my stomach lurch. "What's wrong?"

"You could break my heart. Just know that, yeah?"

I nodded, swallowing a thick lump in my throat. "I know."

"When I say 'I love you' I don't mean that I love what being with you does for my career, or I love how often you're willing to shag. I mean I love *you*. I love making you laugh, and seeing how you react to things, and getting to know the little things about you. I love who I am with you, and I'm trusting you not to hurt me."

Maybe because he was so tall, and broad, and constantly smiling and impossible to offend, Max *seemed* so formidable, as if nothing could actually break him. But he was only human, too.

"I understand," I whispered. It was so strange to be on the other side of messing up, and to be the one who was given another chance.

He kissed me and then stepped back, slipping out of his jacket and hanging it on a coatrack in the corner. I spotted his camera on a shelf in the opposite corner of the room and walked over to pick it up. I stared down at it, found the ON button, raised the camera, and adjusted the lens.

I aimed it at where Max stood, watching me and tugging at his bow tie.

"I love you, too," I said, zooming to take a close-up of his face. I clicked a few more pictures in rapid succession as he stared hungrily at me. "Undress."

He pulled his tie away from his collar and dropped it, eyes growing darker, and began unbuttoning his shirt.

Click.

"A warning," I murmured from behind the camera as he pulled his shirt open. "I'll probably need to lick every inch of your chest tonight."

A smile tilted his mouth. *Click.* "Fine by me. I might insist you lick a little lower, too."

I took a picture of his hands at his belt, his pants on the floor, his feet as they stepped right in front of mine.

"What do you think you're doing?" he asked, reaching to take the camera away from me.

"Taking pictures for *my* bedroom."

He laughed and shook his head. "Get on the bed, Petal. Apparently you need a reminder of how this works."

I climbed back, feeling the cool sheets as the mattress dipped below me. He reached down, adjusted my leg, studied me.

Click.

"Look at me," he murmured.

The light from the Manhattan skyline slipped across my body, illuminating a strip of skin on my ribs. His finger ran up the inside of my thigh as I looked up at his face, partially hidden by the camera.

Click.

I exhaled, closing my eyes and smiling.

New life. New love. New Sara.

Acknowledgments

Not a single word of this book could have been written without the support of our husbands, Blondie & Dr. Mister Shoes. We are constantly shocked by the coincidence that the two of us happened to find the two best men on the planet. Thank you for everything you do to support this crazy gig.

Our agent, Holly Root, is most likely made of magic and cupcakes and stardust and unicorn tears. We aren't sure, of course, but it just seems impossible that someone so amazing could come from this humble planet.

Thank you to Adam Wilson, our hilarious editor and the name we most love to see in our margins. The list of our favorite Adamisms is getting so long we had to start a spreadsheet. Thanks for putting up with our ridiculousness, and for making us want to do it right the first time.

Thanks to Mary McCue and Kristin Dwyer, our publicists at Simon & Schuster Gallery. Your excitement and support already have buoyed us immensely

343

and we kind of just want to sit across your desk and gaze at you adoringly. To everyone at Gallery: Jennifer Bergstrom, Ellen Chan, Natalie Ebel, Julia Fincher, Liz Psaltis: thank you for everything you've done to edit, promote and support *Beautiful Bastard* and *Beautiful Stranger*. Simon & Schuster must be a fantastic place to work because you are all gems.

To our writing buddies and readers: Erin, Martha, Kellie, Anne, Myra, Amy, Tonya, and Moi: thank goodness you loved it the first time around because we don't think we could have rewritten it in a week. HA! HA! ::drinks:: We don't love our books until we've fixed what you say is wrong with them.

Alison and Anya, many thanks for your help with NYC, even though it may horrify you to know what we've done with the information. (Who are we kidding—you're aware.) Helen, thank you for taking the time to help with the Britishisms. And Ian: yay for getting drunk with Lo often enough that she can imagine every single curse word in your accent! Spangly, your help in the art world was invaluable because, if left to our own devices, we would have referred to only the *Mona Lisa* and imagined sculptures made from beakers and nail polish. Lauren Suero, thank you eternally for all your work on the promo side. You are a wealth of knowledge (and awesome shoes).

More love than we can express to our readers, both

old and new. Thank you for cheering us on and for your continued support. We couldn't do any of this without you. If you prefer to keep your panties intact, at the very least we hope you get ravished in a library.

And finally: Christina, you are the calm to my wild. Lo, you are the wild to my calm. Doing this together is the most fun. Let's have cake.

Beautiful
BASTARD

A Novel

CHRISTINA LAUREN